"I DON'T KNOW MYSELF, MY MIND, MY THOUGHTS. AND THAT SCARES ME."

"It's horrible," she said to the man, meaning it.

He breathed out, the sound jittery and tentative, as if breath itself were likely to disappear.

As Fabian watched him, listened to his words, she felt something happen in her body. At first it was like she was going to burst into panic, but then the push of adrenaline turned into warmth, filling her body with feeling, and then she was washed with a slight desire, the same that she'd had the day before as he'd slept against her body while she read to him on the sofa. Her mouth opened before she could think, the same problem she'd had in school, but instead of smarting off to a teacher, she said, "Do you want me to stay here with you? I mean, sleep here with you?"

Without pause, he said, "Yes."

BOOK YOUR PLACE ON OUR WEBSITE AND MAKE THE READING CONNECTION!

We've created a customized website just for our very special readers, where you can get the inside scoop on everything that's going on with Zebra, Pinnacle and Kensington books.

When you come online, you'll have the exciting opportunity to:

- View covers of upcoming books
- Read sample chapters
- Learn about our future publishing schedule (listed by publication month *and author*)
- Find out when your favorite authors will be visiting a city near you
- Search for and order backlist books from our online catalog
- Check out author bios and background information
- Send e-mail to your favorite authors
- Meet the Kensington staff online
- Join us in weekly chats with authors, readers and other guests
- Get writing guidelines
- AND MUCH MORE!

**Visit our website at
http://www.kensingtonbooks.com**

Fangs But No Fangs

KATHY LOVE

BRAVA

KENSINGTON PUBLISHING CORP.
http://www.kensingtonbooks.com

BRAVA BOOKS are published by

Kensington Publishing Corp.
850 Third Avenue
New York, NY 10022

All Kensington titles, imprints, and distributed lines are available at special quantity discounts for bulk purchases for sales promotion, premiums, fund-raising, educational, or institutional use.

Special book excerpts or customized printings can also be created to fit specific needs. For details, write or phone the office of the Kensington Special Sales Manager: Attn. Special Sales Department. Kensington Publishing Corp., 850 Third Avenue, New York, NY 10022. Phone: 1-800-221-2647.

Brava and the B logo Reg. U.S. Pat. & TM Off.

ISBN-13: 978-0-7582-1134-7
ISBN-10: 0-7582-1134-1

First Brava Trade Paperback Printing: February 2006
First Brava Mass-Market Printing: July 2008

10 9 8 7 6 5 4 3 2 1

Printed in the United States of America

For Emily.
You can read this in fifteen years,
but by then, I bet you won't want to.

Acknowledgments

Thanks to the Tarts.
Thanks, Janet, for the "tying one on" info!

Thank you, Mom and Dad, for
the month-long writing boot camp.

Thank you, Lisa, Chris, Sheryl, and Karen.
I so appreciate the great feedback.

Thanks to Sandie of the Underground, who I
missed last time. Sorry!

I really want to thank a few of my best writing buddies
who have made this whole adventure tons of fun:
Julie Cohen, Christie Kelley, Janet Mullany, Kate Dolan,
Beth Ciotta, Jordan Summers, Arianna Hart,
Julia Templeton, Mary Stella,
Sue Fickel, and Suzanne Walter.
You are the greatest!

I also want to thank all the wonderful
authors at Romance Unleashed,
with special thanks to:
Lori Devoti, Kathleen Long, Kristina Cook, Kate Rothwell,
Flo Fitzpatrick, Teresa Bodwell, Jessica Trapp,
and Sally Mackenzie.

You were the first of the group I met, and you made me feel very welcome.
And to all the ladies there—you keep me sane. Thanks.

Thanks Jul for the last minute read through.

And, finally, thanks Kate. You were so right.

Chapter 1

The pink flamingos had to die!

Christian groaned and slammed a flattened, musty pillow over his head, trying to block out the grating noise. But the endless whirring would not be silenced. Add the *clack, clack, clack* of the little man sawing wood, and the noise was almost unbearable.

He threw the pillow aside and sat up on the sagging mattress. A spring poked at the back of his thigh, although he barely registered the stab.

He shoved up from the bed and walked to the window, or rather stepped to the window, as the square room was about the size of one of his Monte Carlo bungalow's walk-in closets.

Grime hazed the small rectangular window, but he could still see the offending noisemakers. He wished he could grow accustomed to them like he had his lumpy bed. But the racket never seemed to end.

The goddamned lawn ornaments would be the thing that finally drove him stark raving mad.

An enormous assortment of ornaments rose from the neighboring trailer's lawn like a twirling and spinning army of kitsch. Flowers, flamingos, other random animals, their petals, wings, and appendages whirling deafeningly in the breeze. And then there was that little man with the saw like an army sergeant, bobbing away, clacking endlessly, spurring the others on. Damn, he hated that little man.

He even hated the ornaments that didn't move. The gnomes. The plastic geese. The wooden cutout that was supposed to look like a lady with an unusually well-endowed backside, bending over among the bedraggled flowerbed.

Christian closed his eyes for a moment, but the menagerie of tastelessness just appeared behind his closed eyelids in full, swirling color.

Giving up the hope of peace, he left his closetlike bedroom to enter a dark, paneled hallway that was just wide enough for the expanse of his shoulders. As he passed the bathroom, the toilet, which seemed to have a will of its own, gurgled to life in greeting. The hiss of water was a welcome distraction from the saw man.

He walked out to the narrow galley-style kitchen, which was large enough for a stained and nicked counter, ancient appliances, and a kitchen table with metal legs and a speckled gray and white top. The cracked linoleum chafed the soles of his bare feet.

He walked over to the computer, which sat on the kitchen table, and pressed the power button. The hard drive hummed to life. Christian then wandered over to the ancient fridge and grabbed a packet of his nightly meal. Blood, pre-measured into small pouches. Eight ounces, just the right amount to keep him from going absolutely mad, but not enough to feed his preternatural abilities.

He dug around in one of the kitchen drawers until he found a straw. Puncturing the plastic, he swallowed a groan—the image of his fangs puncturing the fragile barrier of human flesh flashed through his mind. Damn, he missed that.

Why was he so antsy tonight? So uncomfortable with his developed routine? He made himself go over to the typed out and bulleted list on the fridge, held with a Red Cross

Blood Drive magnet. His twelve-step program. Based on the A.A. program, the steps changed to fit his own particular problem.

He read them again, and chanted the steps over and over to himself as he headed to his computer. He clicked onto the Internet and his site came up: Being Human.

Tonight, he didn't check the comments on yesterday's blog entry, although he did notice thirty-three people had posted. It was truly amazing what people would waste their time reading. Of course, he was the one who was wasting his time writing it.

"Therapy," he reminded himself as he pulled up the entry form to record tonight's thoughts.

And tonight he needed therapy. He could barely remain in his rickety, vinyl-covered chair. Why the hell did he feel like he was going to crawl out of his skin? Nothing was different than it had been for nearly a year.

Especially the lawn ornaments. He gritted his teeth and began to type.

> *It's official. Shady Fork Mobile Estates is hell.*
>
> *That being said, and I think I may have said it before, this place is no less than I deserve. But that doesn't mean I have to like it.*
>
> *So why Shady Fork, you ask? The world is filled with many, equally suitable hells. Well, I'd like to have a deep, very existential reason for you. Something about trying to better understand the plight of human suffering (and believe me, there is plenty of that in this delightful little neighborhood). Or maybe my . . .*

He glanced around at the darkly paneled walls, brown and gold carpeting, and tweed furniture.

> *. . . sumptuous abode was chosen to show myself the depths to which I have fallen. Which it does quite*

admirably. But the fact is, this was where I ran out of gas. Well, near here. And I figured that was a sign, right? So maybe my reason was a little existential. There you go. Who knew?

So back to my progress living as a human. So far on that count, I think I'm doing . . . okay. No slips into my natural behavior. No real feedings in 252 days. (Not that I'm counting.) I've stopped using any of my abilities that would be deemed "unnatural." I have to say getting around is a real annoyance—and far too time-consuming. An ironic statement for someone who has all the time in the world, I know. I think I may have complained about this in previous posts, too. I guess I was spoiled.

Outside the trailer, angry voices rose above the drone of the lawn ornaments. Christian didn't even bother to listen. It was practically a nightly occurrence. Shady Fork was like living in an episode of *Cops*—a form of reality entertainment he hadn't even known existed until he moved to this lovely place.

He shifted again in the uncomfortable chair, trying to find a measure of comfort. Comfort. He'd once lived in luxury. Lavish mansions, five-star hotels, waitstaff and limos, theater, parties with the rich and famous. Fast cars, champagne, the finest of everything. But that was another life. He wasn't that Christian Young anymore.

He frowned at the computer screen, unsure what to write next. The voices outside rose again, then quieted. He stared for a moment longer at the blog, then shoved out of the chair and paced the small living room. His fingers twitched as he considered taking a drive. The sleek, silver Porsche Carrera GT was the one extravagance he'd allowed himself to keep. But guilt strangled him. Why should he enjoy anything? He didn't deserve to, not after what he'd done.

"No," he muttered to himself. He wasn't that same vampire. He couldn't rectify his past deeds, but he could control the now. He could control his vampire nature. He'd done it for almost a year and he'd continue to do so. But instead of picking up the car keys from the scratched end table near the door, he returned to his computer.

Back to the reasoning behind living in a trailer park in the Blue Ridge Mountains. The reason I stay here is because it's a totally different place than what I knew. And I am a totally different being. As the blog title says, I'm working on being human.

Just then a loud scream pierced the air. A terrified sound, very different from the usual drunken shouting. He rose out of his seat and strode to the window. Pulling back one of the thick shades that covered his window, he didn't see anything. Then, across the rutted dirt road that served as the main entrance for the trailer park, he saw movement in the tall weeds. The head of a woman appeared behind a small bush.

He recognized the woman crouched in the high grass. She was the neighbor who lived in the trailer directly across from his. He'd never spoken to her, or any of the residents of Shady Fork for that matter, but he'd seen her a time or two, walking late at night. He'd wondered what she was doing wandering the desolate mountain roads in the late hours of the night. Of course, he'd never wondered enough to actually ask her.

Now, he wondered what she was doing crouching in the grass at—he glanced at his watch—three in the morning. Had she been the one who screamed?

She started, peeking toward her trailer, then she ducked back into hiding. Christian followed her quick look. A man exited her front door. The rangy silhouette clutched the railing of the steps with one hand, staggering, and waving something in the other hand.

"Come out, come out, wherever you are," the man shouted, his voice thick with a twangy southern accent.

The grass swayed, just a bit, but his neighbor didn't reveal her hiding spot. The man half-walked, half-fell down the steps, using the railing to steady himself. Once on the ground, he managed to keep his balance and started searching.

"Come on, Cherry," he called, his voice almost wheedling. "Come out."

When she didn't, he swiped a hand through his hair and roared, "Now! Goddamn it!"

He stepped farther into the thigh-high grass, raising whatever he held in his hand out in front of him. Light from the bare bulb on outside the trailer glinted on the object. A blade. The man headed in the exact direction of Cherry.

Christian didn't even register what he planned to do until he threw open his front door and hurried out into the road.

"Hey there," he called.

The man stopped, dropping the knife down to his side. Now Christian could see the tangle of greasy hair, the shine of sweat on his pasty skin, and the crazed glitter in his dark eyes. But the tall figure was just barely a man. He appeared no older than twenty or so.

"Can I help you?" Christian asked. The deranged kid obviously needed more help than Christian had to offer, but he thought it best not to provoke him.

"Fuck off, buddy," the kid growled. "This ain't any of your concern."

Christian noticed the grass move again, but Cherry didn't show herself. Wise lady. With his greatly depleted abilities, the likelihood he could reach the kid before the kid reached her was iffy at best.

"Maybe I should call the police?" Christian suggested.

The kid flashed the knife, sneering.

Christian raised an unimpressed eyebrow. He now saw the knife was actually a pocketknife. A large one, but not as menacing as he'd originally thought. Still, well-aimed, the blade could do real damage.

"Maybe you should just go back in your trailer and mind your own damned business," the kid warned, waving the knife again.

"I don't think I want to do that." Although in truth, that was exactly what Christian wanted to do. Instead he leisurely approached the armed youth.

Surprise and confusion played over the kid's face. He lifted the knife higher. Christian continued to stroll forward.

The kid actually backed up, unfortunately in the direction of Christian's neighbor.

Christian stopped. "You need to go now."

He concentrated, trying to use his mind control. The kid blinked and looked even more disoriented, if that was possible. Then he lifted the knife, waving it again in Christian's direction.

"Damn it, dude, don't you get it? This is none of your fuckin' business."

Christian stopped concentrating. Apparently his "being human" plan had been more effective than he'd thought, especially if he couldn't control someone this mentally feeble.

"Actually, I think a knife-wielding . . ." He frowned, trying to decide what to call this guy. Oh, why waffle on the matter? "Imbecile, in my neighborhood, is very much my business. Now, drop the knife." Good Lord, had he just officially named himself the head of the neighborhood watch?

The man wavered, uncertain what to make of Christian. But then he snarled and lunged at him. The pocketknife connected, slicing Christian's forearm as he deflected the strike, which he might add was aimed at his chest. This guy didn't mess around. Christian caught the kid's arm, spinning him and jerking the limb painfully behind his back.

The imbecile swore and dropped the knife. As Christian was about to kick the weapon across the gravel drive, his neighbor appeared out of the bushes and grabbed it.

She stood directly in front of her attacker, glaring at him with dark eyes.

"Vance, I'm not going to call the police. But I swear if I see you again, I will," she said. Her voice had the same accent as Vance's although on her it sounded very different, almost pleasant. She pointed the knife at Vance's chest. "I'm not kidding, Vance. This is the last warning I'm giving you."

Christian raised an eyebrow at that. She had given this jerk other warnings? How many chances had he had before? And was this woman as much of an imbecile as her assailant? The guy was planning to attack her with a knife.

"You bitch," the man muttered almost petulantly. "I need money."

"Then get a job, Vance," she told him, flicking the knife closed and slipping it in the pocket of her jeans.

"Dude, my arm is going to pop out of the socket," Vance complained to Christian, trying to look over his shoulder at him.

Christian couldn't resist tugging his arm up just a tad higher. The kid cried out and swore again.

"Let him go," Cherry told Christian.

"I don't think so. You might not be calling the police, but I plan to." These two had interrupted his . . . blogging. Someone was going to pay for that. Not to mention, they'd gotten him involved. And he had been damned successful at not getting involved with anyone.

"No," Cherry said, her dark eyes pleading.

Why on earth would she beg to help this idiot?

Her attention returned to Vance. "Vance, you have got to get help. I mean it. You are going to end up right back in prison again."

"Just give me some money, then."

"No, Vance. No."

The kid actually kicked the ground like a cranky child. "All right," he finally muttered.

"And don't you dare come back here unless you are clean," she added.

The kid mumbled something under his breath, then nodded.

Cherry stared at him for a moment, then looked to Christian. "Please let him go."

Even though it was against his better judgment, Christian released the kid. Vance shook out his arm, rotating the shoulder, and then like a rabbit released from a trap, he ran down the road toward the highway. Well, more like an inebriated rabbit. A few seconds later, Christian heard an engine start and wheels squealing on tar.

"Thank you," Cherry said, and smiled a little sheepishly. "I appreciate your help."

Christian nodded, still not certain what had actually happened here. "Right. Well . . ." What did humans say in bizarre circumstances like this? "Good night, then."

He had turned to head back to the normal security of his trailer when her hand caught his. He startled at the contact, her fingers small and very warm curled around his.

"Oh my God, you're hurt."

He frowned. Her touch had surprised him, but it didn't hurt. Then he noticed she was staring at his arm. He glanced down and saw a large patch of blood had soaked through the sleeve of his shirt.

"Oh. That." He shrugged. "It's nothing."

He started to leave again, but she didn't release his fingers. Instead she tugged him in the opposite direction.

"Come inside and let me look at it."

Refusal was right there on his lips. Then he looked at her wide smile, and for some unknown reason, like why he came to her aid in the first place, he allowed her to lead him into her trailer.

The layout of the trailer mimicked his own. Except his was actually homier, if that was possible. She led him into the kitchen to the sink.

"Stay right here," she ordered, then disappeared down the

hallway. Christian glanced around the room. No wonder she was roaming around the countryside at night. She didn't exactly have a welcoming home to relax in. The kitchen was devoid of all furniture and the living room only had three metal folding chairs arranged around a beaten-up steamer trunk.

And Vance had come to this woman looking for money? That was very optimistic of him.

"Okay," she said as she returned with a rather threadbare but clean-looking towel. "Let's take a look at this cut."

He watched as she set the towel on the counter and reached for the buttons on the cuff of his sleeve. She *tsked*. "Too bad. This looks like an expensive shirt."

It was, but he didn't say anything. Instead he watched her slender, pale fingers work on the buttons. He frowned. Why did he find the simple action so fascinating?

"I don't know," she said, studying the large amount of blood already drying to the blond hair on his forearm. "Maybe we should go right to the doctor. It's bled a lot."

"No," he said, starting to pull his arm away, but she caught his hand, those slim fingers curling around his.

"Okay," she agreed, "but let me clean it for you. It's the least I can do after you helping me."

He didn't agree, but he didn't pull away. She took the towel and wet one corner with warm water. Carefully, she brushed the cloth over his arm in gentle sweeps.

"Does that hurt?"

He shook his head. No, it didn't hurt in the least. In fact, it was oddly pleasurable. The pressure of her warm fingers on his skin. Her nearness. Not until she looked up at him, a questioning look in her eyes, did he realize she hadn't seen his response.

"No, it doesn't hurt," he said, his voice low.

She stared at him for a moment, then returned to her ministrations. This time, Christian didn't watch what she was doing. He studied her. In the brief glimpses he'd seen of her before, he'd never taken note of her looks. But now, close up, he saw she was a very attractive mortal with dark red hair, almost wine-colored, like a strong merlot. Her features were fragile and pale like fine bone china, with high cheekbones, a straight nose, and the most lush mouth he'd ever seen, deep pink, plump and wide. He wondered how lips like that would feel under his.

He jerked back, disturbed by the direction of his thoughts. He hadn't even considered kissing a mortal in nearly two hundred years.

She immediately stopped cleaning his arm and stared up at him with wide eyes, brown flecked with gold. "Did I hurt you?"

He shook his head, his eyes again dropping to her full lips. He breathed in deeply. "No."

She hadn't hurt him, but something about this woman was addling his brain. What the hell was he thinking finding her attractive? He didn't find mortals attractive. Ever.

She regarded him closely, and he wondered for a moment if he was vamping out in some way. Had his irises widened, making his eyes totally black? Or had his skin pulled taut over his bones? Was a fang hanging out of the corner of his mouth?

Not that she looked frightened. She actually looked . . . concerned?

He was, too. His reactions were not normal.

She dabbed at his arm again, her touch even gentler. Little raspy caresses of the towel, which felt . . . nice. Yes, he was definitely acting, or rather reacting, strangely.

He took in another deep breath to steady himself. A rich, spicy scent like warm honey and cinnamon filled his nostrils. Her scent. His body reacted, his muscles tensing, his fingers twitching. And his cock hardened, both tense *and* twitching in his pants. What the hell?

"Are you sure this doesn't hurt?" she asked again.

He started to shake his head, but then he remembered he

actually had to speak, since she was looking at his arm rather than his face.

"No."

"I'm almost done."

Thank God. He breathed in again, and her luscious scent assailed him, stronger and more tempting than before.

Were his vampy powers coming back? He'd truly believed he had them under control, practically ineffectual. But his acute sense of smell was working fine. Although the scent he smelled wasn't the rusty, salty scent of blood. The heat and spices were just her.

But what caught him more off guard than her scent was his reaction to it. He was aroused. And he'd never been aroused by a mortal unless it was caused by the hunger.

He ran his tongue over his canines. They were normal. The rock-hard erection in his trousers was not. He always had simultaneous erections. Fangs, cock. Fangs, cock. That was just how it worked. So what the hell was going on?

"There," she said, shifting away from him. "All clean."

He immediately stepped back, hoping distance would calm him. This was just too strange.

Chapter 2

Jolee frowned. Her neighbor was a strange guy. Not that she was surprised. She'd noticed him before. After all, it was pretty darn hard to ignore a hunky model type with designer clothes and a car that cost ten times her yearly income, and that was if she was lucky, living across from her in a run-down trailer park. There was definitely a story there. She'd even invented one or two of her own.

But until tonight, she'd never considered talking to him for two very good reasons. One, he had to be trouble. Again, guys like this one did not live in Shady Fork Mobile Estates, unless they were in deep doo-doo. And number two, she was too smart and too busy to get involved with trouble. Even on a non-romantic basis. She'd had enough of that in her life, thank you very much.

But tonight had really added a new twist to her two-point plan. He'd rescued her. She could have protected herself from Vance if she'd had to. Although it had been really nice not to have to. To have someone stick up for her.

She simply hadn't expected help. She knew full well that people often ignored others in trouble. Like she'd planned to ignore her neighbor. But he hadn't ignored her.

Of course, she *had* been screaming on her front lawn at three in the morning. But then, no one else had come to her aid. And this guy had even gotten hurt protecting her. If he wasn't already sexy as hell that would have definitely added to his appeal. It was rather nice to have a hero around.

"I don't think you are mortally wounded," she said. When his brows drew together in confusion, she pointed to his arm. "Your arm. It bled a lot, but the cut was actually quite small."

"Oh." He glanced down at his bloodstained sleeve as if just remembering the wound. "Yeah, it's fine."

He nodded as if he didn't have any idea what else to say, which apparently he didn't. He started toward the door.

"Can I get you something to eat?" she blurted out, then winced. It was three in the morning. What were the chances he was hungry? Not that she had much to offer him if he *was* hungry. The invitation was just the first thing that popped into her mind. The truth was she didn't want him to leave. He was the only company she'd had since she moved here, aside from her knife-wielding brother, and she was lonely. She didn't even realize how much until now.

He hesitated, then instead of answering her question, he asked one of his own. "Was that kid—Vance? Are you together in some way?"

Jolee blinked and then laughed, although there was not much humor in the sound. There wasn't much that was funny about her family in general.

"No. Definitely not. He's my brother."

He seemed to consider that for a moment, then he nodded. To her surprise, he walked toward her, a leisurely, almost predatory quality to his movements. His unusual, pale blue eyes locked on her.

Her heart pounded violently in her chest as his hand came out and caught a strand of her hair, which had escaped from its ponytail.

"Your hair. I've never seen this color before."

From the corners of her eyes, Jolee watched him rub the

curling lock, testing the texture. Her heart threatened to hop right out of her chest as she imagined those long, masculine fingers touching parts of her body that actually had nerve endings.

"The color is a little unusual, I guess," she said. Not as unusual as his eyes, which were such a pale blue they appeared almost white. She pulled in a calming breath, forcing herself to look away from his beautiful face.

"That's why you're named Cherry," he said, almost like a revelation to himself.

She frowned for a moment, not following the conversation, probably due to the lack of oxygen getting to her brain. Or maybe too much oxygen, given that her heart was in overdrive. Then she recalled her brother using the dreaded nickname when he'd been yelling for her. "That's one reason, among others."

He frowned, puzzled.

"It's not my real name," she added quickly, as she'd rather not go into the fact that her brothers had mainly called her Cherry to mock her morality and the fact that she actually *didn't* want to sleep around like her other siblings. They had found her virginity a great source of amusement.

"My name is Jolee. Jolee Dugan."

He stared at her for a moment, his gaze going from her eyes to linger on her lips. Jolee's breath caught in her throat as he slowly leaned closer. He was going to kiss her, she realized.

Her heart revved again. A thrill tingled over her skin; her own gaze dropped to his mouth. His top lip bowed in the center and the bottom one was fuller, pale pink, soft-looking and yet infinitely masculine. His head descended.

Then, as if he'd been burnt, he stepped back from her. He shook his head slightly as if to clear his thoughts.

"I should go."

She frowned, confused by his sudden and strange behaviors. "Are you all right?"

He studied her with those almost eerie eyes, then nodded. He started for the door. Even with his odd reactions, Jolee didn't want him to leave. Maybe she was more shaken by the incident with Vance than she thought. Or maybe she simply was lonely. Living alone, running a bar essentially by herself, it had been a lonesome time. She wanted to feel like she was connecting with someone.

"You know, you haven't told me your name."

He stopped again, casting a look over his shoulder. He frowned as if the idea of telling his name to her was a foreign concept.

"So, your name?" she prodded. "You do have one, don't you? I can't very well call the neighborhood hero, 'Hey you,' now can I?"

He turned back to her, and he actually looked a little uncomfortable. But then, as if the awkwardness hadn't ever been there, his jaw tensed and his eyes grew frosty like chips of pale blue ice. He lifted his chin, and she fully understood the phrase "looking down your nose." She didn't think she'd ever seen anyone look so arrogant.

"You know, as much as I love breaking up family squabbles, I do have things I have to do."

"Oh," she said, stunned by his cool tone, wondering what she'd said to offend him. She did suppose it was a little annoying to have to break up a fight at this time of night, and he *had* gotten cut in the process. But he didn't have to be quite so haughty about the whole thing. She didn't say that, however. She didn't want to appear ungrateful. She appreciated his help. He had been a hero, and she knew those were too few and far between.

"Well, thank you," she said, following him to the door. She reached for the handle just as he did. Their fingers touched, his on top of hers. Again he jolted away as if the back of her hand was made of molten lava. She dropped her hold on the doorknob, too, startled by his response.

"Sorry," she said, offering him a small smile. Was he reacting this way because he was or wasn't attracted to her? From his deadpan expression, she couldn't tell. "You know, I was thinking, maybe, if you are interested—"

"Your name, Jolee—is that as in French for pretty?"

The question caught her off guard. She smiled wider at the idea, but then she said, "Hardly."

"No, I thought not," he said coolly. He reached for the doorknob. She didn't stop him this time as he stepped outside.

Jolee remained rooted to the spot, unable to react. Finally, she managed to gather her thoughts enough to go get one of the metal chairs in the living room and wedge the back under the door handle. She needed to get a better lock, she thought to herself. A chain lock. Or a deadbolt. Or . . .

She'd nearly been stabbed by her brother over money she didn't have, and now her weird neighbor had just called her ugly. What a great night.

She laughed out loud, the sound more hysterical than humorous. Thinking about better security wasn't going to erase the embarrassment tightening her chest. Here she'd been thinking her neighbor seemed attracted to her, and he essentially told her how unattractive he really found her. Man, was she that clueless?

She shook her head, telling herself his opinion didn't matter. After all, he had to have issues. A person didn't have the clothes and car and cultured voice he had and live in a run-down trailer park. Something was not right with him. Not to mention he seemed more than a little socially dysfunctional. She had enough of that in her own family. She didn't need to go befriending it.

Still, his words and his arrogant look stung. And reminded her that unlike him, she did belong here. No one would be surprised to find a Dugan in a place like this. No one expected her to make anything out of herself. But she was damned well going to try to. And she wasn't going to waste her time dwelling on her snotty neighbor.

* * *

Christian entered his trailer, shutting the door tightly. Then he twisted the lock for good measure.

This was crazy. He was anxious over a mortal. A mortal woman. Why? It had to be this strange agitation he'd been feeling all night. That was the only answer. But what was different? He didn't know. He just knew that he had to get these feelings under control.

But even now, he felt inexplicably drawn to her. He walked over to the window and looked out at her trailer. All her lights were on. He could go back over.

And do what? Be friends? What did he have in common with a mortal woman? He'd given up his vampire ways to reinvent himself. To no longer be the Christian Young who . . . He didn't actually plan to hang out with humans. Okay, Step Eleven: Making Contact, did sound like he was supposed to do just that. But he blogged—and that was contact.

He turned away from the window. He needed to focus on his plan. He went to the refrigerator. He must have been tempted by the scent of her blood. He'd just been hungry. Maybe he needed to up his pre-measured portions of blood to ten ounces from eight. That was probably it.

"Calm down," he told himself, going to the refrigerator to read his list of steps. "Step Three: You must surrender to the fact you do have a problem, and then find a way to deal constructively with the problem."

But you didn't have the urge to drink her blood. He turned from the list, pacing the small kitchen. He'd wanted to touch her. Feel the smooth texture of her skin, taste the softness of her wide lips. And he just didn't have those kinds of feelings about mortals.

He pulled in a deep breath. It had been a fluke. A little unexpected side effect of his strict feeding plan. No big deal. And he wasn't going to see Jolee again. Not to talk to. He'd insulted her to guarantee that very thing. An image of Jolee's surprised, then wounded expression flashed through his mind. A twinge of guilt pulled at his gut.

Why fret over a mortal? They are of no importance.

He looked around as if the voice in his head were real. Lilah's voice, deceptively sweet. The voice of his vampire lover, and evil incarnate.

Why would he think of her now? The vampiress who'd crossed him over, crossed over his brothers, and destroyed his family. He'd forced her out of his thoughts. Yet, he could see her clearly in his mind. Her patronizing look when he'd been horrified by the results of his first feeding, by what he'd done to another human being.

"But you aren't a human being, not anymore," Lilah had informed him. "You are a vampire, and you are mine. That makes you far more important than any mere mortal."

And he'd believed her. He'd become what he was because he'd believed.

Why was he thinking about this? He wasn't that vampire anymore! He wasn't. He'd changed. His self-imposed exile, his routine, his self-therapy. It was all making him . . . better.

Yes, and how Lilah would laugh if she could see him now. Living in a trailer, drinking blood through a straw, hiding from his neighbor.

This is your brilliant plan of redemption?

Again his thoughts took on Lilah's lilting, mocking tone.

No! This was a good plan. It was working. He just needed to be more careful. He needed to adjust his blood intake. He needed to avoid situations where the hunger might appear. He needed to stay calm. His reaction to Jolee was hardly "falling off the wagon."

"You just need to be a little more vigilant. By tomorrow night, you will be fine," he told himself. He shook his head, chuckling derisively. "You also need to stop talking to yourself."

He strode into the living room and turned on the TV. The

chatter of voices filled the room. A comforting sound. A sound that drowned out the whir of lawn ornaments and the drone in his own head.

"At just nineteen-ninety-five the Salad Shooter is already an incredible value. But that's not all you get. We are also including the World's Best Vegetable Peeler, the only peeler you will ever have to buy again. *And* the Super Corer—core apples, pears, even tomatoes with just a flick of your wrist. All this for one low price. But this offer cannot last. Call now!"

Christian stared at the beaming face on the television screen. Another infomercial. He'd seen this one before, but he focused on the adamant pitch of the salesperson as he continued his spiel.

Did mortals really live in a world where the Salad Shooter could make their entire lives better? The overly cheery salesperson certainly implied that, and Christian couldn't help but feel envious of the possibility. He thought of Jolee, wondering what would make her life better. Even thinking about her seemed to make his muscles tense, and his body react. This had to stop.

He strode back to his computer and punched it to life. He sat down, pulled up his blog and added:

Postscript:
I realized I've never asked my blog readers how they are. How is everyone?

There. He'd made contact. Step Eleven successfully completed. Now he could forget about Jolee.

Chapter 3

"**D**amn it," Jolee muttered as she dropped another glass. Her third of the night. At least this one didn't break. She couldn't afford new barware.

"What's got you so preoccupied tonight?" Jed asked.

She smiled at the old man who had sort of come with the bar. He lived in a building, which was no better than a shack, really, out behind the bar. Jolee had agreed that for his rent, he could handle the janitorial duties for the bar.

"Nothing. Just a clumsy night, I guess."

He nodded, but she didn't think he believed her. He was right not to, because everything was on her mind tonight. Vance's attack. Money. Her arrogant, rude neighbor with his snooty airs.

Money was certainly the biggest concern. After all, she'd spent years worrying about her degenerate siblings, and that had never done any good. She needed to expend her energies on her bar. And making it work.

The bar was relatively busy for a Wednesday night, which meant about twenty patrons. And twenty patrons a night wasn't going to keep her in business. But even with that very real worry, it was her condescending neighbor who'd been eating at her. Popping back into her mind over and over. Making her clumsy.

She didn't understand why. Maybe because she'd really hoped they might become friends. But he'd made it clear that wasn't happening. And as disappointed as she was to discover her neighbor was not friend material, she was even more bothered by his insult. So he thought she wasn't pretty. She could handle that. It was what else he'd implied that had cut her to the quick. His mocking comment had also implied she wasn't classy enough to have some fancy French name.

And that bothered her, because it was the same crap she'd heard her whole life. Her family was no good. *She* was no good. But she was more than her last name—or her first name, for that matter. She knew that, and she intended to prove it.

Her confrontation with Vance and her neighbor's comment just had her resolve a little shaken. But both men had shown her she just had to work harder to prove she could be a success.

She looked around the bar she'd owned for almost three months. She could do this. Other people's opinions didn't mean squat. She sighed. How many times had she given herself the same pep talk while growing up? But this time she meant it. Two jerks weren't going to stop her.

She got a new glass and filled the bottom with two fingers of rum, then she topped that off with ice and cola. She repeated the process two more times, setting each drink on a round tray. She picked up the tray and went out to deliver the drinks. Then she cleared some of the glasses from other tables, still chanting to herself that she could make this bar into a successful business. She had to.

"Hey, sweet cheeks, another pitcher over here."

Jolee nodded in acknowledgment without looking toward the table. She set down her tray of empty beer mugs, then turned her back to the long, dark wood counter. Bracing her hands on the edge, she levered herself up onto the nicked wooden surface and swung her legs around to jump down on the other side. She heard a whistle as she performed her little feat of acrobatics, but she ignored it. Whistles and cat calls seemed to come with the territory of being a bar owner. Well, a female bar owner anyway.

She quickly placed the dirty mugs into the sink filled with hot, soapy water, then she turned to grab a clean pitcher. Patsy Cline's "Walking After Midnight" played on the ancient jukebox against the far wall between the doorways of the ladies' and men's rooms.

As she filled the pitcher, she lined up three more glasses and poured shots of Jack Daniels into each. Not only was it busy, but the patrons were drinking. Always good in a bar.

Well, sort of good. As she loaded another tray, she cast a glance toward the table of men who insisted on using that lovely little nickname for her. The five men actually looked a bit more respectable than some of her other patrons in their tucked-in shirts, loosened ties, and chinos. But as they drank, they'd gotten louder and ruder. Several times they had attempted to touch her as she delivered drinks to them.

Patrons did that, but it was usually meant in good fun. A laugh and a flip comment would make things cool again. She hoped the same would be true with these men. They seemed a little more forward, and cockier. And they seemed interested in her.

Even now, one of them in a blue button-down shirt and pressed dark blue pants stared at her as she finished loading her tray. And she knew he wasn't checking on the status of his beer.

"Good night," Jed commented in his gravelly voice, jerking a head toward the very full tray.

Jolee wiped the back of her hand across her brow to push her sweaty hair away from her face, and smiled. "Not bad."

"I'd watch them boys, though," he rasped around the cigarette he was lighting. Again he gestured with his head to the table she was already well aware of.

"Yeah, I am." This was the first night she actually felt like she might have a real problem with her customers. On the whole, her patrons just wanted some cold beer and a little conversation. But those men, they seemed like trouble.

She glanced back at the table. The same guy and one of his pals watched her.

Dale Timmons, a regular since she'd reopened the place, waved to her that he'd like another beer. She smiled to let him know that she saw him. She reached down to the shelf beside her and grabbed a mug, filling it. Before she headed back to the floor, she walked down the bar to give Dale his beer.

"Busy, eh?" Dale, a man in his fifties in his ever-present John Deere baseball cap, smiled at her. As usual, Jolee had the inclination to give the older man a hug—his gray eyes always seemed filled with such sadness, like a lost hound dog.

"Yeah, not too bad, but it could always be busier," she said with an easy smile.

Dale nodded. "It will be. Just give it time."

"From your lips to God's ears." Jolee only had so much time to give. Money had to start coming in.

"When are you getting the karaoke going?" Dale asked, as he had every now and then since Leo's Brew Pub and Karaoke Saloon reopened under her management.

Jolee had specifically bought the bar because the place was equipped with a karaoke sound system, the monitors to show the lyrics, and thousands of songs, just waiting to be sung by talented and untalented patrons alike.

"Well, if I can keep business steady, I should be able to start again soon." Lord, she hoped. "I'd have to hire another person to tend bar while I ran the sound system. And right now, finances are just a little too tight for me to hire anyone."

Dale nodded again. "It'll come."

"Hey, sweet cheeks," one of the men from the questionable table called to her. "Are you going to bring us our beer or what?"

She jerked her head in response, then offered Dale a quick smile. "Just keep coming, Dale, and I'll get this place going again."

Dale smiled, the smile not meeting his sad gray eyes. "Will do."

Jolee picked up the heavy tray and walked the length of the bar to exit out onto the floor. She delivered all the other drinks, leaving the pitcher for last. As she approached, all the men watched her with eager expressions, and she knew the anticipation wasn't for the beer.

"Thanks, babe," the blue-shirted man said as she leaned forward to place the pitcher in the center of the table.

She forced a polite smile, then turned to leave, but the man snagged her wrist, pulling her to a halt.

"Where are you going so fast?"

"I have work to do," she stated, yanking her wrist out of the man's tight hold.

The man held up his hands in a pose of surrender. "No need to get so touchy. We'd just like to chat with you awhile."

A couple of the other men snickered, but Jolee ignored them.

"Well, as I said"—she forced another smile—"I don't have time." Nor the inclination, but she didn't add that. Best to play it polite. Money was money—even from overbearing jerks.

"Oh, come on, it's not too busy. Have a seat." He gestured with his thumb for the man next to him to stand, which he did. The blue-shirted guy nudged the chair back farther with his foot.

"Come on, sit."

Jolee shook her head. "No. Sorry." She started away from the table, furious with herself that these jerks were making her nervous. She'd have to learn to deal with more than this. She knew that.

"Playing hard to get, huh?" The comment was followed by loud chuckles.

Jolee stopped, spinning back to them. "Maybe I am hard to get."

One of the men whistled and nudged the blue-shirted guy. She started back to the bar.

"Well, playing hard to get is fine as long as I get some eventually."

Jolee spun around again, even as her better judgment told her to just go back to the bar. Check on her other patrons. Something.

"What did you say?" she demanded from the blue-shirted guy. He seemed to be the ringleader of the group.

The man looked untroubled by her sharp question. "Nothing to get all het up about."

She glared at them. *Just stay calm. Blow it off. They've been drinking.* But her thoughts didn't calm her.

"I think maybe you gentlemen should leave."

The man smiled, unfazed by her suggestion. She noted that his teeth were white and straight and utterly wasted on him. "That's not very hospitable of you. But you could make it up to me."

He stood up. He wasn't overly tall, about eye level with Jolee, but he was wide with muscled shoulders and a barrel chest.

She stepped back from him, her bottom bumping a chair behind her.

"What do you say? Want to meet me later?"

"Not a chance," she stated, keeping her voice calm even as she gripped the edge of the tray she still held, preparing to hit the jerk with it if necessary.

"And I'd had you pegged as a woman who knows a good opportunity when you see it." The man's eyes raked down her body, making her T-shirt and jeans feel downright indecent.

"Rick, leave her alone," one of his buddies said.

Rick glanced at the other man as if he wanted to argue. But then, to Jolee's relief, he did sit down, although he still watched her with hungry eyes.

"I think you better leave," she repeated, this time to the man who'd called off Rick. She pushed away from the chair and walked away, keeping her pace steady, refusing to let Rick know how much he'd shaken her. She knew they were watching her, but she didn't glance in their direction as she put the bar between herself and the men.

The ache that had been in her chest all night intensified. The jerk had frightened her, but more than that, he'd just been the last straw. Vance, snotty neighbor, and now this guy. Another guy treating her like dirt.

Tears threatened to choke her, but she bit the inside of her lip and swallowed them back. She wouldn't cry. Not about this. Not about anything. Tears didn't solve a thing.

"Have you ever had the feeling that you are the butt of some colossal joke?" she managed to ask Jed after a few moments.

"All the time." He reached for his pack of cigarettes and tamped one out. "All the time," he repeated as he lit the tip.

"Me, too," she said, mostly to herself.

The men left shortly after that, much to Jolee's relief. They even left money enough for their bill and a decent tip, probably thanks to the guy who'd spoken up for her. But Jolee was too distressed by the whole incident to feel any satisfaction over the slight victory. Even the fact that the night turned out to be the best she'd had since she opened didn't lift her spirits.

As she finished washing up the glasses, she couldn't think about anything but that man's behavior toward her. And her neighbor's. Both of them made her feel so small. So much lower than themselves. And no matter how many times she told herself they were both jerks, she still felt depressed.

"The bathrooms are all cleaned," Jed said, coming out of the men's room with a bucket and mop. "And I'm heading to bed."

"Thanks, Jed," she said, still preoccupied with her own thoughts as she placed the last of the dried mugs on the shelf under the bar.

"Jolee girl."

She glanced up, surprised by the old man's nickname for her. He leaned on the mop, his wispy white hair and beard looking a little like a mane. He reminded her a bit of Santa's skinny, chain-smoking brother—if Santa had one of those.

"It was a good night," he said with an encouraging grin that showed the many craggy lines around his blue eyes.

She nodded. She didn't feel good. She felt lousy—and alone. At this point, Jed was about the only person she could call a real friend. But she wouldn't talk to him about her problems. The old guy had his own issues, aging and alone and living in squalor behind a bar.

"Night." He stopped in the doorway to light a cigarette before stepping out into the warm night.

"Jed," she called before he disappeared into the night. "You want a snack to take home with you? I have some extra pretzels and nuts in the storeroom."

"I'm good," he said with a nod. "But I appreciate the offer." He waved and disappeared into the dark.

She wished she had more to offer the old man, but at this point, she didn't have much else herself. Even with this relatively good night, she was going to be lucky to make her mortgage payment this month.

There's always someone with less, she reminded herself.

She crossed the bar to flip the lock on the back door and slide the heavy bolt above the handle closed. She finished turning down the lights in the main room, then she headed to her small office to double-check her safe, an ancient gray block beside her equally ancient desk. Everything was locked tight.

She picked up her tote bag, and fumbled with her few keys to get the right one for the door out of her office. She stepped out the door and then inserted the key in the lock.

She needed an alarm system, another thing to add to the list of improvements she hoped to make at Leo's. Another thing that would have to wait a while.

The night was warm, and thankfully clear. A half moon hung in the indigo sky, and she could easily see her way to the black strip of paved road.

All the same, she rooted through her bag for her small flashlight. Twisting the top of the narrow black cylinder, the small bulb lit, although it barely cast a beam two feet in front of her. The batteries weren't going to last much longer, and normally she wouldn't have wasted them on a clear night like tonight. But she needed the reassurance of the faint glow. It made her feel better. A little anyway.

Usually, she didn't mind the walk home. But tonight, after that man's come-on and Vance's threatening visit the night before, well, she'd just as soon get home as fast as possible.

Chapter 4

Sometimes I don't know if this plan of mine is really about becoming someone different or just trying to erase the past. Do you think it's even possible to erase the past? I don't know.

I know I'm not hurting anyone anymore. But I'm not making any real amends to those I hurt before. A very important step to recovery. Number Nine on the list, actually. Forgiveness.

How do you ever make up for the worst thing you can possibly do to another? You can't. Maybe this plan is doomed from the start. I'm sorry Rhys, Sebastian, Elizabeth, and Jane. I wish I had understood sooner.

On an upnote, I did get my Popeil Solid Food Injector. So if I want to make a roast with chunks of garlic inside it, then I'm all set.

Christian slammed the stick shift into gear, then pressed the pedal farther to the floor. The engine of his Porsche revved and accepted the push for speed readily.

The shadowy trees tunneled around him, a blur of black on either side of him. He barely registered them, instead staring at the road in front of him. The tires spun faster and faster as more and more road disappeared under his car.

He'd allowed himself to drive tonight. To run away for just a while. But the driving, always a reliable source of escape, wasn't working. No, now racing through the dark didn't give him even the slightest measure of contentment.

He told himself that he'd rise tonight and his reaction to Jolee would be gone. A good day of unnatural slumber was the cure for most ailments. But nothing had changed. He still couldn't stop thinking about her.

He gripped the steering wheel, trying to concentrate on the vibration of the vehicle around him. But instead of feeling the purr of the engine, he could only remember the sensation of her softly accented voice caressing his skin.

He pushed the buttons on the armrest, and the windows glided open, allowing the warm spring air to gust through the car. The earthy, rich scents of new foliage mingled with the scent of leather. He breathed in deeply, only to have that smell replaced by the memory of sweet cinnamon and honey.

He growled, the sound lost in the whip of the wind. Why couldn't he get this mortal out of his head? He couldn't satisfy his hunger, not with her. Not with any mortal. So why did he ache for her? He'd even fed more than usual tonight. He could feel the warmth of the extra blood in his body. But that warmth didn't soothe the need deep inside him.

He hadn't been able to stop thinking about her. Jolee. Even now, he wondered if she was home. Was she okay? Did she hate him? Again he saw her face as he'd last seen it, her lovely, dark eyes widened with surprise, then pain.

He punched his foot down until he felt the pedal connect with the floorboard. The trees and road were a dizzying blur all around him. Suddenly her face was in front of him, small in the distance, blindingly pale, eyes wide and stricken. That face would haunt him.

Almost too late, he realized the image wasn't his memory, a tormenting figment of his imagination. She was real. In front of him.

He slammed on the brakes, jerking the wheel. The tires skidded on the tar, rubber melting and burning as he slid closer and closer toward that face. Toward Jolee.

He wasn't going to make it. A wave of panic and helplessness choked him. He was going to hit her. But at the last moment, it was Jolee who reacted, jumping away from the careening vehicle. The car spun, and he lost sight of where she might have gone. Finally the wheels caught and the car rocked to a halt in the center of the now empty road.

Christian jerked the gear shift into neutral and scrambled out of the car. The night was quiet, except for the low rumble of the car's engine. He ran toward where he thought she'd been, searching the dark, his night vision not focusing as quickly as it should have because of his weakened state and his panic.

"Damn it," he shouted, rushing to the side of the road, scanning the ditch, growing more agitated. Then he saw her, a crumpled mass of limbs among some rocks and weeds.

Suddenly he wasn't seeing Jolee. He was seeing another mortal. A tiny woman with short, dark hair and huge green eyes. His brother's woman, the woman he'd killed in a false sense of vengeance. Jane.

Nausea gripped his stomach, but he forced himself to ignore it. He scrambled down the small embankment toward Jolee. Not Jane, Jolee. And she wasn't dead. She couldn't be. He couldn't have killed another innocent mortal.

His eyes better adjusted and now he could see her well. He could see she had a scrape on her arm, blood glistening in the moonlight. The wound seemed to be shallow and not life-threatening. His eyes moved on.

He was more worried about her head, which had hit the rocks. He knelt beside her, holding his hand over her body. He could feel her life energy, strong, warming his fingers. And he could see her heart beat, even at the base of her throat. She didn't seem to be in any distress, but he was still concerned that something might be wrong with her neck or her head.

Unsure what to do, he hesitated. He didn't know much about the care of mortals. Medicine had been pretty archaic back in the days when he might have needed it. But he seemed to recall, perhaps on one of the late-night reruns of *St. Elsewhere* he'd been watching occasionally, that it was dangerous to move a mortal with possible head or spinal damage.

He needed to get an ambulance here. He stood, debating what to do, when Jolee moaned. He dropped back down beside her.

"Jolee, can you hear me?"

She groaned again, bringing a hand up to her temple. She blinked up at him, then blinked again before mumbling, "What? Telling me I'm ugly wasn't enough? You had to run me down, too?"

Relief and then regret swept through his chest. "I didn't see you. I'm sorry."

She struggled to sit up. Christian placed an arm behind her back, helping her. She jerked away from his touch, then winced and rubbed her shoulder.

"Let me see." Christian stood and stepped from rock to rock to reach her other side. He squatted down and gently rolled back the dirt-covered sleeve of her T-shirt. The pale skin of her shoulder was mottled with purple bruises.

"Can you lift your arm?" he asked.

She nodded, but didn't offer to show him.

"Are you sure?"

"I can, but that doesn't mean I want to. It hurts like hell."

Christian would have smiled, if he didn't feel so guilty.

Being careful not to touch the bruise, he pulled her shirt back down over her injury. "I think we should get you to a doctor."

"No," she cried, then more calmly she repeated, "No."

"You could have a . . ." What was an injury to the head called? "A concussion."

"No," she said again. "I'll be fine. Just help me up."

Christian stood, taking both her hands to steady her. She winced again as she levered herself up, but she managed to get her footing and stand. He started to place an arm around her back to assist her, but again, she shrugged him off.

"I'm okay," she insisted, and began to pick her way over the uneven terrain.

Christian stayed close, several times wanting to steady her when she swayed. But she would pause for a moment, get her bearings, then continue on. At the edge of the road, she came to a stop, looking around, her eyes dazed.

"Are you feeling unwell?" he asked. Fearing she was going to pass out, he moved closer to her.

"My tote bag," she said, blinking around. "I had a tote bag."

"Just wait here. Let me look."

She opened her mouth as though she planned to argue, but then she nodded. He found the bag with no problem, in a cluster of wildflowers about six feet from where she'd landed. Luckily, the bag was still zipped.

"Found it," he called to her, as he joined her back on the soft shoulder of the road. He noticed her skin looked even paler than when he first found her, and her eyes were glazed.

"Jolee?"

She blinked at him. He could sense her wooziness, her confusion. He immediately scooped her up, trying to be as gentle as possible, not wanting to jar her injuries.

She stiffened in his hold. "Put me down."

"You are too hurt to walk."

She didn't argue, but she didn't relax against him either. She kept herself positioned as far away from him as his hold would allow, her head angled away from his. He hurried to his car. With her cradled in one arm like a baby, he opened the door with the other. If she was surprised by the feat of strength, she didn't show it as he then placed her in the passenger seat.

Instead she let her head fall back against the headrest and closed her eyes. Her hands lay palm up, limp in her lap.

For a moment, Christian feared she'd lost consciousness again, but then she murmured, "I must be mad allowing myself to be placed in the deathmobile."

Christian nearly smiled again, relieved she was still awake. Of course, she didn't realize quite how accurate that title for his car really was.

He sprinted around the vehicle and got in. He shifted into gear, this time easing into motion, trying not to jerk her too much. Glancing over at her, he could see her color hadn't improved. Her eyes were still shut, although now she had the hand of her left arm cupping the elbow of her right as if to hold the limb steady.

"Are you in terrible pain?"

She didn't respond for a moment, then she said, her voice soft as though she didn't really have the energy to talk, "Is there such a thing as good pain?"

Christian didn't answer. He knew she was attempting to be funny, but he also knew she was hurt badly. He nudged the gas pedal a little more, still trying to keep his driving steady and smooth, but he needed to get her to help.

The drive to the hospital only took fifteen minutes, but to Christian it seemed like forever. Fortunately he knew where it was. To his shame, he'd gone there one evening when the hospital was holding a local blood drive—the lure of fresh blood almost too much for him. He had left before he'd even entered the building. Step 10: Maintenance. Continue to take personal inventory, and when you are wrong promptly admit it and rectify it.

Jolee hadn't said a word or opened her eyes for the remainder of the drive, and he was pretty sure she'd fallen unconscious. He got out of the car and came around to her side. When he started to lift her out of the seat, she opened her eyes only to immediately close them again against the bright lights of the hospital entrance.

But that didn't stop her from pushing at his chest with her good arm. "No hospital."

She squinted up at him, her lush mouth set into a firm line.

"Jolee, you need medical attention."

"I'll be fine."

He easily restrained her, trying to be as careful of her injured arm as he could. "You are not fine. You lost consciousness on the way here. Your shoulder is badly bruised. You need to see a physician."

Jolee's head pounded, her shoulder throbbed, but still she tried to wriggle out of her neighbor's grasp. She couldn't go to a doctor. She couldn't afford that. And without insurance, the fees were bound to be astronomical.

Despite her current pain, she knew she'd be all right. Sore for a few days, but she'd be okay. She was not going to pay a doctor an exorbitant sum just to tell her to take some ibuprofen and tough it out.

But fighting off her neighbor was not easy. She wasn't even sure it was possible. He was a tall man with broad shoulders and lean muscles. But he was even stronger than his model-like physique would imply. It was like trying to wrestle a brick wall. Finally she stopped squirming, too tired and sore to continue.

"This is ridiculous. I told you I'll be fine."

He nodded, not focusing on her, but trying to decide where to go now that they were through the doors. "I have no doubt you will be fine. But you need a doctor to verify that."

"The doctor is just going to tell me to go home and take it easy for a few days."

"Probably," Christian agreed. He frowned up at a sign that read "Emergency" with an arrow pointing down the hall. He quickly strode in that direction.

"So why not skip the middle man and take me home so I

can start taking it easy," she said, her voice sounding a little frantic, even to her own ears.

"Stop arguing," he ordered, his attention still on the signs leading to the emergency room.

She wanted to argue, especially since she didn't care for how he'd just spoken to her, but her head was throbbing. And she knew an argument was pointless. He *was* a brick wall.

Still, she couldn't see a doctor. Her bank account couldn't afford the cost. Even if they billed her. Even if they let her make payments. She had to get out of here.

"Please. Stop."

The desperation in her voice finally got through to him. He stopped instantly.

He frowned at her, his face just inches from hers, his pale eyes alive with worry. "What is it? Am I hurting you?"

His gaze roamed over her body, looking for signs of problems.

"No," she told him, then hesitated. She didn't want to tell this guy she couldn't afford to see a doctor. Not when he'd made it clear he already looked down on her. But she didn't have a choice. As usual, she'd have to set her pride aside, and do whatever was necessary to survive.

"I don't have any insurance," she finally stated flatly.

He stared at her for a moment. Then his frown deepened. "Insurance?"

"Yes, coverage to see a doctor. To help cover the cost of medical care."

He shook his head as if to say he had no idea what she was talking about. How could he not know what medical insurance was? Then she realized that he likely wasn't from the U.S. originally. That would explain his unusual accent. Maybe he had lived somewhere with universal health care.

"Are you Canadian?"

His brows drew even closer together as he stared at her as if she'd gone nutty.

"Canadian?" he finally asked, but didn't wait to discuss the topic further. "Jolee, are you stalling?"

"No. Here you need insurance to see a doctor."

"Well, that's preposterous. You need a doctor, and you will see one."

Jolee almost smiled. Almost. She had to remember this man was a first-class snot. Even if he was being rather gallant at the moment. *Of course, he did nearly run you down with his car.* Although she'd been a little responsible for that, too. She hadn't been paying attention, her thoughts on the run-in at the bar, and what she'd do if Rick and his buddies returned while she was walking home.

"This woman needs to see a doctor."

Jolee blinked to see that he was obviously done discussing insurance, and was now talking to a custodian who pushed a gray mop around the glossy linoleum flooring.

The custodian, puzzled by the odd man carrying a dirt-and-leaf-covered woman, pointed at the alcove labeled "Registration."

Jolee found herself headed to a window where a woman in a white coat, with large-framed glasses and tightly curled hair, looked up at them.

"My goodness," she said, her eyes looking abnormally wide behind her thick lenses. "What happened?"

"She was nearly hit by a car. She needs to see a doctor."

"Please put me down," Jolee hissed, feeling even more ridiculous now that they had observers.

"Have a seat over there," the woman suggested, pointing to the waiting area behind them. "I'll be right out with some paperwork, then we'll get you in to see a doctor."

He didn't look pleased with that answer, but when she pointed again to the waiting room, he did go to the small area, setting Jolee carefully onto one of the metal and plastic chairs.

He sat down beside her, still looking very confused.

"I don't understand," he said. "Why can't you see the doctor, then fill out this paperwork?"

Jolee forced a smile. "You don't go to the doctor much, do you?"

"Never," he stated, and sounded glad of it.

"Okay." The woman appeared with a clipboard. "Just fill out these two forms."

"Does she really need to do this now?"

The woman raised an eyebrow at him. "Yes. Unfortunately. Although if she's too sore to write"—she gestured to Jolee's arm—"then you can help her. I'll be back in a few moments."

The woman marched off, her white shoes squeaking on the newly washed floor.

"Ludicrous," he muttered as he leaned over to peer at the forms.

"See, we should just go," Jolee said hopefully.

"No. Do you need help?"

"No." She sighed. Taking the pen stuck under the metal clip, she started filling in her information. The forms didn't take her long since she had to skip the insurance parts.

Her neighbor shifted in his seat, looking decidedly annoyed. He leaned forward to glare at the clerk. Busy typing on her computer, she didn't notice him. He sat back only to look again seconds later.

"Are you doing all right?" he asked.

Her head felt like it was pulsating noticeably. "I just want to go home."

He stood up, taking the clipboard from where she'd placed it in the chair next to her, and strode to the woman.

He handed the board to her without so much as a word, although Jolee was certain the woman received one of his lofty looks. Not pleasant, as she could attest to.

He came back and took the seat beside her. More time

and more impatient movements from her companion, then the woman appeared.

"You don't have insurance," she stated as though Jolee didn't know.

"No, I don't."

The woman frowned. "You will need to pay before you leave tonight."

Jolee nodded and started to lever herself slowly out of the chair. "I figured. Thanks."

Her neighbor stood and reached in his pants pocket. He pulled out a black leather wallet with a small designer emblem on the edge. He flipped it open. "I have plenty of money."

Jolee saw several cards flick by. Gold, platinum, even blue. All that appeared to be missing was Diners Club™.

"Now can she see a doctor?" he asked impatiently.

The clerk nodded, and disappeared through the swinging doors that led into the ER.

Jolee stared at him as he put the wallet back in his pocket.

"I can't take your money." She couldn't owe any money. Especially to this man.

"Of course you can. I'm the one who nearly hit you. I insist on paying for your treatment."

He did have a point. She supposed his gesture was the right one. She'd insist on paying for anyone she hurt, too, that was if she had any money. Thank God she hadn't almost hit him. He'd be in real trouble.

But she wanted to make sure he understood this made them even. "If you pay, I don't owe you anything in return."

He frowned, then comprehension dawned in his eyes. "Certainly not."

She immediately felt stupid. Of course this man wouldn't expect anything else from her. But not because he respected her. Not because he saw her as an equal, but probably because he found her to be unattractive. She told herself that didn't matter to her, but it did sting a little.

Lord, she must be mad. There she sat, hurting, exhausted, and she was upset because this guy didn't find her attractive.

The clerk reappeared, followed by another woman in a white coat. The new woman held the door open and offered a polite smile. "The doctor will see you now."

"About time," her neighbor muttered.

Jolee couldn't agree more. She wanted this over and to go home. And to avoid her neighbor from now on.

Chapter 5

After much poking and prodding, Dr. Williams, a woman in her fifties with pretty white-gray hair and a no-nonsense manner, told Jolee what she'd already guessed.

"You have a few cuts and bruises. Your shoulder is going to be pretty sore for the next few days. The scrape on your arm is large but not terribly deep. It should be kept bandaged, though. Other than that, it doesn't require any special attention. And you have a pretty sizable goose egg on your head."

The doctor scribbled some notes on her clipboard. "Really, there isn't much I can offer you except some Motrin and rest."

Jolee nodded. She wanted to rest. Her eyelids felt like they had weights attached to them. "Rest sounds wonderful."

"Do you have anyone to stay with you tonight?"

Jolee hesitated.

"I think it's wise to have someone with you for at least tonight. You have a concussion, and while I don't think it's severe enough to require a hospital stay, I do think you should have someone around in case you suffer vertigo or nausea. In which case, I'd want you to return to the hospital immediately."

"Yes, I do," Jolee assured the doctor. "I have someone."

The doctor nodded, then wrote something else on her clipboard. Probably that Jolee was a liar. She was sure the doctor knew—she was possibly the worst liar on the planet.

"Okay, well, since it's so late, I'm going to have the nurse give you some of the ibuprofen to take with you tonight. I'll also include some bandages and antibacterial ointment, and a list of things to watch out for with a concussion."

Jolee offered her thanks to the doctor, and once the woman left, she proceeded to dress. She winced as she wrestled her T-shirt back on. Carrying trays and reaching for bottles on the upper shelves at the bar was going to be a challenge, but at least the injuries weren't any worse. She'd be able to work. That was a blessing.

She finished straightening her clothes and eased off the table, the white paper under her bottom crinkling loudly. As she stepped out into the room, she saw the nurse who'd brought her back to the doctor was at her station. She was on the phone, but she waved to Jolee to acknowledge that she saw her. She gestured for Jolee to go back to the waiting room.

Jolee stepped through the swinging door, and her neighbor stood up.

"Are you okay?"

"Fine," she said, "nothing that time and rest won't cure." She couldn't help adding, "Just like I told you."

He didn't acknowledge her peevish tone, but before he could question her further, the nurse arrived.

"Here are your supplies." She held out a small white paper bag. "And here is the list of symptoms to watch for if your concussion worsens."

The nurse then looked to her neighbor. "Will you be the one watching her tonight?"

"Yes," he said.

"No," Jolee stated at the same time.

The nurse looked back and forth between the two. Finally her confused gaze landed on Jolee. "You do have someone to stay with you, at least for tonight, don't you?"

"Yes," Jolee said quickly, adamantly. "Yes, of course, I do."

The nurse gave her a searching look. Again Jolee was sure her horrible lying skills had given her away.

"Okay," the nurse finally said. "Good. And feel better."

"I will. Thank you." Jolee clutched the items the nurse had given her like a victory medal. She just wanted out of here.

Then the clerk appeared. "I have the bill waiting for you."

Jolee really didn't want to hear the total. She felt guilty that this man had to pay—even though he was the one who nearly ran her down, and despite the fact he could obviously afford it. Or at least could have afforded it at one time. Who knew what the state of his finances was now? He did live in a rusty old trailer across from the most broke woman in the known universe. Odds were, he wasn't any too solvent. But he didn't hesitate; he followed the woman back to her desk. Jolee, wimp that she was, remained in the waiting area.

In a few minutes, he returned, looking unfazed by whatever the bill had been. But his expressions were hard to read, so she couldn't be sure how he felt about the cost.

"You'd be an ace at poker," she said, falling into step beside him to retrace their path back to his car.

"Why do you say that?"

"Those eyes of yours," she said. "Beautiful and unreadable."

Christian didn't pause or glance at her as she walked beside him, but he was shocked to the core. This woman, who he'd obviously done a terrific job of making dislike and mistrust him, had just given him a compliment. Well, a compliment of sorts.

"Actually, I haven't gambled at cards for years." Not since his wastrel days frequenting gambling hells all about London. "Are you sure you aren't feeling lightheaded?"

She obviously must be feeling a little confused to say anything complimentary about him.

"No," she said, stifling back a yawn. "But I am exhausted."

"Well, I'll get you home as quickly as possible." He led her to his car, opening the door for her.

"Don't go too quickly. I don't want you to run down anyone else tonight."

A smile tugged at his lips, but he didn't comment.

The ride back to the trailer park was much like the ride to the hospital. Silent. Jolee had her eyes closed, although this time he was fairly certain she just dozed.

Instead of pulling in her driveway, he turned into his own. When the engine rumbled to a stop, Jolee opened her eyes, peering around.

"Thanks," she murmured, obviously not thinking it odd that he didn't drop her off at her door. She reached for the door handle. Christian also reached for his, jumping out of the car to come around and help her.

Jolee was already standing, using the door to steady herself.

"Thanks, I can handle it from here."

She started across the street, but Christian followed, catching the hand of her good arm.

She stopped and glanced down at where he touched her, then lifted an arched brow. "I said I can handle it from here."

He shook his head. "The nurse said you need to have someone with you tonight."

"Well, you are right across the road, so if I need you—"

He shook his head. "You're going to spend the night with me."

She immediately shook her head, then narrowed her eyes as if the action had caused her pain. "No. I promise I'll come right over to you if I have any of the symptoms."

"No. You will stay at my place." Lord, she was a stubborn little mortal.

Her eyes narrowed again, but this time out of annoyance rather than pain. "You are impossible. No."

He smiled slightly. Well, at least she was thinking the same thing about his disposition.

"The other option is that I stay at your trailer, but as I recall, you have no sofa. I suppose I could share your bed."

Her eyes widened now, flashing. "No! This is ridiculous. I'm perfectly fine to go home and go to bed. I don't need you to stay with me."

"Right then. Off to your bed." He started to tug her toward her trailer, but she dug in her heels.

"You would seriously do this, wouldn't you?"

He lifted an eyebrow. "Yes. It's doctor's orders."

She stared at him for a moment, then sighed. "I will sleep on your couch."

"My bed."

"Couch."

"Bed."

"Oh, for heaven's sake," she muttered. "Fine. I'll sleep in your bed."

He started to tug her back toward his trailer.

"But"—she dug her heels in again; he stopped and looked at her—"you will sleep on the couch."

"Absolutely."

Jolee allowed herself to be led into his trailer. She was so tired, she just didn't have any more fight left in her.

She collapsed, drained, on his couch, while he set down her tote bag.

"You should go straight to bed."

She nodded, too tired to get up. Instead she flopped over on the cushions, the movement hurting her shoulder, but she didn't care. It felt so good to lie down.

"Do you want to borrow something to sleep in?" he asked.

She nodded, barely even aware of what he'd asked. He just needed to go and let her rest.

He left the room and she let her eyes drift shut. But he returned just moments later.

"Here you go."

She opened her eyes and he was holding out a white button-front shirt. Crisp white cotton, obviously tailored. Of course.

She reached out a hand to take it, the cotton softer than any she'd ever felt.

"Thanks." She glanced up at him. He nodded. And for the first time, she realized what he looked like. Blood smeared the shoulder and collar of his shirt. The material was wrinkled, and his hemline untucked. His hair, which was cut to look chicly disheveled, was way beyond that, sticking out wildly.

"You're a mess," she stated.

He glanced down at himself, then smiled, just a faint tug at the corner of his mouth.

A rather adorable smile, she thought as she yawned, and let her eyes fall shut again. *Too bad he probably knows it.*

"My name doesn't mean pretty in French either," he suddenly said, and for a moment, she thought she might have dreamed the comment.

She opened her eyes and he was there. Still messy. Still adorable.

"My name is Christian. Christian Young."

She smiled, sleepiness making her feel relaxed and a little disconnected. "Christian. That's a nice name."

She closed her eyes and slept.

Christian stood over her, watching her. Her breathing came in a low, even rhythm. In. Out. Her spicy scent surrounded him again, the sharper scent of her fear and pain gone. Thankfully gone.

He stared at her face, still pale, but a hint of pink colored her high cheekbones. She would be all right.

He didn't think God would be interested in his thanks, but he thanked him anyway. He hadn't given any credence to God, even when he was alive. Funny, that he should now. Now, when he had no chance of being forgiven by God or man.

Hmmm. He'd never quite believed that he'd be able to do Step Seven of his twelve steps. But there it was, Humility—asking a higher power to remove his shortcomings.

He looked back at Jolee, again seeing another face, the face that had prompted this change in him. The face of a mortal whose only mistake had been to love his vampire brother. Did his brother Rhys still ache for Jane? Of course, he did. Christian could never expect forgiveness from him. Or Sebastian. His baby brother was right to stand by Rhys. Rhys had been right about Lilah all along, that she was evil and cruel and never loved him, but Christian's obsession with her wouldn't allow him to listen. Rhys would never forgive his shortcomings. Never.

Unable to think anymore about what he'd done, he spun away from Jolee and headed to his bedroom. There, he stripped off his soiled shirt, throwing it on the small dresser. The white material landed in a pile. He started to undo his pants when something on the shirt caught his attention.

Slowly he approached the garment, staring at stains, rusty brown against white. Picking up the shirt, he studied the smears. For the first time, he smelled the blood there. Even dried, the blood still contained that intoxicating scent, that lure. He lifted the shirt to his nose, breathing in deeply. His hunger responded, his muscles seizing with the urge to feed. But still his fangs didn't extend.

He threw the garment away from himself. He was only torturing himself. He could never bite her. He couldn't bite at all. But the need was still there, even though his fangs didn't respond.

He left the room, fleeing the need. He was halfway down the hall when realization hit him. The scrape on Jolee's arm had been bleeding when he found her. Her blood had been on his clothing, but until just now he hadn't even smelled it. His hunger hadn't cried out to him until he'd consciously smelled it. There was a time that he'd never have been able to block out the lure of her blood. Were his powers so far gone? Or had he been so worried about her that blood was secondary? He didn't really know.

But he did know he could smell her in the trailer, her spicy, rich scent. A scent that didn't have to do with blood, and only with Jolee herself. He entered the living room. She hadn't moved. She remained curled on her side, her injured arm cradled against her chest. Her dark auburn hair, which had been knotted at the back of her head, had fallen loose. Strands clung to her cheeks. She had a smudge of dirt on the side of her chin, or maybe it was a bruise. Guilt constricted his chest. But no hunger. Even after smelling her blood and reacting to her essence, his hunger had calmed again.

He frowned. But his hunger had responded to her last night in her trailer. His erection, his desire to touch her. That had been the hunger, he was sure of it. Maybe the additional couple ounces of blood had gotten him back under control. Maybe he had found the perfect amount. Enough to satisfy, but little enough to make him as close to human as he could get.

She shifted, her knees practically coming up to touch her chin. She would be more comfortable in his bed. The lumpy mattress was far from luxurious, but it was better than the sunken cushions of the sofa.

He started to lift her, easing one arm under her knees and the other around her back, but she moaned.

"No," she almost pleaded, as if she couldn't stand to be woken again. So instead, he moved her so she was better situated on the length of the sofa, allowing her long legs to stretch out.

He returned to his room and grabbed a blanket. As he covered her, she murmured thanks, but he didn't think she even woke up. He tucked the cover securely around her thin frame. He couldn't recall a time when he'd tucked a person in. Maybe his sister, Elizabeth. But he couldn't recall.

Pain and bitter remorse squeezed his chest. Another mortal he'd hurt. Another mortal he could have saved, if he hadn't been blinded by his own obsession with Lilah. He hadn't killed Elizabeth himself, but for all practical purposes, he might as well have.

Maybe that was why he was so drawn to this mortal. She seemed to need someone. To help her, to save her—he wasn't sure from what exactly, but he was going to make sure he protected her in some way. In the way he should have protected his sister, his brothers, and Jane. And himself.

He sat in a chair and watched Jolee sleep. She shifted slightly so he could see her face. Those lips, her long lashes against her pale skin. Her nose, straight and tipped up just a bit at the end. His body reacted to her, but he ignored the confusing reaction. Instead he went to his computer and to his blog page.

> *I think I have found a way to make up for my past mistakes. I know I can never receive forgiveness from my brothers. Or Elizabeth. Or Jane. But I can receive forgiveness from another human. I don't exactly know where this strategy fits under my step program. She is either Step Nine: Forgiveness, where I make amends to someone I've hurt.*

He glanced at her. He'd definitely hurt her. Both physically and mentally.

> *Or maybe she's actually Step Eight, which I have titled Willingness. I had been using this blog as my connection to others, but I think maybe I need to do more. I think I might need to actually interact, in person, with humans for this plan to be a real success. To show*

my desire to change. Or she could actually be Step Twelve: Service. This step requires me to go out and help others and share what I've learned.

That idea now wasn't as appalling as it had once been. Again he looked over at Jolee. In fact, he rather liked the idea of being "friends" with a mortal. It would be quite a novelty, really.

Jolee breathed evenly, deeply. He didn't understand the strange reactions of his body to her. The urge to touch her. The erection without the fangs. All he knew for sure was he needed to be near her. He didn't understand the need, but she made him feel something other than emptiness and hunger. And he would protect her. That seemed like a fair and safe trade-off.

He turned back to the computer.

Maybe she is a combination of all three. In which case, I dare say I'm being quite successful at this program.

Chapter 6

Jolee stretched, then groaned. Good Lord, she felt like she'd been hit by a Mack truck. She opened her eyes, staring at the ceiling. Then she turned her head, seeing tweed furniture. Furniture she didn't have. Wait, the Mack truck analogy wasn't far off, was it?

That's right. She was in her neighbor's trailer. Christian's trailer. Had he finally told her his name, or had she just dreamed that?

Bracing her good arm against the edge of the couch, she pushed herself up. She looked around, but the room was empty. She couldn't tell what time it was, because thick, insulated shades covered all the windows. The only light came from a bulb left on over the range in the kitchen.

Christian—she was pretty sure he had told her his name— was nowhere to be seen. She swung her legs off the couch and stood. Her whole body ached, so she moved in a stiff, awkward shuffle around the room, trying to find a clock. She checked the living room and then the kitchen. No clocks. She wandered over to the window and lifted a shade. The sky was bright, but from the placement of the sun in the sky it had to be afternoon. The trailer was stifling, the air overly warm and stagnant.

She was tempted to open a window, but it seemed like too much work. Not to mention he must like his place like this, given the heavy blinds. She dropped the shade back into place and moved to the kitchen. She needed a drink; her tongue felt like she'd been licking a bag of flour.

She opened a cabinet searching for a glass but instead she found an odd collection of items. The Eggstractor. A Pasta Plus pot, the items still in their boxes. Meatball Magic? She took down the box, scanning the back.

"No longer do you have to take valuable time making meatballs for dinner, now with the Meatball Magic, it's easy." She frowned at the box. Was making meatballs that difficult? She shrugged and put the box back.

She picked up a white object with a handle and a hole on the other side. "Salad Shooter," she read from the side of the contraption. She put it back, noting the only other doohickey open was the Eurosealer. No dishes. No glasses. Just infomercial gadgets. How odd.

She found a plastic cup that was actually the base of the Master Chopper. That would have to do. The first cup she guzzled down in one breath. Then she returned the cup to the faucet for a refill. Sipping this time, she further inspected his home. She knew she shouldn't be nosy, but after the compilation of items in the cupboards, she was intrigued. The rest of the cupboards were bare. The drawers were empty except for a large package of straws. She frowned. She could see Christian drinking from a martini glass or a champagne glass. Not with a straw. But then he didn't seem like the type to watch informercials either. Or live in a trailer park. The list seemed to be growing.

She went to the fridge, frowning at the typed list held by a magnet.

Being Human:
Step 1: Honesty
Step 2: Belief
Step 3: Surrender
Step 4: Soul Searching
Step 5: Integrity
Step 6: Acceptance
Step 7: Humility
Step 8: Willingness
Step 9: Forgiveness
Step 10: Maintenance
Step 11: Making Contact
Step 12: Service

This guy needed a list on how to be human? That was never a good sign. She read the list again, then shook her head. She opened the fridge and peered in. The only things in there were packets of . . . juice or something. Hence the straws, she guessed.

"Makes my fridge look like a regular grocery market." She glanced back at the cupboard with all the gadgets. "No wonder they all look new. He has no salad to shoot or eggs to eggstract. And forget about the easy meatballs."

This guy got stranger each time she met him. And she hadn't even met him today. God knew what he'd do now.

Aside from the hum of the computer on his kitchen table, the trailer was quiet. Where was he? She took her cup and went in search. The hallway was dark. She flipped on the bathroom light on the way by to see a little better. The door at the end of the hallway was closed, and she hesitated to knock. If he was in there, he was probably sound asleep. The door, just like the one in her trailer, slid on rollers into the wall. She moved her hand to the small round handle and eased the door open just enough to see in.

This room was also pitch-black, except for the light from

the bathroom behind her. The strip of light created by the open door fell directly on him, where he lay on the bed.

He was sound asleep—and naked. Jolee almost closed the door immediately, but she couldn't get her brain to cooperate with her body. The lean sinew of his arms and chest held her captive, all hard curves and latent strength. One of his arms was flung up above his head, palm up. The other hand rested on his flat stomach. His hand was large, broad, with long, strong fingers. Jolee stared at those fingers, finding something oddly thrilling about his hand against his own skin. Spread over that flat, rigid stomach.

An image of his hand moving over his chest played through her mind. Traveling down his stomach, slowly, sensually.

She swallowed. What was she doing? But even as she reprimanded herself, her eyes wandered to the place where his fantasy hand had been heading. One of his legs was sprawled out straight, long and muscular, but the one closest to her was bent, offering him a little privacy.

Thank goodness, she told herself, even as a small wave of disappointment skimmed over her.

She stared at him for a second more, then with a shake of her head forced herself to slide the door shut.

"Pervert," she muttered to herself, then took a large swallow of her water, hoping the cool liquid would extinguish the heat in her skin. It didn't.

She might have been a pervert, but to be fair to herself, he was the most perfectly built man she'd ever seen. That alone was enough to explain why she hadn't been able to look away. Her fun was over, though; now she had to get out of here. The realization that her neighbor not only had a breathtaking face but the body to match didn't change the fact that he was not someone she wanted to associate with. In fact, that knowledge only solidified the fact that he was best avoided. She knew the ego that came with a face like that. She'd already seen his ego once. He might have been kind last night, but she doubted that kindness would last. His hero tendencies seemed to be short-lived.

She hurried back to the living room, looking for her tote and the white bag with her medication. She found both by the end of the couch. As well as she could with the limited movement of her arm, she folded the comforter. Then she saw his shirt wadded up in a ball and half wedged between the arm of the couch and the cushion.

She vaguely remembered he'd brought her a clean shirt to sleep in. She'd apparently balled up the expensive garment and used it as a pillow. She picked up the shirt, shaking it out. The white cotton was badly wrinkled and covered with dirt and bits of dried leaves. There was also a spot on the front that she feared might be drool. She spread the shirt on the back of the couch and tried to wipe off the debris and smooth the worst of the wrinkles. It didn't look much better for her effort.

She sighed, then picked up her bags. Well, he probably wouldn't be surprised. He already thought very little of her. He'd probably expect her to mistreat a custom-made shirt. She just hoped the drool dried before he woke.

She headed to the door, only glancing briefly toward the hallway that led to Christian and his perfect body. He might have a perfect body and face and clothes, but the man had problems, she was sure of that. Problems she couldn't begin to deal with, not when she had her own to sort out. The most immediate of which being how she was going to get through a night of work with this bum shoulder and still pounding head.

She stepped outside, the bright light doing nothing for the headache. Then she closed the door tightly behind her, hopefully leaving the memories of Christian still sleeping in his bedroom.

* * *

For the first time since Christian moved into the hell that was Shady Fork Mobile Estates, he didn't wake immediately irritated. Irritated with himself and with the events that brought him to this *very* low point. Or irritated with the hunger that had to be restrained by a strict diet. Or even irritated with the evil lawn ornaments next door.

His first thought was of Jolee. How was she? A still unfamiliar sense of concern filled him. But mingled with the concern was an even more foreign emotion. He searched for a name for the feeling. It was almost like . . . excitement.

He slipped out of the bed and looked for his pants. Before he even had them fastened, his newly recognized excitement faded. He paused, concentrating on the atmosphere of the trailer. He didn't feel her presence there. The fourteen by fifty-six foot space was empty as usual.

Hoping that his senses were just too weak to perceive her, he grabbed a shirt and strode to the living room. But by the time he reached the main room, he knew she was gone. The comforter was folded in the center of the sofa. Above it, his shirt was spread out against the back of the sofa, the arms stretched out wide. A lifeless welcome.

He ignored the disappointment that smothered the rest of his excitement. She must have gone back to her trailer. That was reasonable. She'd want to shower and change into clean clothes. He tugged on the shirt he carried, then went to get his shoes.

Other than the outside light, her trailer was dark. She could be asleep, he decided as he bounded up her steps. He knocked, but heard nothing from inside. He concentrated, but he didn't feel her presence there either. He tried the doorknob. The whole knob encasement wiggled loosely in his hand. The door clicked open. She really needed to fix that.

He stepped into the dark trailer, still not able to pick up her presence. Spicy sweetness scented the whole place, but it was a lingering scent, not a fresh one. He considered searching through the rest of the trailer, but there was no point. She wasn't here.

He tried to lock the door, which didn't catch correctly, so he left it unlocked, as she had. Then he stood on the stoop unsure what to do next. Where was she? Worry and exasperation mingled inside him. She should be resting. What did she have against following the doctor's orders?

What if she'd gotten ill, and decided she needed to go back to the doctor? Certainly he would have been no help if that happened in the daylight. Had she gone to another neighbor for assistance? Maybe he'd go by the hospital, just to check. He started back across the road to get his keys, when cinnamon and warm honey overwhelmed his senses. The scent was there, a definite cloud of perfume, right in the middle of the road.

The fragrance was the same type as in her trailer, waning, but still strong enough for him to sense. Pleased, he walked a little farther down the road. Her scent grew just subtly stronger. He couldn't believe his dwindled abilities would allow him to find her. Apparently vampires were like dogs and scent was the last thing to go. He did sense her, and he intended to follow the faint trail left for him like an olfactory version of breadcrumbs.

She must have gone wherever she went the other nights he'd seen her walking. As hurt and sore as she was, she'd still gone to her nightly destination. Why? The path led him back up the main road, and he quickly realized that she'd been walking home from this place last night, when he'd nearly hit her. He passed the spot, rubber from his tires lining the road.

Her trail only went a few yards beyond that point, and for the first time, he noticed a building set back from the road. A painted wooden sign was affixed to the roof and lit with lights on the eaves: Leo's Brew Pub and Karaoke Saloon. How multi-ethnic.

Another sign, even bigger than the name, balanced above

that, reading: Member of the National Karaoke Association. Christmas lights decorated both signs and the eaves of the roof. Neon signs advertising different alcohols hung in the windows.

How had he missed this place?

The gravel parking lot to the left of the building had several cars lined up. Music drifted out from the open windows, as did the sound of voices. Suddenly he sensed Jolee's presence; he could feel her in the warm air. Christian frowned. This was where she went every night?

He wandered closer. Peeking in a window, he saw a large open room with more Christmas lights lining the rafters. Several groups of people sat at nicked wooden tables, drinks in their hands. Two men played a game of pool in the far corner. Farther down in the opposite corner was an open space with a booth next to it. There was a monitor affixed to one of the ceiling beams and another large monitor behind that on the wall, facing out into the room. The monitor was dark, and the booth empty. A few more patrons sat on stools at a long bar at the very end of the room. And behind the bar was . . . Jolee.

"Jolee girl, you need to be home in bed," Jed commented, not for the first time tonight.

Earlier Jolee had just laughed off his advice; she'd been hurting but she could handle it. However, after a few long reaches for liquor bottles on the shelves behind her and lifting a couple heavy trays, she was really hurting now.

But she forced a smile and said, "This is the best night I've had. I can handle it."

Jed shook his head. "Well, let me help you."

He'd offered that already, too, and she'd turned him down. The poor old guy was stiff enough after mopping and taking out the trash at the end of the night. She hadn't wanted him overextending himself. But maybe just for tonight.

"No, I'll help her," a voice stated before she could relent.

Jolee turned to see Christian standing at the end of the bar. She walked over to him and whispered, "What are you doing here?"

"The better question is what are you doing here? You're supposed to be resting."

"Well, some of us have jobs," she said pointedly.

He didn't seem to notice the jab. "Surely, your boss would understand that you need a couple nights off."

"I am the boss."

Christian stared at her for a moment, then cast a look around the bar. "You own this place?" Confusion was clear in his eyes.

"What? You don't think a woman can run a bar?"

"No, I just can't imagine why you'd want to." He cast another disparaging look around the place.

Anger rose in her chest, and made her pounding head feel like it was going to explode. "You know what, I really don't need your rude comments. Just because you're a pretentious jerk, doesn't mean you can come in here and criticize my place. So just—"

"That *was* rude. Forgive me."

She snapped her mouth closed and glared at him. "Thanks for stopping by. Now you can leave."

"Nope," he said as he unbuttoned the sleeves of another tailored shirt and rolled them up. This shirt was dark blue and made his pale blue eyes even more striking. The pushed-back sleeves revealed his leanly muscled forearms. She noticed the cut from Vance's knife was totally gone. It must have been even smaller than she'd thought. She also noticed how good his muscles looked. Damn it.

She forced her gaze back to his face and demanded, "What are you doing?"

"I'm going to help you." He braced his arms on the bar and swung himself over to her side with the agility of a gymnast.

"There's an entrance down there," she pointed out grumpily.

Not that she hadn't done the same thing many times, of course certainly not with his grace. And with the way her shoulder felt at the moment, she wouldn't be doing it again anytime soon.

He offered her a small smile, nothing more than the quirk of one side of his lips, but it still made her breath catch.

"I'll remember that next time."

"Well, actually if you want to hop right back over the bar and leave, that's fine."

"No." His amazing eyes held hers. "Let me help you."

Her gaze roamed his face. He looked sincere and even a bit desperate.

She wanted help. She needed it. "For tonight."

He nodded.

"All right." But Jolee had the feeling that she'd just agreed to a whole lot more than just tonight.

Chapter 7

"A man shouldn't be that pretty," Jed stated as Christian carried another tray of drinks to a table. The woman at the table obviously didn't agree as she looked Christian up and down, a hungry look in her overly made-up eyes. The two men with the woman seemed to be in Jed's camp.

Jolee glanced back at Jed. The old man still grimaced at Christian like his looks were disgusting rather than perfect.

Jolee had to agree. It was a little disgusting. Mainly because she found herself paying more attention to him than the drinks that needed to be made.

She focused on what she was supposed to be making—a gin and tonic. She turned and started to reach for the bottle of gin from the second shelf of lined-up liquors. When suddenly Christian was there, getting the bottle for her. The muscles in his shoulder rippled under the expensive material of his shirt as he lowered his arm and turned to hand the bottle to her.

"Thanks," she said, keeping her voice cool even as tingling warmth stole over her skin.

His gaze roamed over her face. Then he smiled, another of those darned irritating half-smiles. His eyes glittered as if he was fully aware of her real reaction to him.

"How are you feeling?" he asked, his velvety voice low and full of innuendo.

She gritted her teeth. She hated that her darn body responded to his looks, and she really hated that he was aware of that fact.

"Fine," she said curtly, returning to the empty glass on the bar.

But even as she focused on mixing the drink, she could feel him behind her. Just inches away. Heat again sizzled across the skin of her back. She determinedly ignored the sensation, adding mixer to the glass and placing it on the tray with the others.

"Ready," she said, sliding down the bar away from him, making sure to avoid any contact with him.

He didn't speak as he took the tray and headed back out to the floor. She didn't allow herself to watch him, instead busying herself with the orders of the patrons seated at the bar. The place was definitely hopping. A wonderful change, and if she wasn't in pain and forced to accept help from the man she'd decided to avoid, she'd be skipping around to fill all the drink orders, but as it was, she was walking gingerly and cursing her luck.

"Hi," a female voice said as Jolee was reaching for another mug under the bar. Jolee popped up, her head only grumbling a little, to find the woman who really enjoyed a good blue eyeliner.

"I have a question for you." She smiled, actually appearing a little sheepish.

"Shoot," Jolee said.

"Does the guy waiting tables work here every night?"

"No," Jolee said, not hiding the relief in her voice. "He's only helping me out tonight."

She couldn't handle him near her every night. She wiped an arm across her damp brow. She'd spontaneously combust.

"Oh," the woman said, disappointment clear on her face.

"I was going to tell all my girlfriends they had to come up here and check him out."

Jolee gave her a regretful smile. "Sorry."

"Me, too." The woman headed back to her table, although her gaze was again on Christian.

He stood at another table, his back to the bar. And if Jolee wasn't mistaken, the woman was staring at his behind. Jolee followed the woman's gaze. It was a fine behind.

She groaned. *Stop this! Now!*

She grabbed up a damp rag and pressed the cloth to her cheek. The cool moisture felt good on her overheated skin. She could not be attracted to a man who, if it wasn't for the guilt of nearly grinding her under the wheels of his sports car, would still be treating her like . . . well, something else he might find under the wheels of his car.

"Where'd you find the pretty boy anyway?" Jed asked, scowling like he'd swallowed something bitter.

It took Jolee a moment to realize he was talking about Christian.

"He's my neighbor."

He grunted. "Well, he'd like to be more than that."

Jolee chuckled. "Hardly." She reached for his beer. "I think I need to cut you off."

He snatched the mug away from her. "When he lays his eyes on you, he looks downright hungry."

Given the state of his refrigerator and cupboards, he probably was hungry.

Jolee shook her head. "Believe me, you're imagining things. He's here out of guilt. Nothing more."

Jed frowned like he was unconvinced and reached for his cigarettes.

Christian walked up to the bar, placing an order slip on the wooden surface. "These mor—people really drink."

He glanced over his shoulder at the crowd and shook his head.

Annoyance rose up quickly in Jolee's chest. Both at his

comment and his taken aback look. And had he been about to refer to her patrons as morons? He'd definitely been about to call them something.

"These mor—people"—she mimicked his accent—"are spending their good money to have a good time. They don't need your judgment." She snatched up the order slip.

Christian appeared completely unfazed by her outburst. His gaze searched her face. "Are you feeling all right?"

She ignored him and started filling his orders. She could feel him watching her, but she didn't return his look.

"Jolee," he said, his accent making her name sound beautiful.

She clenched her teeth. *Stop it! Stop being attracted to this man.*

"Jolee," he repeated, and she did look at him. "What's wrong?"

"You think you're better than everyone. That's what's wrong."

He actually seemed surprised by her response. "I was just making an observation. I've never served drinks in a bar or, well, anywhere before. I didn't realize how much work it is. I certainly meant no offense."

She studied him for a moment and couldn't detect anything but honesty in his words. Honesty. Number One on his twelve step list, if she remembered right. Was this all just an act? His attempt to be normal?

She immediately felt guilty. He'd been busting butt all night to help her. She should be thankful, at least for that. "Oh. Okay. Sorry to get snippy."

"That's okay. I deserve it." He offered a slight smile, then took the new tray of drinks and headed back to the floor.

She frowned, watching him. He sure ran hot and cold. She didn't know what to make of him, which part of him to trust. The noble guy who came to her aid or the distant guy who acted strangely and looked down his nose at her.

Tonight he hadn't acted condescending or haughty. He'd

stepped right into the role of replacement cocktail waitress. And he was rather . . . good.

And despite all her thoughts about him thinking he was better than others, and now her declaration to him about his behavior, he really wasn't like the people here. He might not be any better than her customers, or herself, but he sure wasn't like them.

He placed a mug in front of a burly man in a dirty tank top that barely covered his beer belly. Christian nodded politely at the man, then strolled on to deliver the next drink. He sure didn't look like a waiter at a run-down bar, more like the host of a ritzy party. Even serving beer.

The woman who'd asked if he was a regular waiter called him over to order another drink. She seemed to be having a difficult time making up her mind. She giggled and touched Christian's hand. The men with her appeared unimpressed with her behavior, while Christian's expression was somewhere between exasperation and mild fear.

Jolee suddenly realized having him work here tonight had actually worked out well on two counts. She had needed the help. Her shoulder had already stopped throbbing. And the experience just might have humbled him a bit. It *was* rather amusing to watch someone who was obviously used to being the one waited on, wait on others.

The woman finally made up her mind, and as Christian turned to leave the table, the woman pinched his butt. Jolee giggled. Oh, this was definitely worth her unwanted attraction to him. He had to be in hell.

And Christian had thought his trailer was hell. This place was sheer agony. Loud mortals, the even louder twang of music playing from a blinking machine against the wall, and the stale smell of beer and smoke. Under all that was the unrelenting scent of blood, prodding his hunger. Teasing it.

Mocking it. That alone would have been difficult to handle, but all together, the experience was just excruciating.

And now, a woman with the cosmetic discrimination of a clown had just grabbed his ass. His first inclination had been to turn and bite her offending hand like a mad dog. Lord, how he had fallen.

Then he saw Jolee across the room, a wide smile on her lips. The first smile he'd seen since the night he'd insulted her. Suddenly the pinch and the other assaults to his senses didn't seem to matter.

"What are you smiling about?" he asked as he reached the bar.

"That a woman just pinched your behind." She smothered a giggle, but her dark eyes danced.

All annoyance fled at the sight of her amusement. He smiled, too. "Glad I could be of some enjoyment."

"She came up earlier to see if you were a regular waiter here." She stifled another giggle.

"Well, that could be arranged." Good Lord, had he just offered to continue working in this hellhole?

Jolee's smile faded. "No. I do appreciate tonight. But by tomorrow I'll be able to handle things."

He didn't believe her, but he didn't push the subject either. He was unwilling to ruin the small measure of camaraderie they'd achieved. Instead he nodded and picked up two more drinks that needed to be delivered.

He finished placing them in front of people who frankly didn't need them, then he returned to Jolee. Anxious to see that smile again. To talk to her. But she was down at the far end of the bar, talking to someone else. He started to clear some of the empty glasses on the tables, giving a wide berth to the she-clown with the roving hands, when he sensed Jolee's agitation.

Over the haze of all the other emotions and scents in the room, hers found its way to him, sharp and unmistakable. He strolled in her direction, watching her as she spoke to the person at the end of the bar. He couldn't sense fear or panic, only a vivid sense of anxiety and . . . displeasure. Was this guy giving her a hard time?

Stepping behind the bar, he walked the length to stand near her—some distance away, but where he could hear what they were discussing.

"Baby, I thought you'd be happier to see me," the man said.

"Mark, how did you find me?"

"Vance."

"News sure does travel fast."

"This place is pretty nice." The guy ignored her comment and rose up on the rungs of the barstool to look around.

Christian shot the man a quick look. Oily brown hair curled up around the edges of his baseball cap. Light brown eyes topped with large shaggy eyebrows. And a mustache. Christian could smell the grease and cigarette smoke clinging to the man's faded T-shirt and jeans.

"Real nice," Mark said, dropping back on his seat. "You look like you are doing all right for yourself, Jo."

"Why are you here, Mark?"

"Can't your old beau stop by for a visit? Maybe a beer?"

Christian frowned. This unpleasant creature had been a boyfriend of Jolee's? His Jolee.

He paused. *His Jolee.* He could hardly call her that. When had he even begun to consider her that? Yet he realized that he didn't want to think of that man touching her smooth pale skin with his dirty hands. Or kissing her lush lips. Why on earth would he care? He knew the fact that he wanted to touch her skin and taste her lips was due to his hunger. No other reason.

"One beer," Jolee told Mark and turned to go to the tap.

She saw Christian. She smiled, but not the joyous grin of earlier. She slipped past him, her slender body not making contact with his, but he felt her delicious heat passing over him. A few moments later she slid back by and set the beer in front of Mark. She started to leave him again, but Mark caught her injured arm.

Christian straightened as she winced.

"What happened?" Mark asked, still not releasing his hold. A thumb with dirt under the nail rubbed the edge of the bandage on her arm.

"Just a little accident."

Christian raised an eyebrow at that description. But she wasn't about to give this guy the whole story; she obviously didn't want to talk to him.

"Mark, I do have to get back to work."

To Christian's surprise, he let go of her arm. "Sure. I'm good." Mark drank down half his beer in one swallow.

She slipped back past Christian, going to fill a mug for a man in a green baseball hat at the other end of the bar who'd waved to her.

"Are you okay?" he asked on the way by her.

She nodded, giving him a quick smile that didn't reach her eyes. She turned her attention to topping off the mug. "Sure. Just a guy from my hometown."

He noted that she didn't refer to him as a past boyfriend. He could tell she was still anxious, but he didn't question her further, instead he returned to the floor to take orders.

The evening continued smoothly with both of them working steadily until about one-thirty most of the patrons had left. Including the woman with the groping hands, to his relief. Only the pool players, the old man who'd occupied a barstool near the tap all evening, and Mark remained.

Christian cleared tables, putting glasses and trash into a gray tub. Not a pleasant job. Jolee worked behind the bar, washing glassware. Probably not a great job either, he decided.

"Jolee," Mark called to her. "I'll take another."

Christian had noted that the one beer Jolee told him he could have had turned into several.

Jolee didn't shout back, nor did she pour him another. Instead she walked back down the bar to speak to him in a hushed tone.

Mark, who had obviously had enough beer, didn't feel the same compulsion. "You're cutting me off. Just like when we were a couple, eh? Always trying to control the situation."

Christian picked up the tub and went behind the bar, placing glasses into the sink.

"Mark, don't make a scene. You've already had too much to drive," Jolee pointed out calmly.

"I can sleep in my truck. Or I can sleep at your place. Can't I, darlin'?"

Jolee shook her head. "No, Mark."

Mark fixed an angry stare at her. "Too good for me now? Vance said you moved away because you thought you were too good for the likes of us."

"That isn't why I left, Mark."

Christian found the man's words interesting, given that she'd just made the same accusation about him earlier tonight. That he thought he was too good. He wondered why she did leave. Moving to Shady Fork couldn't have been that much of an improvement from her hometown. Then he looked at Mark.

Well, maybe it was.

"Mark, you're drunk. Just go out to your truck and sleep it off." She started to walk away, but like earlier, Mark caught her arm. Except this time he gave it a sharp jerk.

Jolee cried out.

Instantly, Christian was at Jolee's side, his fist knotted in the front of Mark's sweaty, worn T-shirt. "Let her go."

Mark, startled and disoriented from the beer he'd drunk, stared down at Christian's hand, then back up to him. Finally he asked Jolee, "Who the hell is this?"

"Let her go," Christian repeated.

Mark did. Jolee stepped back.

"Is this why you left?" Mark demanded.

Jolee didn't respond.

Mark turned his bleary-eyed glare on Christian. "Don't get too riled up about her. She ain't worth it. She's a slut. All the Dugans are lous—"

Christian didn't let him finish, driving a fist right into his insulting mouth. Mark fell against the back of his stool, hanging there, limp and barely conscious. Christian didn't check Jolee's reaction. He jumped over the bar, threw the senseless man over his shoulder, and headed toward the door.

"Christian," Jolee finally called after him.

He turned to find her staring at him with wide, shocked eyes. But he noted she didn't look overly concerned with the unconscious man.

"I'll be right back. As you said, Mark needs to sleep it off in his truck."

He exited the building, but not before he heard the old guy on the stool by the tap say in a gravelly voice, "I like that guy."

Chapter 8

Christian had returned, assuring her that Mark was fine and situated safely in his truck. Embarrassed by the whole incident, she'd taken the coward's way out and hidden in the back, working on cashing out the money for the night.

As she punched the numbers into her giant, nearly antique calculator, she couldn't believe the past few days. Could anyone else from her life back in Sawyersville show up? Obviously moving three hours away wasn't far enough.

The worst part was Christian had to step in both times. She didn't want to know what he was thinking of her. But it couldn't be good.

Although, he had been furious about Mark's accusation. She didn't really understand why. The things Mark said weren't nice, they upset her, but why did they upset Christian? After all, he barely knew her.

She blinked, realizing that she'd just been staring at the calculator's gray screen, not really seeing what she'd done. Then she blinked again. That total couldn't be right. She pushed the clear button and started to enter the numbers again, assuming the old machine had a glitch. Or more like she and her wandering mind had.

She hoped that by the time she was done with the money, Christian would be gone. The bar was closed now. He certainly didn't need to stick around. And she didn't want to face him. She didn't even know what to say.

She hit total, then stared at the gray screen. The same amount as before stared back at her. Aside from Mark, she'd had a great night. More than a great night. A fantastic night. If she continued to have nights like this, she would be able to afford to hire someone to help out part-time.

She had Christian to thank for tonight. He'd saved her here, too. He'd been a great waiter. She should go out there and thank him. For everything. But still she hesitated.

What if aloof, condescending Christian was back? She didn't know if her thoroughly injured ego could take more insults. Now he'd really have cause to believe the worst in her. A drugged-out brother. Mark saying she was a slut. She did come from a rough background, but she wasn't like them. And she couldn't deal with Christian thinking she was.

She put the money in the safe, double-checked the lock, closed her accounting book, tidied her pencils and pens into neat rows in her desk drawer, then she realized she couldn't delay going back into the barroom any longer.

She walked in to find the whole place cleaned, and everything ready for closing. Even her side work was done. Glasses washed and put away. The bar and tables wiped down. To her further surprise, Christian and Jed sat at one of the tables, having a drink together.

"There you are," Jed said.

Christian looked in her direction, too. But she couldn't read his gaze. Just those eerie, beautiful eyes, watching her.

"The place looks great. Thanks."

Jed nodded. "Join us in celebrating a good night."

She appreciated the gesture, but all she could think about were the things that had happened that didn't merit celebration.

She glanced at Christian, then shook her head. "I'm pretty tired." She smiled warmly at Jed. "Can I take a raincheck?"

Jed bobbed his head. "Of course you can. You know where to find me."

He stood, his movements stiff. He picked up his package of cigarettes, then extended his hand to Christian.

"Good to meet you, young fella."

Christian nodded, a peculiar expression on his face, another look Jolee didn't understand. He accepted Jed's hand, shaking soundly.

"Nice to meet you, too, Jed."

Jed said good night to Jolee, lighting a cigarette as he walked slowly toward the rear exit. He paused to add, "I hope to see more of you around here, Christian."

Christian nodded, but didn't commit one way or the other.

Her heart sank, and she reprimanded herself for the disappointed feeling. She should be pleased that he didn't seem anxious to come back here. All night she'd told herself that was what she wanted.

She followed Jed to lock the door behind him. "You sure you don't want a snack to take with you? I got an apple in my bag. And pretzels and peanuts, of course."

Jed shook his head. "You worry about yourself, Jolee girl. Rest that arm."

She promised she would, then closed the door and flipped the locks into place. She hesitated before turning back to Christian.

He now stood, still watching her.

"Th-thanks for tonight," she said, feeling nervous and uncertain about being here alone with him. She still wasn't sure about him. About his variable behavior. And his eyes, always studying her, yet she could never read the emotions there. Unnerving, to say the least.

"I'm glad I could help," he said. He walked toward her, his steps unhurried and graceful.

She fought the urge to step back as he stopped only

inches from her. His eyes seemed to devour her. His gaze first locked with hers, drifted to her mouth, then down her body.

"Is your shoulder all right?"

Huh? What shoulder? Did she have a shoulder?

She nodded absently, then forced herself to stop staring at him. Reacting to him. Those eyes, his strong sculpted lips, his hair, all disheveled and lovely.

She had the strangest sensation that he wanted to touch her, but she dismissed the feeling. She'd made that mistake before, she wouldn't again. She was obviously experiencing transference, perceiving that he wanted to touch her, when in fact it was her hands that shook with yearning.

Did she really want him? How could she when she didn't understand him at all? Well, obviously she could. But there was a lot of difference between physical attraction and emotional attraction. And she wouldn't act on the physical. Not that he'd want her to. She was sure he didn't.

She looked away from his questioning eyes and cleared her throat, hoping that would help her find her voice and gain a little control.

"Yes, my shoulder's fine," she finally managed. "It feels a little stiff, but okay. Thank you for your help. I couldn't have handled tonight without you."

She hoped that he understood that applied to Mark, too. She didn't want to talk about the incident any more than necessary; even now she felt her cheeks heat with embarrassment. She stepped past him, her hip bumping a chair in her effort not to touch him. The chair legs scraped on the wooden floor, making a loud squawk. The noise only seemed to agitate her more, and she hurried over to grab her tote bag from behind the bar.

"Ready?" she asked almost too pertly.

He didn't seem to notice and nodded.

She turned down the lights, double-checked the lock on the front entrance, then walked back to her office. Christian picked up the mugs that he and Jed had used and placed them in the sink, then followed.

She felt him as soon as he entered her small office. A solid presence behind her as she dug through her bag for her keys. She didn't look at him, anxious to be out of the confined place. All night had been about sharing tight spaces with him. She needed more room. Or at least her sanity did. He was making her crazy. So close. So beautiful.

She opened the office door wide with her good arm. "You first."

He exited, and she noticed that he seemed to take the same measures not to touch her. She didn't know if it was relief or disappointment that made her knees feel strange and quivery.

She pulled in a steadying breath, then grabbed her tote and stepped outside to lock the door.

Christian leaned against the side of the building, watching her. Those eyes still unfathomable. She slid the key in the lock, on the first try, thankfully. Then she scanned the parking lot for Christian's car. Only Mark's big feed truck sat in the patch of dusty gravel. She could hear his loud, liquor-induced snoring from there.

She knew he'd be gone by morning. He'd be too embarrassed to hang around. He'd also be sporting a swollen lip and a heck of a sore jaw in the morning. She tried to feel sorry for him, but couldn't muster the emotion. She didn't advocate violence, but Mark had had that coming for a long time.

"Where's your car?" she asked.

"I walked here."

"Why?"

He shrugged. "Just had the urge to walk."

"How did you know this is where I was?" She hadn't thought about that earlier. She'd been too surprised to see him, and then too distracted by him.

He shrugged again, one of his half-smiles tugging at his lips. "I just had a feeling."

She considered him for a moment, then started walking toward the road. He fell into step beside her. She could feel him at her side, not even a foot away. The warm spring air seemed to crackle with her awareness of him.

"Why did you leave your hometown?" he asked suddenly.

She stumbled, and his hand came out to steady her.

"Are you all right?"

"Yes," she said, then eased her elbow from his hold. Heat burned her skin where he'd touched her. Those strong fingers against her bare elbow.

She swallowed, steeling herself against the reaction and in an attempt to give him an answer. She didn't want to tell him about her life. Especially not her life back in Sawyersville. Not where her last name was synonymous with so many terrible things. He would never consider her an equal then.

"I just wanted to see more of the world." That was true.

"So you came to Shady Fork?"

He had her there, although she didn't appreciate the dryness of his tone.

"There are places much worse than Shady Fork, believe me. Not to mention the fact you live in Shady Fork, too."

"Good point," he agreed easily.

They fell silent, and she hoped that was the end of that line of questions. It wasn't.

"So was your hometown one of those worst places?"

She sighed. What could she say? She had the feeling he'd know if she was lying, and in truth, why bother. She could answer this question honestly, and not have to go into detail.

"Yes, Sawyersville was one of them." There, answered. On to a new subject.

"What was so bad there?"

She stopped, the gravel crunching under her worn canvas sneakers as she spun to face him. "Do we have to talk about this?"

"No," he said easily, as though the topic really didn't interest him that much.

"Good." She started walking again. She didn't want to tell him about her dysfunctional family. Or the things her family was accused of—most of them true. And all the names she'd been called and the ways she'd been treated, because of their behavior. Although he already knew one of the names.

"I didn't intend to offend you. I just thought we might become"—he seemed to struggle for the right word—"friends."

She stopped again with another crunch of gravel. "You want to be friends?"

She couldn't be more shocked. But as she said the word back to him—*friends*—her heart leapt, doing a tiny, hopeful hop in her chest. She didn't trust this man, yet she still wanted his friendship? Was she that desperate? She didn't even have to think a second about the answer. Yes, she was. Desperate and lonely.

Friends? That was what he'd decided he wanted last night. But now that he'd said the word out loud, it seemed almost silly. What did he know about being a friend? He hadn't had a mortal friend in nearly two hundred years, and to be honest, he'd never had a female mortal friend, even when he was mortal himself. Sure, he'd enjoyed female company, but being friendly had always held another connotation.

Aside from his sister, who he'd treated more like a pet, and at times a pest, what did he know about being friends with a woman? He didn't.

Yet he heard himself tell her, "Yes, I'd like to be friends."

"Why?"

She would have to ask that.

"I—I'd just like to get to know you better." He did want to know her better, he realized with a little surprise.

She frowned, and then without a word, turned and started down the embankment.

What the hell was she doing? He followed, wondering if somehow the injury to her head was just now showing signs of damage. The moon was bright, and for the first time he noticed the narrow path winding through the tall grass. She stayed on the gravel trail, following it into a field. She stopped at an old wooden fence.

He could sense animals nearby, farm animals obviously, but whether they were sheep or cattle, he didn't know. He should; he was sure the two animals were easy to tell apart, but since he'd avoided all things rustic until now, he wasn't sure.

Jolee leaned her elbows on the weathered railing, staring out at the pasture colored in shades of gray, monotone but bright from the moonlight.

"Jolee?" He came to stand beside her, studying her profile rather than the pastoral scene.

"I love how you say my name," she murmured, not looking at him.

Her words pleased him. He didn't quite understand why, but they did all the same. Then she glanced at him, and he could see the uncertainty in her eyes, he could sense indecision on her skin.

"But I keep telling myself I shouldn't."

"Why?"

"I don't want to trust you," she said.

She shouldn't. He wasn't the trustworthy sort. But greedy creature that he was, that didn't stop him from wanting her trust.

"Why not?"

"What do you think of me? Honestly?"

He frowned. What did she mean?

She must have seen his confusion, because she added. "I mean, one minute you're running to my rescue like a knight in shining armor. But then the next you treat me like dirt." She didn't sound accusatory, but rather just stating the facts.

Those were the facts. He had done both. Although he'd never claim to be a knight in shining armor. He was far too tarnished.

"The other night, when I was rude to you, I was having a bad . . ."

"Day," she supplied.

"Well, it's been considerably longer than that, but yes."

She looked back out at the pasture, and he could tell misgivings still warred inside her.

"You're right," he said. "I am sorry to be so confusing. I confuse myself."

"Why?" She turned now to face him. Her eyes had lost their look of uncertainty and now contained only concern. Concern for him. He could sense the emotion in the air. A warm, stroking sensation, caressing his skin. Comforting.

He was amazed at how she changed her feelings so quickly. She only had to believe someone else needed help, and all her self-preservation disappeared. Eventually, someone was going to really hurt her, and that was why he needed to stay close.

"I haven't had many friends," he admitted. None, to be exact. "I suppose I don't know how to react at times. But I think you could help me."

Hadn't he just told himself that he needed to stay near this woman to protect her? Now he was the one asking for help. From a mortal. He waited for the rush of disdain for himself. For being weak and pitiful. But the flood never came. He only felt hopeful, and maybe a little uncertain. Again she stared out at the field, apparently considering his words.

Some distance away, just beyond a cluster of trees, a flock of sheep came into view, all huddled together. Their white coats seemed to glow in the moonlight.

Finally she sighed. "I just don't know, Christian. Part of me does want to be your friend. Very much. But the truth is I don't have a great track record with guys, platonic or otherwise. I'm a little gun shy at the moment."

"Because of friends like Mark?"

She nodded, not making eye contact. "Among others."

"I'd like to think I'm not like Mark."

She smiled at that. "No, you definitely are not like Mark."

"Did you leave your hometown because of Mark?"

"No," she said, and for a second he thought she wasn't going to continue.

"We dated years ago. Nothing very serious." She turned to face him, wrapping her arms around her midsection as if to shield herself. From a chill or from his judgment, he wasn't sure.

"He has always shown up every now and then, although I never expected him to come find me here. For some reason, he can't seem to let me go. I guess because I broke up with him. He wasn't used to being the one dumped."

Christian raised his eyebrow. "Please tell me that's because he didn't have anyone else to dump him before you."

Her eyes drew together and her jaw set, and he knew that he'd made a faux pas.

"What does that mean?"

"I . . ." He knew he should drop the subject right here. He wasn't so clueless in communication that he didn't know when he was digging a hole for himself. "I can't imagine the type of woman who'd want him."

Or maybe he was.

Her frown deepened. "Well, I dated him. What type of woman do you think I am?"

Hole getting wider, getting deeper.

"I think—I think you are a woman who wants more. Who can have more."

Her brows relaxed. "Do you?"

Yes, he did. He realized he didn't really know her. He didn't know what motivated her. He didn't have any idea what she really wanted. She owned a bar. She lived in a nearly condemned trailer park. None of which necessarily spoke of a person who was hungry to escape a difficult existence. But he knew she was searching for more.

"Yes, I think you want more, and I don't think there is anything wrong with that."

If he expected her to be pleased by his statement, he didn't get the response he wanted.

She sighed and gazed back out at the sheep. "I don't know. Sometimes I think it's impossible. That some people aren't destined for anything better. It's too hard and . . . disappointing."

"But it's worth the hardship. You need dreams and goals."

Good God! What was he, a vampire in self-imposed purgatory, doing telling a mortal that she needed dreams and goals? He, who'd spent his entire existence focused on one goal, one dream. Lilah. Only to discover she hadn't been worth his obsession. She hadn't even been remotely who he'd thought she was. And he was counseling Jolee. It was quite ridiculous, really.

She glanced over at him, then smiled, a broad smile that outshined the bright moon above her.

Suddenly his counseling seemed a stroke of genius.

"You're right. I know you are. I'm just having a moment of self-pity. Ignore me."

There was no way to ignore her, not when she smiled like that. He forced his gaze to her eyes, dark, but sparkling in the moonshine.

"Believe me, I've been known to corner the market on self-pity."

Her smile turned sympathetic. "Well, if you promise to ignore mine, I'll ignore yours."

"Deal."

She smiled wider, this time in the direction of the sheep. They had moved closer. One bleated. Another answered.

He leaned his arms on the fence, watching them with her, feeling a strange measure of peace.

"Why did you hit Mark?" she asked suddenly.

"I didn't want him talking to you like that. You don't deserve that."

She glanced at him, and then before he realized what she

intended to do, she hugged him. Her good arm coming around his neck, her injured arm around his back.

The hug was quick, impulsive. But her scent lingered after her touch was gone. The brief contact with her body heated his skin as he absorbed her warmth.

Need flared. He wanted to pull her back against him and taste her heat, but he didn't. He stepped away from her instead. She gave him a smile that said she was embarrassed by her actions. He sensed she was regretful, too.

He started to speak, hoping that would calm his longing and her awkwardness.

But she spoke first. "It's very late. We should go."

She started back up the narrow path to the road.

His hunger flashed as he noticed how her jeans molded to her backside and displayed her long legs. The effect of her arms around him still burned his skin. He pulled in a deep breath, willing away his yearning, his need.

His cock hardened, almost painful against the zipper of his pants. But his fangs remained retracted, even as the hunger surged through him.

Behind him, he heard the fretful bleating of the sheep, and felt the minute vibration of the ground as the flock fled. They sensed him now, his need making him a distinguishable predator.

Jolee stopped at the road and waited for him.

At one time he wouldn't have let her walk away. When he'd wanted to feed, he'd done so, no hesitation, no remorse. He would have fed from her, satisfying himself. And he could have satisfied her, too, with his bite. Now, he couldn't do either. He was neither a man nor a vampire.

Now, he was just standing in a field in West Virginia, making the sheep nervous.

Chapter 9

Jolee waited at the side of the road for Christian, feeling utterly stupid. Why had she hugged him? The embrace had been an impulse, and as soon as she'd wrapped her arms around him, she realized she shouldn't have. She liked the feeling of his hard chest against her breasts and the muscles of his shoulders under her fingertips. The brief touch had made her incredibly aware of everything about him, and she had practically ignited with desire.

Christian had looked uncomfortable with the gesture, too, but not because he wanted her. She was sure of that. He'd said he wanted to be friends. Not have her throw herself at him.

Although the hug was meant in no way to be a come-on. She'd just felt happy that he'd been there tonight. That he didn't seem to believe Mark's hateful words, and he'd felt strongly enough about her to stop them.

A warm hum joined the lingering low burn in her belly. Having a champion was so novel to her. She could defend herself. She'd done so for years, but tonight she hadn't had the energy for Mark's attack. She was sore and tired and emotionally worn out. And Christian had been there.

He started up the path. She noted the sheep, in the distance behind him. They were bleating and running in the opposite direction from them, but she didn't give their behavior much thought. She was far more worried about what Christian was thinking than what the sheep were.

As he approached, she couldn't tell his thoughts. The darkness shadowed his face, but she knew bright sunlight wouldn't have helped. She was sure his poker face was back in place.

Neither spoke as they started down the road toward the trailer park. After a few steps, he changed positions, shifting to her other side so that he was on the outside, near the road. Being protective again, she realized. She didn't want to lose that. Not yet.

But still neither said a word until the silence threatened to suffocate her. She didn't want the night to end this way. She'd had too much stress, too much angst of late to let go of something nice in her life. And Christian's friendship would be nice. Her attraction to him was torture, but she could control that. She wouldn't let it ruin a friendship. She needed a friend more than a lover.

They turned into the trailer park, and she knew she had to say something. Part of her thought she should let the hugging incident go and talk about something completely different. But another part of her wasn't listening. That part appeared to be running her mouth.

"I hope you know that hug was only intended as a thank you."

"I know," he answered, his voice low and a little husky. He didn't look at her.

"Because I realize you just want to be friends. And that's what I want, too."

He didn't respond, which only spurred her on like a nervous, chattering schoolgirl.

"I wouldn't hit on you, because I know that you don't find me attractive and, well, I wouldn't hit on you anyway, because I'm really not like that. So—"

Christian stopped and caught her fingers, tugging her to face him. "I enjoyed your hug. And I know you only meant it to be a gesture of thanks."

Relief calmed the tightness in her chest. "I'm glad. I—I just don't want you to think that anything Mark said was true."

"I don't."

She smiled and suppressed the urge to hug him again. Talk about learning nothing from past mistakes. Instead she squeezed the hand that held hers.

"Good."

They continued on, their hands still linked as they strolled to their places. Neither seemed in a hurry to get there.

"Jolee."

"Hmm?" she responded, glancing at him.

In the light from their trailers, she could see the strange expression on his face. His pale eyes were intense as he pulled her to a stop and searched her face, scrutinizing each of her features.

He reached up and touched her cheek, his fingers cool against her skin. "I don't think you are unattractive."

"You don't?" She knew it was a rather inane response, but she was so distracted by his sudden touch, and what it was doing to her insides, the brief question was the best she could do.

"I don't," he murmured.

As if in slow motion, his head lowered. But not until his mouth met hers did she truly believe he was going to kiss her. She whimpered, startled by both the occurrence and how wonderful his lips felt pressed to hers, cool like his fingers but leaving fire in their wake as they moved, carefully, gently sampling her.

The kiss wasn't one of domination or uncontrollable passion. It was slow and gentle, even a little uncertain. But that didn't temper her response. If anything, his tentative caresses fired her desire far more than the wildest kiss. His mouth worshipped her as if he were touching something fragile and precious. She imagined him lavishing that same considerate attention on her whole body. Her toes curled in her sneakers.

She moaned, the sound vibrating between their lips. Then his mouth was gone. In fact, he broke all contact, his hand moving away from her cheek, his fingers releasing hers.

No, her body cried out. She didn't want to stop. Never had anything felt that perfect, that right. But instead of voicing her protest, she took a deep breath and opened her eyes.

Christian stood a few inches from her, his gaze not on her, but on the ground. His artfully messy hair shielded his face, making it impossible to see his reaction. Was he upset? Did he regret kissing her? Or was he as shaken by the perfection of the touch as she was?

"Christian?"

He stared at the ground a second more, and the muscles in his shoulders relaxed as though he was forcibly calming himself. Finally he raised his head. His eyes looked even more intense than usual and a little wild. The pallor of his skin was deathly pale, and his cheekbones and jawline appeared more pronounced.

"Are you all right?" she asked, taking a step toward him.

He looked away again.

"I have to go," he said. His voice sounded rough and deep, all his smoothly accented words gone.

"What's wrong?" She started to reach for him, but he jerked back as if her slightest touch would burn him.

"I can't talk now." He stumbled backward toward his trailer, all his usual grace gone.

"I will see you tomorrow," he added, almost as an afterthought.

She nodded, although she wanted to follow him and demand to know what was wrong. Really wrong. How could he go from kissing her so gently to looking like a half-crazed maniac?

He spun and bounded up his stairs, closing the door with a sharp bang behind him. She stayed in the middle of the road, dazed. What had just happened? She considered his paleness, his wild eyes, his sudden anxiety. She'd seen all those behaviors before.

No, she didn't want to go there. Especially not after he'd just given her the best kiss of her life. Not after she'd just reacted to him like she had no other man. But she'd known right along something had to be wrong with Christian. Very wrong for him to be here in Shady Fork. And she did know what those kinds of symptoms—paleness, acting crazy, and anxiety—meant. Vance had looked just the same way the other night.

She'd been stupid to forget. He might be beautiful. And often quite gallant. And very possibly the best kisser in the world. She also knew she'd been right about him. He had a problem. She just hadn't known exactly what the problem was. Her chest tightened and her throat felt like she couldn't pull in enough air as the truth hit her. And she absolutely knew what a drug problem looked like.

Christian paced back and forth in front of the window, his agitated movements hidden from her by the darkness of his trailer and sheer curtains. She remained in the road, staring at his trailer, bewilderment clear in her dark eyes. He continued to pace, trying to calm the need raging in him. Willing her to go into her trailer and take temptation out of his sight.

She finally climbed her steps and disappeared inside. But her absence didn't lessen his yearning. He ached with it, every muscle in him tense and throbbing. Why had he kissed her? He hadn't even realized his own purpose until his mouth was pressed to her lush, wide lips.

Since crossing over, he'd never had the inclination to kiss a mortal. He'd always believed vampires who seduced their victims by using kisses and caresses to be masochistic fools.

Why bother to seduce, when he could just take what he wanted? So much more efficient.

Or were those Lilah's beliefs, and he just followed them without question because that was what he did? Good little lackey that he was.

Lilah believed that a vampire should only find sexual satisfaction with other vampires. They were superior to mortals by the virtue of their strength, abilities, and wisdom. They should not defile themselves by mating with a creature that was lesser. He'd believed her, not only because he did consider himself above mere mortals, which he had, but because that belief meant that she was his and his alone. She might have gone to others to feed, but she derived no real sexual pleasure from the experience; her love was his alone. Of course, that had been yet another falsehood he'd believed because he'd wanted to.

He spun again to stalk back across the room. His cock pulsed, rigid, insistent. His need and uneasiness weren't lessening. The memory of Jolee's soft, velvety lips against his, responding to him, caressing him in return, played vividly through his mind, over and over.

He couldn't recall a kiss ever being like that. Breathtaking pleasure created by the mere touching of mouths. Lilah only used her kisses as an enticement or a lure to get what she wanted. Kisses given with no warmth or gentleness, only manipulation and domination. At the time, Christian had found her calculating teases to be captivating. Now he couldn't recall why.

Jolee's sweet response and gentle surrender was infinitely more thrilling. A kiss accepted and returned purely out of enjoyment. He'd never experienced anything so magnificent. Her scent and heat clung to him, still brilliant and warm. Desire vibrated through him. He bit his lip, expecting his fangs to pierce it. They didn't. Instead, his cock pulsed against the restraint of his zipper.

He growled, disgusted with himself. What the hell was

going on with him? He should be able to control the desire. With the hunger fed, he shouldn't have any reaction like this.

He went to the fridge and took out his last packet of blood. His meal for tomorrow night. He went to the drawer and grabbed a straw, stabbing the plastic. Blood rose up in the white tube, then drained back down. His cock seemed to mimic the action.

He drank, draining the small bag in mere moments. He waited. Waited for the blood to hit his system and calm him. But it didn't. His cock still strained, his body still ached.

"Shit!"

Something wasn't right. Had he rationed himself too long? That had to be it. If he was going to be around Jolee, he had to satisfy this need. He couldn't lose control and kiss her again. He couldn't have her thinking that he was interested in her in a romantic way. That was way beyond his knowledge. Even having a friendship with her was going to be a stretch. He hadn't exactly had much practice on that front.

But he was going to be her friend. She needed him, and in truth he needed her. Aside from the occasional erections, he had done all right being pseudo-human. If he fed more, he'd have total control again.

He had to find a solution to his attraction problem tonight. He considered going back to Mark and trying to feed from him. But he didn't think he could. Even if his body cooperated, the smell and greasiness of the man would be enough to nauseate him. He considered the sheep, but that was just too disturbing to be contemplated for more than a split second.

That left the hospital. He needed more blood. Drinking larger amounts didn't mean he'd destroyed his plan. After all, a bag wasn't alive. That was why he'd turned to the pouch in the first place. And just to prove he'd become a kinder and gentler vampire, he'd always taken the expired bags. And to think he'd once sent back wine for poor vintage. Now he was searching for the day-old blood. But he had to do what he had to do, and he couldn't risk acting unpredictably around Jolee, or worse, frightening her.

He needed more.

With that decision made, he waited for the hunger to flare again as it always did in the anticipation of being satisfied. Yearning still prodded him, but he didn't feel the great eagerness he'd expected. In fact he felt more drawn to see Jolee again than to feed. The rationing had affected his reactions as well as his preternatural abilities. That would explain the kiss. He'd been ravenous for Jolee, but because he couldn't feed from her, he'd . . . kissed her?

The explanation seemed a little far-fetched, but it was the only one he could find. He liked Jolee, that alone was a huge oddity, but to be attracted to her?

No, his reaction to her touch, to her lips, that was the hunger. And he planned to satisfy that. Tonight. Then he wouldn't see her as anything other than a nice mortal.

He grabbed his car keys. He really hoped the clerk with the squeaky white shoes and clipboard had been a blood donor.

Chapter 10

Was she ever going to have a night when she didn't come to work obsessing about something? Jolee finished putting the change in the register, washed her hands, and then started filling metal buckets with peanuts from a large plastic tub under the bar. But the task didn't get her overactive mind off her current fixation.

Christian's kiss.

Why had he kissed her? And why had she allowed herself to react? She'd known, from the moment she moved into her trailer, he had to be in some sort of trouble. The car, the clothes, all of it screamed something wasn't right. But last night, she'd let herself forget. All because of a pretty face and a few good deeds. And a kiss.

She sighed. God, that kiss.

See, that was why she was in this mess. But she wasn't even going to ask him about the kiss when she saw him again, because they had to discuss something more important. His addiction. If he was an addict, he needed friends. She believed that. But he needed help more. She was willing to do what she could. Although she knew from Vance that she couldn't help him unless he wanted it.

Last night, as she hadn't been able to sleep, she realized what the list was on his fridge. A twelve-step program. She hadn't put that together at the time. She didn't understand why he titled it "Being Human." But she did know that was what it was.

So he seemed to already want help. And she would offer any help she could. But she wasn't going to be involved with him in a romantic way.

Involved with him. She didn't even know if that was what the kiss meant. It could have been simply a kiss designed to show her she was an attractive woman.

She paused, a fistful of peanuts forgotten in her hand. How would he kiss if he was actually into her? Her poor heart couldn't handle even the thought.

She blinked, frowned at the peanuts, then dropped them in the bucket. Hadn't she just told herself she wasn't going to get involved? No more thinking about kisses. She picked up the tray now loaded with filled buckets and started distributing them to the tables. Glancing at the door, she wondered if it was going to be another busy night.

Then she wondered if Christian would stop by. She told herself it was best if he didn't, but that didn't stop her from hoping he would. She couldn't talk to him here, but at least she could see how he looked and how he acted.

The back door opened, causing Jolee to jump.

"Sorry," Jed rasped. "I didn't mean to scare you."

She smiled. "You caught me daydreaming."

Jed gave her a knowing smile as though he knew exactly who she was daydreaming about, then he headed to his usual barstool.

"How's the arm?"

"Much better," she told him. It was still stiff, but overall, she felt pretty good.

She glanced at her watch. It was five, and she crossed to flip on the "Open" sign and unlock the front door. She opened this early for the happy hour crowd, which she hadn't actually gotten yet. But she was ever hopeful. Then she went around putting up all the windows. It was a warm evening, and she didn't have air conditioning. Well, she did, but that was on the fritz when she bought the place. Another expense to deal with, later.

"Well, let's hope tonight is like last night," she said, going to the bar to pour Jed a beer and herself a glass of ice water. She took a long sip, then sighed.

Then she looked at the closed door.

By 8:30 P.M., Jolee was starting to consider two possibilities. The bar wasn't going to be as busy as last night, not even close. And she was starting to doubt whether Christian would stop by. Maybe he was embarrassed to see her. Maybe he was unwell. She tried to tell herself his absence was just as well. Herself didn't buy it.

She filled a mug for Dale, one of her half a dozen or so patrons, and strolled down the bar to place the beer in front of him.

"Slow night," he commented.

"Yep, should have been here last night. It was hopping."

"Well, it's early yet."

She nodded. It was Friday night; it should be much busier than a Thursday night.

With everyone set with drinks, she left the bar to wander to the jukebox. She sighed, dropped a quarter from her apron in the slot, and then punched in "Sundown" by Gordon Lightfoot. The tune seemed appropriate as she watched the light fade to black outside the window. She meandered back to the bar, taking a seat next to Jed. Well, this wasn't the first long, profitless night they'd shared, and she guessed it wouldn't be the last. She'd been too quick to hope the bar's business was changing.

Just like she'd been too quick to be attracted to Christian. She didn't think she was a reckless person. As she glanced at her dead bar, and longed to see someone who was probably very bad news, she decided she might be misjudging herself. She glanced over to the booth where the karaoke waited silently. She had a huge selection of songs, and even without people to sing them, the music would be a nice change from the jukebox. She'd heard every song on that old machine at least twenty times.

She slid off her barstool and walked over to the booth. The sound system was elaborate, with three different CD players and knobs and buttons that ran the monitors and speakers. She pushed the "on" switch and the system hummed to life. She then flipped through the books of CDs. Country, rock, disco, even gospel. You name it, she had it.

Well, nothing released within the past six months, because she didn't have the funds to keep the lists updated, but still hundreds of choices. She picked out one, a Neil Diamond classic, and more importantly, a song she didn't have on her jukebox. She put the CD in and pressed the play button, then adjusted the volume. "Crackling Rosie" began, upbeat and fun. The lyrics appeared up on the screens, clear and crisp. The few patrons turned from the bar to look at her and then to the screens. Reading along.

She smiled at everyone and shrugged. "Just thought I'd see how it's working."

The bar was slow enough that she could probably run back and forth to play songs and serve drinks. At least it would keep her mind occupied. She was tired of her thoughts tonight. She fixed the microphone, attaching it to the stand beside her in the booth. And she plugged the socket into an outlet marked "microphone" with red labeling tape.

The microphone shrieked to life, the deafening, high-pitched noise making her and everyone else jump. Jolee quickly brought it out of the booth away from the other equipment.

"Sorry." She winced as she placed the stand on the stage.

The Neil Diamond song ended, and she picked another. An old country song she remembered from her childhood, also not on the jukebox. Then she went back to the bar, taking three of the karaoke songbooks with her.

She placed one near Dale and another farther down the bar.

Then she walked over to another of her regulars, an odd little man who came to have his pitcher of beer every Friday and Saturday night. He never spoke, except to place his order, then he sat in the corner, watching the other patrons. She put a book on his table.

"If you feel the urge to sing a little something," she explained.

He just stared at her with his slightly bulging dark eyes. Then he nodded, and that was the end of the conversation. She smiled to herself as she walked away. He might be odd, but he was loyal.

She checked drinks, and then went back to put on another song. The songs did sound a little strange, since they were just the music without the main vocals, but she didn't mind and neither did the patrons. They read along with the lyrics, and looked content to do so. The music certainly lifted her spirits. She wasn't achieving quite the atmosphere she wanted, but it was closer.

"Do you sing?" Dale asked as she came by to check his beer.

She hesitated. Wasn't that why she'd wanted this particular bar? Wasn't it her way of fulfilling a dream that was too far out of her reach?

"I do," she admitted, though it was difficult. She loved to sing, but she still heard the voices from the past telling her she wasn't good enough.

"Sing us something, Jolee girl. You should be the first one to break that contraption back in." Jed nodded for her to go on up.

Her gaze roamed from one customer to the next. They all watched her with encouragement in their eyes, even the odd, quiet man at his table in the corner.

She smiled nervously, but went back to the booth.

What did a person sing for the very first song in her own bar? She flipped through the CDs, nothing jumping out at her. Then she saw a song. Not necessarily a song she'd normally pick, although she knew it well and liked it. And the lyrics seemed to fit how she felt tonight.

She slid the CD out of the plastic sleeve. "The Game of Love" by Santana, featuring Michelle Branch. Maybe not the classic she thought she'd sing, but why not? Maybe it would be therapeutic in some way.

A song about a woman's confusion with love, and how one situation with her man leads to another more complicated situation. Very appropriate, given every time she and Christian were together the relationship seemed to change and become something very different than either of them planned.

She placed the CD in the player, then left the security of the booth to stand before the small group at the microphone stand.

She breathed in, trying to calm her nerves. This was what she'd hoped to do from time to time as she ran the place. She loved to sing.

The intro started and her fingers shook as she held the mic. The words appeared on the monitor. She glanced at the customers in front of her, then she started, her voice warbling on the first lyrics.

The music was upbeat with Carlos Santana's distinctive guitar rifts. She liked the beat and eventually she was lost in the music, rather than her nerves. By the first chorus, her voice rang out with more strength and confidence.

She stopped watching the lyrics, and allowed herself to look at her tiny audience. Jed tapped his fingers on the bar. Dale grinned and nodded. The two guys playing pool leaned on their sticks and watched. Even her reticent patron in the corner tapped his sneaker-clad toe.

She smiled, feeling wonderful.

By the middle of the song, her confidence soared, she sang the lyrics with feeling, shimmying with the beat. She felt better than she had in days. Well, aside from the breathless, incredible moments when her lips had been pressed to Christian's. But she knew after this song was done, she wouldn't feel confused and deserted and irritated with herself.

After the bridge, she glanced up at the monitors to be sure she started in the right place. The words scrolled out in front of her and she sang along. She looked back at the room, a dramatically pleading look on her face as she questioned why her love didn't come see her anymore. But she didn't see her supportive audience. She only saw him.

Christian stood in the doorway, a bemused look on his face, his eyes locking with hers.

Christian had heard the singing as he stepped out of his car, a mellow and mesmerizing voice. He didn't recognize the song, but something about the voice was so familiar, so transfixing. Still, he'd been stunned when he opened the bar door and saw Jolee on the small stage at the end of the room, singing as though she'd done so for years.

She faltered just slightly when she spotted him, but she recovered and finished the song. The few patrons clapped and cheered. Instead of coming over to him, she placed the microphone back in the stand and went to the booth. She didn't look in his direction as she busied herself with the equipment.

He frowned, wondering why. Was she upset because of the kiss? He suspected she might be. He'd said he wanted friendship, then he'd kissed her. His actions would have confused him, too, if he didn't know his erratic behavior was caused by blood lust rather than regular lust.

Now that was satisfied, and he could behave like a normal—vampire. He grimaced slightly. Normal vampire, that was an oxymoron, wasn't it? Well, he could act marginally normal anyway.

He nodded at Jed, who sat on his usual barstool, his customary cigarette hanging from his lips and dangerously close to his bushy beard. The old man nodded back with a shrewd glint in his blue eyes. What did the old guy think he knew? Christian didn't stop to ask, continuing straight to Jolee.

"Hi," he greeted her, amazed at the peace he felt just being near her.

"Hi," she said. Her cheeks were flushed, and he knew the blush wasn't solely from the thrill of performing. Why would she be embarrassed? She had a . . .

"You have a beautiful voice," he told her as the thought completed in his own head. "I shouldn't be surprised; you have such a pretty speaking voice."

She glanced up at him, the blush along her cheekbones turning rosier. "Thank you."

He smiled. She looked pretty tonight too, her thick, dark red hair pulled into a loose bun at the back of her head. Several tendrils had escaped and clung to the graceful length of her pale neck. Her green T-shirt was snug, showing the narrow curve of her shoulders and the swell of her breasts.

He frowned, confused as to why he would still notice such things. Plenty of blood hummed in his veins. He should be back to himself. The self that wouldn't be distracted by a mortal's appearance.

She put another CD in the player, then exited the booth. She moved carefully around him so her body made no contact with his. So they were back to this, he thought, disappointed by her distance. Although he should be glad. After all, he didn't want her upset because she thought he was interested in a romance. That would be awkward.

He followed her behind the bar, and she whirled around when she realized that he was there. "What are you doing?"

"Helping you."

"What? Why?"

"Because you need the help."

She glanced around at the practically deserted room, then raised an arced brow. "I think I can handle the rush."

He had to admit the bar's patronage tonight was a far cry from last night, but she did need the help.

"You need someone here, if for no other reason than security."

She bristled at that, coming to her full height, which brought her level with his nose. She grabbed his wrist and pulled him down the length of the bar to the far end where the other patrons couldn't easily hear them.

"I can handle things here just fine. I've been taking care of myself for a long time."

He didn't doubt that—although he did wonder how she'd made it as long as she had unharmed. She had this desire to trust people. The need was there, warm and gentle, in her dark eyes.

"But you do seem to have a number of shady men showing up on a regular basis," he pointed out, ignoring the fact that he might fit that description, too.

She narrowed her eyes. "Only two, and I could have handled them if you hadn't been here."

He hoped so. He hated to think of what might have happened with either man, if he hadn't been there.

He nodded but crossed his arms over his chest. He wasn't leaving.

"Plus I do have Jed here every night." She gestured to the elderly man. Jed leaned on the bar, his chin propped on his hand, and he appeared to be dozing. A cigarette still dangled from his lips.

"I don't think Jed's going to be much help unless the troublemaker gets close enough to him for Jed to burn the guy with his cigarette."

She gave Christian a disapproving scowl, but then

stepped over to pluck the burning cigarette from the old man's mouth.

Jed jumped, and Jolee crushed out the end in the ashtray.

"You need to be careful with those," she warned.

Jed grunted, taking a sip of his beer as if nothing had happened.

She came back to Christian, the stern yet caring look she'd used on Jed replaced by a determined frown. "You are not working here. First of all, I can't afford to pay you."

"I don't need money," Christian stated easily.

"And secondly, I know about your problem."

Christian froze. She knew his problem? That he was a vampire? Impossible. He hadn't lost complete control during his bouts of attraction to her. She couldn't have seen anything.

"What problem?" he asked.

"You look much better today," she said quietly, "but I know you're using drugs. I can't have an addict working for me."

Drugs? An addict? He wasn't an add—

Well, if she'd seen him last night, she'd sure think he had some sort of addiction as he slinked through the hospital in search of the blood bank. He'd definitely looked like someone who needed a fix. Especially when his shape-shifting ability had failed him, and he changed from shadow into solid form with a bag of B negative hanging out of his mouth. He shouldn't have attempted using his powers in his weakened state.

Fortunately the janitor who'd spotted him had his own drinking problem. He'd just groped in his pocket for his flask, taken a swig, and hurried on. But if that wasn't risking all to feed an addiction, then he didn't know what was. But he wasn't the type of addict she suspected. Of course, blood addiction wasn't generally anyone's first guess.

"I don't use drugs. I never have." Okay, there was an incident in an opium den in China, but that was more than 150 years ago, so that really didn't count now.

She regarded him closely, skepticism still narrowing her eyes. "So why did you look so pale and shaky last night?"

"I hadn't eaten."

Her unconvinced expression stated that she thought that was a lame excuse. Ah, but ironically the truth.

"So you were just hungry?"

Just hungry didn't quite do justice to preternatural hunger, but it was going to have to do.

"I'm—" He struggled to find the right term. "Hypoglycemic." *Thank you, St. Elsewhere.*

"A sudden drop in blood sugar makes you that pale and disoriented?"

Why did he have the feeling she wanted to use a more descriptive word than disoriented? Deranged, perhaps.

"Yes," he said. Drop in blood sugar, drop in blood. Close enough.

Chapter 11

Jolee considered Christian's explanation. She also studied him closer. Tonight, he looked wonderful. His skin tone was golden and healthy. His pale eyes were clear and alert, no signs of disorientation. And of course, there was his perfect physique. Right now, he certainly didn't look like a drug user.

And now that she thought about it, even when Vance had gotten a fix and he wasn't in the throes of withdrawal like the other night, he still appeared pale and spacey. He certainly didn't look like a Greek god.

She wasn't sure how hypoglycemia affected people, but she did know the disease caused a decrease in blood sugar. She could believe that a rapid drop could affect a person quickly and violently. That was how Christian's strange spell had come on. Suddenly. The rest of the time he seemed fine.

She gave him a weak smile. "Sorry."

He shrugged as if being accused of drug addiction was an everyday occurrence, and not remotely insulting.

"So can I get to work now, boss?" he asked, giving her one of his adorable, quirky smiles.

"Christian, I can't pay you."

"And I told you I don't need money."

"Then why are you here?"

He reached for a mug, pulled the tap and poured a perfect glass of beer. "Because I'm just a natural. Who knew bartending was my calling?"

He placed the perfect beer in front of Jed. Then he came back to her, his expression so endearing, it was hard to even recall her point.

She refocused. "Not here, here. Why are you in Shady Fork? You obviously do have money. I can tell by your speech that you're well-educated. Why a trailer park? Why Leo's Brew Pub and Karaoke Saloon?"

His smile faded. He didn't say anything for a moment, his eyes almost looking regretful. "I'm here because I needed to isolate myself for a while."

Isolate? What did that mean? She frowned, and he must have seen her puzzlement.

"I have a lot of things to sort out," he explained. "And I had to get away from my world. But by no means will anything from my world affect your life."

She nodded, even though she still didn't understand.

"I need something to do. And I like it here." He glanced around. "Although I'm not sure why."

Instead of being offended, Jolee laughed at his bewildered expression.

"It just grows on you, I guess."

He stared at her for a moment, his poker face back. "It does."

She wasn't sure, but he didn't seem to be referring just to her bar. She was probably just being hopeful. Now that he wasn't a drug addict, or at least he claimed he wasn't a drug addict, did she think she could have a relationship with him?

No. He was still running from something, and even though he said it would never affect her, he certainly didn't sound like Shady Fork was going to be his permanent residence. He could leave at any time. Not a good choice for a relationship.

"So am I hired?"

She hesitated.

Then the man from the table in the corner approached the bar. He placed a piece of paper on the scarred wood, sliding it toward her.

The paper had a sequence of numbers and the title of a song. She stared at it for a moment before she realized he was requesting a song to sing.

"You want to sing?" she asked, unable to keep the surprise from her tone.

He nodded, then turned to go back to his table.

"See," Christian said, "you need me to tend the bar. You need to run the karaoke."

Jolee picked up the paper, then smiled, realizing his help was indeed the perfect solution.

"Are you sure?" she asked.

"Yes."

Despite the soreness Jolee must still be feeling from the accident, she practically skipped up to the booth. She called the man who'd brought her the paper up to the microphone.

The slim man in a baggy T-shirt and denim shorts walked up to the mic, his movements stilted. Tube socks made his thin legs look even skinnier, the white material pulled all the way up, his bony knees just visible above the tops. He stared out at the room, his face impassive as he waited for Jolee to put on the correct song. The first notes of a song Christian vaguely remembered from years ago began to play. Then the title appeared on the monitor. "Hitching a Ride" by Vanity Fair.

The fact that this man would choose something so bouncy surprised Christian. Then the man began to sing, the perky, pleasant voice he recalled from the original replaced by hoarse, voice-cracking shouts like those of a fanatical punk singer.

Christian actually stepped back, blinking. What the hell?

He glanced at Jolee, expecting to see amazed horror on her face, too. Instead she watched the crazed performance with a giant smile.

Christian grimaced, his gaze returning to the man, who now waved a leg around and twitched in some sort of convulsive dance. And still, he screamed in a guttural rasp that even made Christian's throat feel raw. Yet, in some way, the strange performance was sort of entertaining. Christian found himself smiling, and even clapping when the song was over.

The man then calmly replaced the microphone in the stand and walked back to his seat as if the shouting and twitching had never occurred. He sat down and took a sip of his beer.

Christian shook his head. Mortals were just too weird.

"Wasn't he great?" Jolee grinned as she came up to him to fill a glass with water. Obviously the man's performance had her throat feeling scratchy, too.

"He was something," he said, more interested in the twinkle in her coffee-brown eyes and the huge grin on her lips.

Damn, she was pretty.

He paused, wondering again why he was aware of her. He shouldn't be, but then the observation was hardly a major concern. She *was* pretty—as far as mortals went.

"Jolee," the man in the green baseball hat at the end of the bar called. "I'd like to sing one."

"Sure, Dale." She grinned back at Christian as though the man's request was some great success. Then she touched his arm, her small, work-roughened fingers like heated velvet on his skin.

He stepped back from her, shocked at the intense longing that surged through him from the simple touch. He breathed in deeply, trying to dispel the fierce need building within him, but that only made him more aware of her warm, spiced scent. This reaction should not—could not—be happening. He'd fed, and fed well. He should feel calm, not filled with . . . desire. Did he not feed enough?

She noticed his reaction and her smile disappeared. "Do you need something to eat?"

He frowned, wondering how she guessed his thoughts. Then she turned and leaned down to rifle through her tote bag. His gaze dropped to the curve of her ass cupped by her faded jeans. His fingers twitched as he imagined cupping his hands there, too. She straightened up and spun back to him. His eyes snapped up guiltily to meet hers.

"Here you go." At first, still dazed by his lascivious thoughts, he didn't see that she was offering him something, and when he did, it took him a second to recognize what the item was in her hand. An apple?

She shook the fruit at him. "Take it. I don't want you getting sick."

He accepted the apple, feeling a strange combination of lust and tenderness. Only Jolee would want to feed him when he was considering grabbing her ass. Of course, the throbbing erection in his pants was imploring for even more than a grab.

"Are you all right?"

He nodded, still baffled by his reaction to her.

"You're sure?"

No. But he nodded again.

"Eat that," she ordered as she headed down the length of the bar to talk to Dale.

He stared at her, then glanced down at the apple. If only that would help his situation.

"She's making you crazy, isn't she?"

Christian glanced over at Jed, who sported another of his shrewd grins. How could a man who had nearly ignited himself with a cigarette be so perceptive? Although while Jolee was making him crazy, it wasn't in the way Jed thought.

He looked back to her. She was talking to Dale, her face animated, her eyes flashing with excitement. Then she exited from behind the bar. Christian watched the sway of her slightly flared hips. Again his cock jumped. His fangs, however, didn't react at all.

He frowned.

This just didn't happen. His lust was only tied to his hunger. One did not happen without the other. His cock pulsed again, just like the times before that. As if to say, yes, it did.

"Here's our very own Dale, singing 'Country Roads.'"

Christian turned his attention to Jolee, who was smiling in Dale's direction as he took the microphone. Dale began to sing a song Christian didn't recognize, but the older man had a surprisingly melodic voice. Jolee beamed across the bar at Christian, obviously impressed by the man's talent. But all Christian could focus on was his reaction to her. To that smile, and hair, and pale skin.

Damn it. He wanted to have sex with Jolee.

Chapter 12

"Wasn't tonight great?" Jolee sighed as she leaned forward to wipe down a table.

Christian grunted and tried to stop his eyes from roaming to her ass. Yeah, great.

She began moving dirty ashtrays and small metal buckets containing peanuts and shells to a large tray. Even though her movements were efficient, they gave the impression of being unhurried. Her long arms reached gracefully for another bucket, her long legs extending as she stepped to the next table. Her hands looked elegant, even as she brushed them together to dust the ashes off her fingertips.

"I realize I didn't make much money, but I'm just so pleased that people actually sang. And had fun."

Fun. He guessed tonight was fun, if one labeled torture as a good time. Sadly, he wasn't referring to the karaoke.

She picked up the tray and brought it back to the bar, emptying the ashes and peanut shells into the trash.

"I really think it will attract more customers. Even though it's treated like a joke, people really enjoy karaoke."

She carried the emptied dishes down to the sink where he was washing mugs. He didn't look at her as she stopped beside him, waiting her turn at the sink. He breathed in her wonderful scent, and felt her warmth stroking his skin.

"A guilty pleasure, you know."

Christian's head snapped up. "What?"

"Karaoke," she said, with one of her indulgent smiles. "It's sort of a guilty pleasure for people."

"Oh, right." He busied himself again with the mugs, some of which he was pretty sure he'd washed already. How could he be feeling this? He wanted to groan out loud with frustration. And she stood altogether too close to him, completely oblivious to the fact he wanted to . . . Argh! He didn't even know what he wanted to do.

"Maybe I should make up flyers or something saying that karaoke has returned to Leo's. Maybe something like"—her arm brushed his as she framed an imaginary flyer in the air with her hands— "'Just when you thought it would never happen again. It's back.' Or 'Never say never. Karaoke is back at Leo's.'"

She was kidding, right? *Just when you thought it would never happen again? Never say never?* He knew she couldn't possibly know of his past feelings about mortals and sex. But someone, somewhere had to be playing an enormous joke on him.

"Those might not be very good," she decided, her arm brushing his again as she dropped her hands back to the bar. The brief, innocuous touch sent ripples of yearning straight through him. How could this be?

Then she nudged him with her shoulder. "Come on, Christian, don't tell me my grand karaoke promotion is boring you."

"No," he murmured.

"I can tell it is." She smiled indulgently, still oblivious to the fact that he raged with need for her.

"That's okay," she told him, not referring to the emotions eating at him. "I need to go cash out anyway."

She then looped an arm around his back, giving him a quick squeeze. "Thanks for your help. I really do appreciate it."

He nodded, keeping himself rigid, afraid if he moved at all he'd grab her against him . . . and what?

She disappeared into the back, and he let out the breath he had pent up deep in his chest. Just when he thought he'd discovered the lowest level of hell, he seemed to find another one far lower. This was torture.

"Just go for it, boy," Jed said from where he leaned on his mop in the doorway of the men's room.

Christian must have been so engrossed in every detail of Jolee that he didn't notice the old man watching them.

"I don't know what you're talking about." Christian scrubbed a mug with unnecessary fervor.

He heard Jed amble toward the bar.

"Sure you do. You watched her all night like you'd like to eat her up. Or maybe just a nibble here and there, eh?" Jed wiggled his bushy white eyebrows.

Christian tried to look apathetic, but the imagery that went along with that description was far too intriguing and accurate.

"We're just friends," he told Jed, determined to stick to that arrangement.

"She'll be more than friends," Jed informed him.

"Why?" Why would a sweet mortal like Jolee want an eternally damned vampire like himself?

"Take a gander in that mirror over there." Jed gestured to the glass behind the bar, which was mostly concealed by bottles. "I still say you are prettier than a man has any business being, but I reckon a lady likes that."

Christian didn't know how he felt about Jed's comment on many counts, but he had pointed out the truth. Vampires were abnormally attractive, and maybe Jolee would fall for his looks, but that was all he had to offer her.

"And you look out for her," Jed added with a nod of approval. "Looks and a protectin' nature. That'll get you far."

Christian would have laughed at the old man's take on relationships if he didn't feel so troubled by the fact that he even wanted her in the first place. This shouldn't be a problem. He should be able to find Jed's words amusing, rather than having possibilities.

"What are you two talking about?" Jolee said when she walked out of her office.

"Talking about this and that," Jed said, then yawned. "But this old geezer needs to hit the sack. Old bones—something you two wouldn't know about."

Christian raised an eyebrow. Oh, he had old bones, all right. And they shouldn't be attracted to Jolee.

Jed wagged his eyebrows one more time at Christian, then left.

Christian concentrated on finishing up the dishes.

"Jed has really taken a liking to you," Jolee said after she wished the old man good night and locked up behind him.

"Jed is a nice mo—man," he said, placing the clean mugs on their shelves under the bar. He was surprised, but he did really feel that way. He was also a bit of a meddler, but he meant well, Christian supposed.

"Okay, done," he said with relief as he rinsed out the last of the ashtrays. He needed to get some space between himself and Jolee so he could figure out how to end this pesky attraction. She took the cleaned ashtrays and returned them to the tables.

"Okay." She sighed. "The place looks great."

He tried to look at the place, but his eyes were on her. As they always were whenever she was near.

She smiled at him, pride and happiness in her eyes. "Let's go home."

* * *

Jolee slid into the passenger seat of Christian's car. He had, of course, offered her a ride home, but she could have sworn he was reluctant to do so. She chose to ignore it. She was too happy at the moment, and happiness had been a rare commodity of late.

This time, since she had been mostly senseless the first time, she really looked around his impressive car. The dashboard lit up with different buttons and knobs and an expensive sound system.

"Wow, I feel like I'm in Batman's car." She grinned at him, but he didn't smile back. Not even one of his half-smiles. In fact, he looked rather annoyed.

"I'm sorry. That was just a joke."

"Yes, I got it."

She sighed, not sure what had him in a mood. He really could be ridiculously moody. She supposed it could be his hypoglycemia. In which case, he needed to be more vigilant about keeping food with him.

"I think maybe you should carry crackers with you," she said. "Or maybe juice. There is always orange juice at the bar, so you can drink that anytime you need to."

He glanced over at her, his brows drawn tight over his narrowed eyes. "What are you talking about?"

"Food. You obviously need to eat. Look at you now, getting all grouchy for no good reason."

"I'm not grouchy."

She shrugged, but didn't believe him.

They pulled into the road to their trailers. He maneuvered the car into her driveway and waited for her to get out.

"Do you want to come in?" She knew it was well after two A.M., but she also knew from many nights of walking home late at night that he was usually up anyway. Although she wasn't quite sure why she even wanted him to come in.

No, that wasn't true, she did know why. She wanted to spend time with the Christian who'd arrived at Leo's tonight.

The one who insisted on working at the bar. The one who stood by her, even when she thought she didn't need him. The one who'd kissed her last night.

She knew she should just disregard any of her feelings involving attraction. She'd told herself several times through the course of the evening that she wasn't going to be interested in him in any way aside from a friend. But her traitorous mind always returned to their kiss.

Their kiss had been the kind a woman would remember years from now when she was old and gray. The type of kiss that she'd always thought only happened in fairy tales. Not real. But now she knew there were kisses that made the earth move and fireworks explode. She'd also be lying if she said she didn't want more. But she would settle for friendship, because the truth was she needed that just as much, if not more than, any kiss, even an earthshaking one.

"I don't have much in my fridge, but I could fix us something," she offered.

Christian shook his head. "I need to get home. But thank you."

She nodded, feeling a little forlorn. The reaction confused her. She'd really enjoyed work, even though it had remained slow. The karaoke was a success. The customers joined in. She actually felt good, but for some reason, she didn't want to be alone. Maybe because she wanted to share her joy with someone. Despite her disappointment, she smiled anyway and opened the car door.

"Good night, then. See you tomorrow?"

He nodded, although there was bleakness in his eyes that made her wonder. She wished she understood this man.

She slammed the door shut and headed into her trailer. Following her nightly ritual, she walked straight to her bedroom, turning on lights along the way. As frugal as she tried to be, electricity was one thing she splurged on. She didn't like darkness, especially in this old run-down place. For some reason it made her uneasy.

She reached her bedroom, a tiny square room at the very end of the trailer, just like Christian's. An image of him lying on his bed flashed in her mind. All smooth skin and hard muscles.

She glanced at her bed, covered with a Strawberry Shortcake comforter that she had gotten for five dollars at a yard sale when she moved here. She told herself it was such a good deal she couldn't pass it up. But secretly, she also wanted it. Strawberry Shortcake had been popular when she was younger and she'd never had any of the toys. She pictured Christian lying amongst the pink bows and red strawberries. Even pink bows wouldn't detract from the sheer masculinity of him.

She stopped looking at her bed and twisted the silver knob on her radio. A pop song from the sixties filled the silence. Not as good as real company, but the tune was cheerful and made her feel less alone. She opened the top drawer of her dresser and pulled out a pair of pajamas, light blue boxer-style shorts and a matching camisole top. A picture of a sassy-looking fairy decorated the front of the top with the word "Naughty" scrawled underneath in glittery script. Another bargain purchase.

Christian would seriously wonder about her taste, and her age, if he saw the bedspread and the pajamas together. She chuckled. Well, that wasn't likely anyway. Christian certainly hadn't shown any signs of being interested in her tonight. In fact, he'd kept plenty of distance between them. She had to forget his kiss or she was going to make herself insane.

She changed into her PJs, assuring herself she just wouldn't think about him anymore tonight. Naked on pink bows and red strawberries. Kissing her with gentle, worshipping brushes of his lips.

Groaning, she tugged on her top. This wasn't working. She marched to the bathroom to wash her face. With very cold water.

She'd just finished drying her now tingling cheeks when there was a loud, almost impatient knock on her front door.

Startled, she threw the towel over the rack by the sink and hurried to see who was there, hoping it wasn't Vance again. Relief swept over her as she saw Christian's handsome face in the window.

"Hi," she said, both surprised and curious about why he'd changed his mind.

"Can I come in?"

"Of course." She stepped back, holding the door.

He entered, his hands in the pockets of the black pants he'd worn to work. He also had on the same black silk shirt from earlier. A night of bartending, and he still looked like he'd walked out of a designer clothing ad.

He even had the sexily pensive expression down as he strolled into her almost empty living room and glanced around. Finally his gaze found its way back to her.

She crossed her arms over her chest, feeling self-conscious in her cotton pajamas with her freshly scrubbed face. The fact that he was just staring at her with those contemplative eyes didn't help.

"Are you all right?" she finally asked.

"I don't think so." He shook his head slightly as if to clear some vision or thought from his mind. His eyes focused on her, his gaze wandering over her.

Her body reacted, even though she didn't get the feeling that his look was one of desire. He appeared almost pained.

"What is it? Do you need to eat?" she asked, stepping closer to him.

He blinked, his attention now focused back on her face. "If only that would help."

She took another step closer. What did he mean? Did he need to go to the hospital? His color looked fine. His eyes, while troubled, were clear. He didn't look crazed like he had last night, only distressed.

"Is there something I can do? Do you need to go to the doctor? I'm not great with stick shifts, and your car is a little . . . intimidating, but I can drive you if you want."

"A doctor wouldn't help."

The dullness of his voice alarmed her. "Christian, what is wrong?"

He shook his head, the strangest look of incredulity on his face. "I want you. Sexually."

Chapter 13

Christian hadn't planned to admit his desire. In fact, he'd made up his mind that he couldn't feel this way, period. He'd told himself he would see Jolee again, and somehow his bizarre reaction to her would have disappeared.

When he'd gotten back to his trailer, he'd decided his attraction still revolved around his hunger. Maybe he'd overfed this time. And as soon as she was out of his sight, the yearning had calmed some. He still thought about her as he had for days, but he hadn't felt so tense, and so . . . well, aroused. All signs that his hunger was finally leveling out, and he'd be able to think clearly around her. Then, like a fool, he'd decided to test his theories by seeing her again, tonight.

Well, his theories had failed. Miserably.

She'd opened the door, and his longing had returned, instant and fierce. Of course, the situation wasn't helped by the fact that she was barely dressed. All long, graceful limbs and pale skin.

He'd tried not to look at her. He'd tried to tell himself that he didn't want her. But it hadn't worked. He couldn't take his eyes off her. Her bare shoulders, the lovely line of her neck.

Her breasts, firm and high under the thin material of her top. Her long, lovely legs, bare and smooth. Her feet with high arches and small toes. Pretty feet.

He nearly groaned. Never. Never had he admired a woman's feet. Not even Lilah's, and physically, she'd been perfection. She had been an ancient vampire, and centuries of existence had faded all her mortal flaws.

But remembering Lilah's physical attributes didn't blot out the beauty of Jolee. He found the woman's feet fascinating, for God's sake! Even the chipped, hot pink polish on her toenails.

He was doomed.

He forced his eyes back to her face.

Her dark eyes were wide as she stared at him. "You want me? Sexually?"

Her eyes narrowed, and he realized that rather than being shocked like he was, she was angry. In fact, she was furious. The emotion needled roughly at his flesh.

"I didn't intend to," he explained. "I don't even understand why I do." He muttered that more to himself than her.

A sudden flare in her anger distracted him from his own confusion, the feeling unpleasant on his skin.

"Well, don't knock yourself out trying to figure it out. Because I'm not interested."

He frowned. He'd been certain she was. He'd tasted her desire on his lips when they'd kissed. Hadn't he? Or was that just his own desire? He really wasn't sure anymore.

"I don't want to be attracted to you," he explained, trying to apologize in some way. "I just can't seem to control my thoughts." He glanced down, giving the erection in his pants a significant look. "Or my body."

Jolee's eyes widened slightly, then she frowned and muttered, "Well, try."

She stomped over to the door and opened it, giving him a look that eloquently said, *Leave.* Another emotion swirled around him—hurt. The emotion was faint, nearly over-shadowed by her anger, but definitely there, and also un-pleasant in a different way.

Suddenly awareness hit him. He was a complete ass. She was attracted to him, and he, while admitting his attraction, was also insulting her. His words had been rather rude, now that he thought about it. She thought his dismayed reaction was because his attraction was to her in particular. Which wasn't the case. It was because he was attracted to any mortal, although he could hardly tell her that. But he did need to tell her something. He couldn't tolerate the feeling of her pain; the sad and injured emotion was far worse than the prickly sensation of her anger. But more than that, he couldn't stand that *he* had caused her pain. Another rather shocking revelation.

"I didn't intend to upset you," he said, trying to figure out how to explain.

"Really? What part of your lovely admission did you think wouldn't upset me? The part where you only want me sexually? Or the part where you don't want to want me at all?"

"I don't just want you sexually," he heard himself say. Was that true? If it was, what did he want from her?

She frowned, obviously confused by his words, too. "Then what do you want?"

"I—" He didn't know. How could he know? This was madness. "I don't know. Since I met you, I've had feelings that I thought were long since dead in me." He wanted to continue, but couldn't sort out what the hell was going on inside himself. He wanted her sexually—he shouldn't. He wanted her friendship—he shouldn't. He wanted to protect her from anything that might hurt her—he shouldn't. Unless that anything was himself.

He looked away from her, a frustrated growl sounding deep in his chest. He heard the door shut and her feet padding toward him. Her fingers touched his arm, seeming to burn

him through the material of his shirt. But he didn't pull
away.

"Christian."

Damn, he loved the soft, slow lilt of her accent. He didn't
even have to look at her to feel aroused. Her voice alone
made him crazy with wanting her. But he did look.

She stared at him with those warm brown eyes, coffee
sprinkled with cinnamon. "Please tell me what you're thinking."

He closed his own eyes, willing all the emotions roiling in
him away, but it was hopeless. "I—I don't want to want you,
because I can't offer you anything in return. I'm not a man—"

He sighed, wishing he could just leave it at that. He wasn't
a man, he was a vampire, and that was the reason he couldn't
be with her. But he had to go on. He had to make her understand that all this was his fault. A flaw within him, not her.

"I'm not a man who can give you the type of relationship
you deserve. I don't—know how."

She studied him for a moment, then asked, "What kind of
relationship do you think I deserve?"

"You deserve a man who can give you everything."

She considered that. "And you can't?"

"No."

"What can you give?"

He shook his head. "Nothing."

After a moment, she nodded. "Well, that *is* a little less
than I'm willing to accept."

He knew she meant that as a joke, but he moved his hand
to capture the one at her side. He squeezed her fingers. "You
shouldn't accept anything less than everything."

She smiled, but her eyes were sad. "So what do we do?
Stay friends?"

He wanted that, but he didn't know if he could. "I don't
know."

"I'd like it if we could."

He nodded. "Me, too." Although if he were wise he'd

leave tonight. Get in his car and drive as fast and as far as he could before sunrise.

"Maybe we should just sleep on all this and see how we feel in the morning," she said. "Maybe it will all feel different tomorrow."

"Yes." God, he hoped so. Even just holding her fingers, he was trying to find solutions as to how he could be with her. He wanted her so badly.

But he released her and walked to the door.

She followed some distance behind. Just as he was about to step outside, she stopped him. "Christian?"

He looked back at her.

"Why did you tell me this?"

"I never meant to, it just came out."

She nodded, though she clearly didn't understand, any more than he did. "Well, if it makes you feel any better, I've been trying not to be attracted to you, too."

He didn't answer—but no, it didn't make him feel in the least bit better.

Jolee watched him leave, not stopping him this time. She had no idea what that conversation had been about. It was almost as if he'd had to admit his feelings. As though if he admitted them, they'd disappear. Sort of like admitting anger or hurt. Once the emotion was labeled, the emotion could be worked through and begin to fade. In this case, she was afraid admitting they wanted each other would only make the situation more difficult to ignore, more of a temptation.

But he had openly admitted that he couldn't give her anything aside from a physical relationship, and she wouldn't accept that. She didn't want to settle.

Christian did have a rather tactless way of getting to the point, but in some strange way, he was more open than most men she knew. He never seemed to stop intriguing her. What had happened to him to make him feel that he couldn't love again? She wondered if there had been another woman—maybe there was still a woman. Maybe that's why he was here. He was running away from someone. All the more reason to forget any feelings for him.

She wandered to her window. Lights flickered in the windows from his television. All the things they'd shared, and they were right back to where they were before they met.

She wandered back to her bedroom. She pulled back her comforter and crawled underneath it. She knew sleep was going to be a long time coming, but she didn't have much else to do.

She wished things could be different, but they couldn't. She was sad, but not surprised. Her life had been filled with disappointments and things just out of her reach. She wasn't shocked that Christian was one of them.

Chapter 14

"Where's Christian?" Jed asked as he ambled into the bar and pulled himself up on his barstool.

"I don't know," Jolee told him honestly. "I guess he's at home." She had woken today with a renewed promise to not fixate on a man who had openly told her he didn't have anything to offer.

She'd dated plenty of those types, and she was done. That alone should be enough to keep her mind focused on the things that were important. The success of the bar and success for herself. She was silly to think this was the time to date anyone anyway. She didn't have time to give to a relationship.

Of course, that didn't explain why she kept looking at the door, hoping Christian would walk in. She told herself that the unconscious reaction was because she hoped to have karaoke tonight. Not that she truly believed Christian would show, no matter how many times she checked the door. Why should he? She wasn't paying him, and their relationship was awkward at best. She could hardly blame him if he stayed away. She should thank him, really, for keeping temptation out of sight. She looked at the front entrance again, despite her train of thought.

Thunder rumbled in the distance. Luckily the storm had held off long enough for her to walk to work without getting soaked, but heavy rain had been falling for the last half hour or so. The stormy weather didn't seem to be affecting business. The bar was already busier than last night, and it was only a little after seven. Groups of revelers crowded several of the tables, and a bunch of young men hung out at the pool table, laughing and ribbing each other. The room was filled with an energetic, almost electric undercurrent, as though the impending storm had everyone a little restless.

Another clap of thunder boomed, closer this time. She glanced out the window at the storm-darkened sky. She blew out a breath, and wiped the back of her hand across her damp brow. She sure hoped a nice, fierce storm would cool the temperature. Humidity weighted the air, leaving her skin warm and sticky. The heat made her uncomfortable and fidgety, too. But it also kept the patrons drinking.

She finished loading a tray with drinks and headed out onto the floor. With the heavy tray balanced on her still sore arm, she zigzagged through the tables, stopping here and there to deliver drinks.

"Thanks, darlin'." A man with sparkly blue eyes and a nice smile grinned at her, accepting his beer.

She nodded and smiled back absently. She hurried to the next table, her arm getting a little shaky under the weight and the ache in her shoulder. She started to shift the tray a bit to make it a little more stable when the lopsided weight disappeared out of her hand.

She whipped around, confused why she wasn't hearing a horrendous crash as the drinks hit the floor, only to find Christian holding the tray, sporting a disapproving expression.

"You shouldn't be carrying this."

"Well, I have to get drinks out," she informed him, trying not to be pleased to see him.

"Well, I'll carry the drinks. You go start your karaoke."

She raised her eyebrow at his bossy tone, but did as he said, walking to the booth. She hated to admit it, but she really was pleased he'd decided to come tonight. And not just because she'd be able to run the karaoke.

Christian finished delivering the drinks with some difficulty, because he had no idea who they were intended for, then went back to the bar.

Lightning flashed outside, then more thunder.

"I knew you'd show up," Jed said with a smug smile.

"Oh, you did, did you?"

He nodded at Christian. "I did."

Christian shook his head, chuckling at the old man's conviction. Jed was so sure that he and Jolee were going to be a couple. Too bad they were going to have to disappoint him.

He glanced at Jolee. She wore her customary T-shirt, this one lavender. But instead of being tucked into her usual jeans, the shirt tied at the side. A glimpse of flat stomach showed between the edge of the shirt and the waistband of her denim shorts, and her legs went on endlessly from below. He forced himself to look away.

He was here for only two reasons. To help Jolee, because she did need the help, no matter what she said. And to prove a point to himself. He scanned the room, praying that the subject he needed would be there to help him prove the new point he'd considered. Sure enough, he spotted a rather attractive, petite brunette standing near the pool table.

She happened to look over at the bar just as he spied her. He smiled, and she gave him a tentative smile back. But there was definitely interest in her brown eyes.

"What are you doing?" Jed muttered, looking back and forth between Christian and the woman.

Christian shrugged. "Just smiling at the pretty lady."

"Yeah, well, *your* pretty lady is over there." He nodded in the direction of Jolee, who was still getting the sound system ready for karaoke.

Christian's body responded as soon as he glanced at her, but he forced himself to look away. "She's not my lady, Jed."

Christian busied himself filling a mug of beer for Dale, who was on his regular barstool at the end of the bar. He heard Jed grunt in disbelief as he walked down the bar to serve the beer.

Well, Jed might not believe him, but he planned to prove it to himself. He intended to prove that Jolee wasn't anything special. That his newly discovered attraction to mortal women could happen with any woman. Not just Jolee. Then he could stop fixating on her. He didn't plan to act on his attraction with any mortal, but once he knew that his feelings weren't specific to Jolee, then maybe he could just get over the whole thing. He was obsessing about her, because at the moment she was a novelty. Soon, she'd be one of many mortal females who turned him on.

He walked up to a group seated near the pool table.

"Can I get you anything here?" he asked, although his gaze was on that little brunette. She was watching him, too, glancing surreptitiously over her shoulder.

The group ordered another pitcher. Christian nodded to acknowledge he'd heard, then he approached the pool table.

"Hi," he said, coming to stand beside her.

"Hi." She smiled at him. A pretty smile, although her lips were rather small. Not wide and full like . . . He focused on her body. Full breasts and flared hips. The perfect hourglass figure in her short skirt and tank top. But her legs were rather stocky and her ankles thick. Not those long, go-on-forever legs like . . .

He gritted his teeth. This wasn't working.

"Can I get you a drink?" he asked.

She smiled at him, a coy little curl of her thin lips. Not straightforward and wide like . . .

Damn it!

"I'll take a raspberry wine cooler, sugar," she said in a high-pitched, almost squeaky voice.

He nodded, not even bothering to smile in response. This mortal woman was not going to be the one who proved his case. If anything, she'd made it even clearer that there was so much special about Jolee. But there were bound to be other women here tonight who would attract his interest.

"Hi, everyone," Jolee said into the microphone, her sweet, mellow voice rising over the chatter of the patrons.

He nearly groaned as his body reacted instantly. *Boom.* Like the clap of thunder overhead.

Jolee glanced skyward, then smiled. God, that smile.

"As long as the weather permits, karaoke will be going on, so please come on up and join on in. I'll be around to put out songbooks, as well as pens and request forms. Just bring the forms to me here at the booth, and I'll get your songs on for you. Thanks."

Christian forced himself to stop looking at her and headed back to the bar. He refused to let that voice get to him. Instead he filled a pitcher, setting it on the bar. Then he went to the cooler to the left of the tap, sliding the top open as he searched for a . . . Did the brunette want a raspberry or a strawberry wine cooler?

He settled for the wild berry, twisting off the cap and tossing it in the trash can. He picked up the pitcher and headed back out to the tables.

Jolee was bringing a songbook to the table next to the one that ordered the pitcher. She laughed at something one of the patrons said. The rich, musical sound filled the air, surrounding Christian, warming his entire body.

He cast an irritated look in her direction, but she didn't notice. She talked animatedly to a man who regarded her with hungry eyes and a wolfish grin. Let her become interested in the man, he told himself. He shouldn't care. After all, he'd already rejected her. Sort of. Kind of. Well, whatever he'd done, he would still be better off if she wanted someone else.

He glanced over at the table again and was relieved to see she had moved on, placing books on other tables. Although the man she'd been talking to still watched her, his eyes roaming down her body.

Irritation gripped Christian. He heard a small snap and saw that the plastic handle on the pitcher had cracked in his hand. He quickly set it down on the table, surprised by his own reaction. The men at the table didn't notice as they refilled their glasses.

At least he hadn't squeezed the bottle in his annoyance, he thought thankfully as he brought it over to the petite woman. Crushing glass bottles tended to garner a little notice.

The brunette gave him another coy smile as she accepted her drink, her fingers brushing his as she did so. And he felt . . . nothing. He returned to the bar only feeling frustrated. He wasn't having any luck with his new theory.

A loud clap of thunder shook the bar, and at the same time the door opened. A group of four women ran in, laughing as they shook the rain from their hair and clothes.

That had to be a sign, right?

The foursome chattered, scanning the room for an empty table, until they spotted him. Then they elbowed and whispered to each other and finally approached the bar, taking seats just a few feet from where he stood. One of these women had to have the ability to arouse him with just a few softly spoken words or a rich laugh. He was sure of it.

Jolee glared across the room to where Christian stood with a line of women seated in front of him. Two of the women leaned forward on the bar, offering generous glimpses of their attributes. The women had been there since they walked in nearly two hours ago. Christian had only left them to distribute drinks, then he was right back, basking in their attention.

She stopped watching them and concentrated on the woman at the mic singing a good version of "Redneck Woman" by Gretchen Wilson.

The woman finished, and Jolee applauded along with many of the other patrons. She noticed Christian and his harem didn't applaud. They were too busy flirting outrageously.

She rolled her eyes and turned her attention back to her work.

"Hitch, come on up here and sing us a song."

Her loyal customer, who sat in his corner with his pitcher of beer, approached the microphone. She smiled at the odd man, finding him rather endearing, even when she didn't get a smile back.

She'd jokingly called the man Hitch after his amazing rendition of "Hitching a Ride" last night, and since then, he'd signed his name that way on his request forms.

She put on his song, and he started another of his amazing, shouting performances. She watched him for a moment, then glanced back to Christian. He was still there—still with the women.

She slipped out of the booth and marched behind the bar.

"Christian, can I speak to you for a moment?" she asked, although she hoped her tone told him her request was really an order.

He nodded and followed her down the bar away from his harem. The women watched him leave, displeasure clear on their faces.

Good, Jolee thought, let them be annoyed. She was. And she didn't want to be, and she shouldn't be. After all, she definitely didn't want to be with Christian if he was this fickle, and so openly looking for just a physical relationship. She stopped and faced him. He crossed his arms over his broad chest and regarded her with those aggravatingly un-readable eyes.

"I don't care if you chat with the patrons," she told him, "but not at the expense of the other customers."

"What do you mean?"

"Just what I said. I don't want my other customers ne-glected because you are too busy flirting."

"You are jealous," he said with one of his half-smiles.

She clenched her teeth. His little smile was no longer cute, just very, very annoying. "I couldn't care less who you talk to—or flirt with. Just do the job that you *had* to have and I'll be perfectly happy."

He raised an eyebrow in response but didn't say anything. She felt like screaming at his cool reaction, but instead she spun and stalked back to the sound system, just as Hitch fin-ished roaring his way through another British Invasion classic.

She wouldn't let Christian get to her. What was the point? His behavior tonight made it pretty clear that he wasn't wast-ing any time being upset about the fact that she wouldn't have a casual fling with him. She glanced in his direction. He was back with the women, although he appeared to be excusing himself. She didn't care. Well, she did just a little, but that was only because he'd told her that she'd made him feel something he hadn't for a long time. Obviously his idea of a long time and her idea were two very different things.

"Hey there."

Jolee looked up to see one of the men who had been try-ing to flirt with her all evening.

She smiled. "Hi. How are you? Having fun?"

"I am," he said with a big grin. "But I'm wondering when we get to hear you sing. You do sing, don't you?"

"I do," she said. "I guess I could sneak in a song."

"Just for me?"

"Sure. Just for you." Maybe singing would make her for-get that Christian was really making her miserable.

* * *

Christian noticed the moment the guy who'd been watching Jolee all night got up and approached her in the booth.

As usual, jealousy twisted his gut, just as it had all night, every time that guy talked to her. Here he'd accused her of being jealous, and he was the one who couldn't stand watching her talk to him.

But the man quickly returned to his seat, although he still watched her as if he'd like to be doing far more than just looking. Christian glanced over to the bar where the women stared at him with the same avarice as Jolee's admirer, but he didn't feel any satisfaction at their hungry gazes. The point of talking to them wasn't to make Jolee jealous. The purpose was to see if he could be attracted to one of them. And he couldn't. Not even the tiniest twinge of lust. He could feel the hunger when he looked at them, but no desire.

"Well, I guess it's my turn at the mic tonight," Jolee said, drawing his attention back to her. She put a CD in the player, then came out from behind the booth to stand at the microphone on the stage.

Her hair had started to loosen from her usual bun, tendrils clinging to the dampness of her overheated skin. She looked flushed and a little disheveled, like she'd just made love.

Christian pictured himself against her warmth, her body tight against him, her long legs circled around his hips, her lush mouth pressed to his. He pulled in a breath, trying to dispel the image.

The music started and Jolee began singing a song that asked did he want to dance with her. Her voice started out sweet, coaxing her partner to join her, but her plea became more persuasive, more seductive as the song progressed.

Christian watched, mesmerized. The words of the song might have referred to dancing, but the way she sang them implied so much more. His already aroused body ached with each of her honeyed pleas. Desire pulsed through him, responding to her voice, to the way she held the microphone, the way her mouth moved with each verse. Her hips swayed, her eyes closed.

She was no longer talking about dancing, she was talking about making love. No matter what the lyrics said.

He knew it. He glanced around. And so did every other man in the room. But no other man was going to get that chance. Only he was going to make love to her.

Chapter 15

Rain pattered on the roof of the bar. The steady sound didn't block out the deafening quiet inside the bar. Occasionally Jolee could hear the clink of glasses or the slide of a chair, but otherwise just the rain.

She sat in her office, forcing herself to concentrate on the money and receipts. This was her most successful night to date—a successful night, period. The kind of night that would assure her a profitable business and a nice income. She knew she should be thrilled. Instead she just felt irritated and ready to be somewhere else, namely at home in her bed.

More glasses clinked in the barroom. Christian washing glasses. She'd told him to go home, that she'd handle closing, but he'd insisted he would stay.

"You can't walk home in this weather," he'd said. But she would enjoy the cool rain on her skin. Although it would probably turn to steam as soon as it touched her. She was that furious.

Christian was enough to make any woman insane—and infuriated. First he spent most of the night flirting like a sailor on leave with every woman in the bar. Then the last part of the night, he'd been hovering around her, shooting daggers at any man who so much as smiled at her. He'd even been snappy with her as if she'd been the one flirting all night. As if he had any right to be snippy in the first place. He was the one who said he wasn't interested in a real relationship.

Argh! Men!

She hit the total button on the calculator with more force than necessary, then she wrote down the total in her accounting ledger. She just wanted to leave. She knew running away wasn't going to fix her problem, but it was the best course of action tonight. She was hot and sweaty and miserable. And she'd had it up to here with Christian Young.

Thunder rumbled again in the distance.

"Jolee."

She jumped, spinning in her chair toward the door.

Jed stood there. "Sorry to startle you. Just pokin' my head in to say good night."

Jed was leaving? Leaving her alone with Christian? Not good.

"It's really raining," she pointed out. "Maybe you should wait until it lets up a little."

"It's fine. I'm not about to melt. Plus, I need to rest."

"Are you okay?"

Jed waved a dismissive hand. "Hell, I'm all right. Just old."

She gave him a sympathetic grin. "I could walk down to your cabin with you."

"Now, I ain't that old. I reckon I can make it there myself. Stay right here. Christian's almost done with the side work anyhow."

She nodded. Well, the sooner she could leave the bar, the sooner she'd get out of Christian's presence.

"Good night," she said.

Jed nodded and disappeared out of the doorway. Jolee continued to watch the door, listening to Jed say good night to Christian. The old man also muttered something about "getting his head out of his ass," but Jolee wasn't sure who that comment was directed toward. She shook her head, then returned her attention, or as much of it as she could, to cashing out. After about ten minutes she was done, and she didn't hear any more noise coming from the barroom.

She spun the combination lock on the safe, tested the handle to be sure it was secure, then stood. She listened for a moment, but heard nothing aside from the steady drumming of the rain on the roof, and another clap of thunder.

Reluctantly, she walked to the doorway. She was annoyed with herself that she was nervous. Christian should not make her nervous. He shouldn't make her feel anything. All she had to do was go out there and tell him she was ready to leave. She didn't even need to make small talk. Just, ready? Let's go.

The lights were already turned down when she entered the bar, and she didn't see him right away. Then she spotted him, sitting in a chair at one of the tables. His head rested in his hands as though he was upset or had a terrible headache.

"Christian?" she said, unable to keep the concern out of her voice, despite her earlier irritation with him.

His head popped up and he gazed at her, a hopeless look haunting his eyes.

"What is it?" she asked, stepping farther into the room.

He stood, the simple movement amazingly graceful. He didn't speak.

"Are you feeling unwell again?" she asked.

He shook his head, still not moving, still not speaking.

Honestly. Did this man ever make it through a night without some incredibly weird behavior pattern?

"You know what?" she finally said. "I'm beat. I'm hot, and I need a shower. I need to eat. Then I need to sleep."

He nodded, and for a moment she thought he was going to agree and follow her. But again, he just stood there.

"All-righty then." She started back into her office to

gather her things, and then she was leaving. Even if she had to walk. She didn't care about that look on his face. She didn't care about why he'd acted the way he had tonight. She just wanted to go home.

Lightning flashed, then the thunder boomed as if to tell her that walking was a bad idea. She ignored the warning. Then, from behind her, Christian spoke, and she couldn't ignore that.

"You sang beautifully tonight. I found you captivating. All the men did."

In the doorway, she slowly faced him. What? Why was he telling her this? Was toying with her becoming a game to the man?

Argh! She felt like screaming. Why was he doing this? And why did her body react, her heart doing a little jump at his compliment. But thankfully, she didn't show him her reaction. Instead she mumbled, "Thank you."

She made a move to go into her office, and again he spoke, stopping her.

"I can't seem to stop wanting you."

She marveled at the offhand way he said things like that. How did he do it? Act like this was just how it was, oh, and he'd taken out the trash, too.

"Well, as I think I told you before, try."

This time she did stride into her office, getting her tote bag and her keys. She started for the door, her only thought to leave, when she realized she had to lock the door after him. But before she could go back and demand he leave, he appeared in the doorway, his tall, muscular form silhouetted against the faint light in the barroom.

She gestured to the door. "I need to lock up."

To her surprise, he crossed the room and stepped out into the damp night. The rain fell lighter now, just a little heavier than sprinkles.

She found her key, then followed him outside. The cool rain felt good on her warm, sticky skin. As good as the rain felt, it was going to be a long walk home in the dark wetness. Another bolt of lightning streaked across the blue-black sky, promising a bigger storm to come. She would be wise to just bear his presence a few more minutes and catch a ride with him. Then she could finally be alone, where she'd likely still obsess about this man. But at least she could do so in private.

She'd just reached Christian's car when he caught her wrist, tugging her to a stop. "Jolee, I think we should talk."

She frowned at him. "About what?"

"About us."

She laughed, the sound humorless. "There is no us."

"I think there is."

She stared at him, shadows playing across his perfect features, his pale eyes vivid even in the dim light.

"I'm really starting to believe you are crazy."

"Me, too," he agreed.

His hand came up to caress her cheek, his fingers gentle and reverent over her damp skin. His eyes held hers, so intense they seemed to glow. Lightning lit the sky again, creating new shadows on his striking face, intensifying the brilliance of his gaze, adding to the strangeness of the moment.

"Why are you doing this, Christian?" she asked softly, not wanting to react to his touch, but quivering inside despite her effort.

"I can't control myself. Not when it comes to you."

His head lowered, and she knew she had to stop him. She had to stop this insanity now. But his lips found hers, cool and moist from the rain. They moved over hers, tasting the rain on her. Again she was hit by the sweetness, the perfection of his touch. She responded despite herself, slanting her lips to meet his. He pulled her closer, deepening the kiss.

Thunder clapped loudly, and with the harsh noise, reality returned. She pulled away and he let her go, his arms falling loosely to his sides.

"Why are you doing this?" She knew she sounded frantic,

but she was, so why hide it? This had to stop before she did something she regretted. Before she got hurt.

"I told you straight out that I don't have any interest in a fling. Go back to your throngs of admirers. I'm sure you'll find one who wants you. *Sexually.*"

"I'm sure I would, too," he agreed easily, which made her want to scream. How was she attracted to this conceited, socially inept, domineering—

"I wanted to be attracted to one of them," he stated.

She shook her head, unable to believe he was doing it again. Being so . . . clueless.

"I do not want to hear about your problems finding the perfect one-night stand."

He frowned. "I never intended to have a one-night stand with any of them. I just wanted to prove to myself that I could be attracted to someone other than you."

He swiped a hand through his damp hair. "But I wasn't. The whole night I only thought of you. Wanted you."

The words shouldn't have brought her joy. After all, what did they really mean? But they did. She was obviously going mad right along with him.

She tried to remain sensible, even though all she could seem to center on were his hungry eyes, the cling of his damp shirt to the muscles of his shoulders and his chest. The lingering heat of his kiss on her lips.

"I—I don't understand what you want from me, Christian."

"I want to be with you. You're the first thing I think of when I awaken. You're the last thing I think of before I sleep. I've tried to stay away from you. God knows, I have. But I can't do it. Your smile. Your sweetness. Everything about you keeps drawing me back."

Her insides quaked. No one had ever said anything like that to her before. But could she trust he wasn't just giving her a line? Men knew the right things to say. They knew how to manipulate a woman into doing what they wanted.

"Jolee, say something." His voice was uncertain, none of the self-assurance from earlier laced through the words.

"So what do you want? What can you give?" She needed to hear exactly what he thought the rules of the relationship would be. He shook his head, looking oddly forlorn, like a bewildered child who didn't know the answer, but knew it was very important.

"I don't have a clue how to be a . . . boyfriend, but that is what I will try to be." Again he looked miserable. "Jolee, I just want you."

She studied him, trying to ignore the thundering beat of her heart. He looked truly wretched, as if he didn't believe he could convince her of his sincerity. Finally, he looked away from her, his defeated expression telling her he truly believed he'd lost. That more than anything convinced her. She had to take a chance. She understood how he felt; she couldn't seem to stay away from him either. She didn't want to.

She caught his face, gently turning him to look at her. Her fingers shook as she stroked his wet cheek.

"I want you, too," she whispered. She did want him, more than she'd even let herself believe.

"I just don't know . . ." She shook her head. "I just don't know if I can trust you. I'm scared."

He caught her hand, holding her fingers. "I'm scared, too."

"Have you been hurt?"

He didn't answer for a moment, then he murmured, "Yes. Yes, I've been hurt."

He closed his eyes, and she got the feeling his admission made him feel weak. Like he didn't want to remember it.

She stroked his cheek, amazed at the smoothness of his skin. To her surprise, he nuzzled his cheek against her open palm as if he was desperate for her touch, for her compassion.

She stepped closer, holding his face between her hands. He opened his eyes, staring into hers. She saw desire in their depths, along with pain and uncertainty. All the same emotions that were in conflict inside herself. Slowly, she lifted her head to kiss him. She didn't want to feel the pain and uncertainty. She only wanted the desire. The closeness that desire could give them.

At first he remained motionless in her arms, and she simply caressed him with her lips, loving the moist softness of his lips in contrast with the strong line of his jaw under her fingertips. Thunder crashed above them, but unlike last time, neither one of them broke the kiss. Instead Christian's arms came around her, pulling her tight against his chest. One hand cupped the back of her head, while the other splayed across the middle of her back.

He took control of the embrace, his lips sculpting to hers, powerful, sensual. His teeth nibbled her bottom lip, and she moaned, finding the tiny nips infinitely erotic. Hot and raspy, his tongue traced the seam of her lips and she opened for him, her tongue mingling with his as they tasted each other's moisture and heat. She moaned again. His kiss grew more passionate, more intense. An all-consuming embrace that promised nothing but more pleasure. Like he would tenderly devour her whole, and she'd never feel anything but absolute delight.

She moved her hands from his face, sinking one in his hair, the wet strands clinging to her fingers. The other hand gripped his shoulder, muscles rippling under her fingers as his mouth continued to consume her. Before she even realized it, Christian had walked her backward, her bottom hitting the cold, rain-drenched hood of his car. She jumped, a surprised noise vibrating in the back of her throat as the cold, wet metal touched the backs of her bare legs.

Christian broke the kiss, staring at her, disoriented, concern shadowing his eyes. "Did I hurt you?"

"No," she assured him with a dazed grin of her own. She brushed a hand on the top of his car. "Cold."

He started to step away from her, but she caught his shirt

and pulled him back. A faint voice in the back of her mind told her this was going too fast. They needed to get to know each other better. They needed dates and chances to talk. They were out in the rain, for heaven's sake! Then his lips returned to hers, and she was no longer listening.

His pelvis pinioned her against the car, his chest pressed tight against hers. The friction of their bodies created a burning heat that overshadowed any coldness. All she could feel was Christian. And nothing had ever felt better.

His fingers glided slowly down her sides, exploring each rise and indentation of her ribs through her shirt, until those huge hands spanned her hips, holding her firmly. Then, without his lips leaving hers, he lifted her and set her on the hood of the car. His hips slid between her legs, keeping her from slipping down over the slick surface. She didn't pause at the sudden shift. She just allowed her hips to cradle him, the rub of him so intimate against her, so excruciatingly thrilling.

His hands found the hem of her shirt and slipped underneath, long, strong fingers stroking over her skin until they reached her breasts.

He lifted his head, gazing at her intently as if waiting for her to tell him it was all right for him to continue. Her breasts ached. Her nipples strained, swollen and taut against her bra, begging for his touch. She didn't even consider telling him no. Instead she guided his hands upward, gasping as his palms cupped the sensitive flesh.

He rasped his thumbs over and around her hardened nipples, pleasure swirling through her with each pass, each twirl.

"Oh my God, Christian," she whimpered, arching against him as he squeezed her, teasing the oversensitized buds.

He frowned as if he wasn't sure if her cry was one of pleasure. "Is that good?"

She nodded adamantly. How could this man not know that he was driving her mad? She wiggled against him, her body wanting more. More of his touch. More of him.

"I want to see you," he murmured, his voice low and rough. "I want to see the paleness of your skin. I want to know what color your nipples are. How they taste."

Her breath hitched in her throat at his words. God, she wanted that, too. She was on the hood of a car, in the parking lot of her bar, in the rain—and all she could think about was his beautiful mouth on her bare skin.

"Yes," she said, agreeing to anything he wanted to do to her.

Christian had no idea what he was doing. He was acting totally on instinct. And every instinct in his body told him he had to touch this woman. With his hands. With his mouth. He had to explore every inch of her.

He watched her, not wanting to do anything that didn't please her, and he saw only desire darkening her coffee-colored eyes. Rain clung to her lashes, to her lips. He leaned forward and licked the drops from her lush skin.

She whimpered, her legs squeezing his hips.

He groaned, too, his erection throbbing against her. This was madness, he knew it, but he couldn't stop.

He carefully peeled Jolee's T-shirt up over her head, dropping the wet garment onto the hood of his car next to her.

She sat before him all perfect pale skin. Her rounded breasts tilted upward slightly under the pink cotton of her bra, the shadow of her dusky areolas and hardened nipples visible through the wet material.

He stared, wondering if he'd ever seen anything as beautiful as this woman, rain-soaked, aroused, and waiting for his touch. He dropped his head, drawing one of those tight buds between his lips. She cried out, her hands gripping his shoulders, her hips grinding against his. He started to pull away, to be sure she was finding pleasure, when her desire swirled around him like the electrical snaps of the lightning above. He sucked harder and received another broken cry.

With amazement, he realized he could make her come with just his mouth on her breasts. It was a heady, powerful realization. Especially given he hadn't pleasured a mortal in nearly two hundred years. Her arousal fueled his. He cupped a hand behind her head, then pressed her down on the silver metal. She held tight to his shoulders, pulling him with her.

Her lips found his, tasting him hungrily.

He lost himself in the thrilling sweetness of the kiss, until the touch threatened to drive him mad. He waited for the madness to trigger his hunger, but it didn't. All he felt was intense desire, overwhelming and so fierce. And here he was feeling so damned proud he could excite her so easily. She had amazing power over him.

He pulled away and moved his hands back to her breasts, testing the shape of them in his palms. She writhed against him. He found the tiny clasp of her bra nestled in the valley of her breasts, and flicked it open. The scraps of material fell away, leaving her bare.

He caught her wrists, spreading her arms wide, and he simply looked at her. Eating up the wanton sight of her. Rain beaded like glittering jewels on the pale mounds, clinging to the rosy tips. He leaned forward and licked the droplets from her pink, swollen nipple.

Her hands knotted in his hair, her body squirming against his, her hips bucking his. He slid his hands down her body to the button of her shorts. He tore his lips away from her beautiful breasts, watching her again as he worked the button undone.

She remained spread across the hood, watching him in return with heavy-lidded eyes. Her desire snapped around him, flicking at his skin, pleading for more. And he wanted to give her more. He wanted to give her everything.

He slowly worked open the zipper and he pulled down the shorts just enough to see her pink panties, and to slip his fingers down inside them. Jolee bucked wildly at the scant touch, his fingers just brushing the tight curls of her sex. He caressed her again. He had forgotten how a woman's hair felt against his fingertips, springy and a little coarse. And how slick and smooth and hot the skin was just beyond.

He stroked her again, this time finding the bud nestled at the top of her sex. He started to swirl a finger around the tiny nub, testing how much or how little pressure to use, when Jolee rose up, pressing his hand between their hips, grinding against him.

"Oh my God," she breathed against his neck, digging her fingers into his back. "Oh my God."

She cried out, her muscles tensing. Just as her release began to scent the air, spicy and awe-inspiring, he felt the sharp edges of her teeth bite into his flesh.

Roughly, he jerked out of her embrace, backing away from her, seeing another woman in her place.

"Lilah."

Chapter 16

Jolee didn't believe it was possible for something so wonderful to turn horrendous in mere seconds. She covered her bared breasts, searching frantically for her T-shirt, which was in a clump right beside her. With one arm still shielding her breasts, she snatched it up. The material, sopping wet from the rain, remained in a clinging ball. A broken, frustrated cry escaped her as she struggled with the stupid thing, shaking it with one hand, trying to straighten the sticking cotton.

Christian caught her hand, gently stopping her frenzied struggle. She jerked her hand out of his loose grip, but also let the knotted shirt plop back to the hood. Refusing to meet his gaze, she tried to decide what to do, what to say. She was such a fool.

She recoiled as something damp but warm settled over her shoulders, and she realized Christian had taken off his own shirt and placed it around her shoulders. She started to shrug the garment off, but then thought better of the idea. Her pride was not worth remaining naked.

She slid down from the hood, turned her back to him, and fastened her bra. The wet cotton chafed her still sensitive nipples, another reminder of what she'd just done. She was a thousand different kinds of fool. Maybe more.

With trembling hands, she struggled with the buttons of his shirt. Then his hands were on her shoulders, trying to turn her to face him. She pulled away, still not looking at him. She couldn't. She didn't want to see the beautiful face that had so easily sweet-talked her. She'd really believed he was being honest with her. That he wanted a relationship— with her. She never would have let things get that out of control if she believed otherwise. Damn it.

She gave up on the buttons and clutched the front closed with her hand. On unsteady legs, she found her tote in a puddle where she must have dropped it when he'd first kissed her. Rain had soaked the top and mud seeped through the bottom.

"Great," she muttered. She slung the ruined bag onto her shoulder, this time not the least bit worried about his expensive shirt, and started shakily toward the road.

"Jolee," he called, his voice low and filled with worry. His deceptive voice.

She heard his feet splashing in the puddles as he followed her.

"Please, wait."

"No."

"You can't walk in this weather."

She laughed, the sound brittle. "Well, you didn't think the weather was too much of an issue a few minutes ago."

She continued toward the road. Suddenly her legs, which were still wobbly, came out from under her, although it was with the help of Christian. He scooped her up as if she weighed nothing at all and strode back to his car.

She struggled, kicking her legs, pushing at his chest.

"Put me down!"

He acted as if he didn't even hear her. She shoved his chest with all her might, but he didn't even seem to notice. With shocking ease, he held her, opened his car door, and placed her inside. Even in her fury, she couldn't help being a little impressed by that kind of strength.

"Stay there," he warned, then closed the door. She debated getting out and running. But what would be the point? He'd probably just catch her again. No, she'd sit here quietly and get a ride home. Just as she should have earlier. She never should have listened to him.

He came around to the driver's side and slid in. He didn't say a word as he started the car's engine and sped out of the parking lot, gravel grinding under the wheels.

Within minutes, he pulled up to her trailer. Before the car had even come to a full stop, she opened the door and jumped out, racing up her steps and into the trailer. She locked the door, then crossed into the living room, her breaths coming in shallow puffs as she tried to calm down. Tears burned her eyes, and she blinked to keep them at bay. She would not cry about this. This would not be the thing that finally broke her. He wasn't worth her tears.

And as angry as she was with him, she was angrier with herself. She was so, so stupid. The episode in the parking lot had been as much her fault as his. She'd been the one who kissed him again. The one who trusted him. Trusted him, even after he'd told her straight out that he had nothing to give a relationship.

He'd told her he'd been hurt. And it wasn't as though she hadn't already deduced there must have been another woman. She had even wondered if there was still another woman. Well, there obviously was—Lilah. And it didn't much matter if she was a *had been* or a *still was*. If he was calling out her name when he was with another woman, Lilah was still very much in Christian's mind.

A sharp rap sounded on the door. She didn't move, didn't look toward the sound. It was Christian, of course, and she didn't want to talk to him. Not now. Likely never.

He pounded again, this time the thin particle board shaking under his resolve. Still she didn't move.

Not until the rattle of the doorknob did she realize that the stupid lock probably wouldn't hold. She spun around, ready to grab a chair and wedge the back under the handle, but Christian was already in the room. He stood only a few feet away from her, and she wondered at his speed. She hadn't even heard him open and close the door, yet here he was in her living room.

"Leave."

He shook his head. "No. We have to talk."

"I don't see any point. Please just go."

He crossed his arms over his chest.

"That damned lock," she muttered.

"You need a new one," he agreed automatically, then added, "Although I would have kicked the door in anyway."

She didn't doubt his words. The idea that he would do such a thing should have scared her, but it didn't. Scared or not, she didn't want him here.

"Christian, I can't do this. I don't want to do this. I just want to go back to before I met you."

"I want that, too. But it isn't going to happen."

She knew he was right, of course.

"But I can start forgetting you now," she said. "Tonight. Please, please just go."

She knew she was pleading, but it didn't matter. The only thing that mattered to her right now was getting him out of her sight. She couldn't look at him. She couldn't think about how she'd reacted to his touch. How easily she'd given herself over to him. While he was imagining another woman.

"I can't leave," he told her flatly. "I can't leave you hurting. Not because of me."

"I'll be fine," she assured him, amazed at her sudden bravado, especially since, on the inside, she felt like curling up and dying. "You can't change what happened. And you can't change the fact that I was a fool and believed that you could give me something that you yourself said you couldn't. We just need to stop this, now."

He nodded, and for just a moment she thought he was agreeing to leave, and to leave her alone. Instead of triumph, she just felt more miserable.

But he didn't leave. His gaze roamed around the room as if he was searching for something. Finally his eyes stopped on her.

"I met Lilah a long time ago."

Jolee opened her mouth to tell him she didn't care. She didn't want to hear, but she couldn't bring herself to say a word. She did want to know.

"She was beautiful and charming and seductive, and I fell for her the first moment I spoke to her. And she seemed to feel the same way."

Despite her hurt and anger, she didn't doubt it. There was something about this man that was so captivating, so alluring, and it went beyond his stunning good looks.

"I believed she was the love of my life, my soul mate."

Jolee's heart twisted in her chest, amazed that she could feel this much pain about the fact he had loved another woman. She had no reason to feel so hurt—it wasn't as if they were in love. But she couldn't help wondering what it would feel like to be loved by this man. As he said, to be the love of his life, his soul mate.

"My family didn't accept her," he said, his expression faraway and troubled. "My oldest brother, Rhys, specifically tried to tell me that she wasn't what I thought. That she didn't love me. I didn't listen. I just cut them off. I wouldn't allow anyone to come between me and Lilah. We were destined to be together, and in my mind, everyone was just jealous of what we had."

He laughed then, a cold, low laugh that made her shiver. "Jealous of what we had. It wasn't until it was too late that I realized we had nothing. Absolutely nothing."

Despite herself, Jolee asked, "What happened?"

Christian didn't know how to answer that question. He couldn't tell Jolee about all the horrible things he had done at Lilah's bidding. All the pain he'd inflicted, because that pleased her. Excited her. The times he'd bitten mortals, violently, brutally, just to arouse her. Blood was the only thing that did excite her, and she loved to watch his attacks. In his madness to keep her pleased, he gratified her as she asked. Through bloodletting, through biting. And her appetite for both were boundless.

Love through vicious cruelty. Why hadn't he seen then what she was? Why couldn't he have seen the truth sooner? Before what he'd done to Jane—and to his brother. His brother.

Christian forced his attention to Jolee. To this slender mortal with dark, sad eyes and lush lips who was just beginning to remind him of everything that was good and showing him again that passion didn't have to hurt. That arousal didn't wound. That satisfaction didn't have to end in pain. He couldn't lose Jolee. He knew she was somehow tied to his redemption. He had to have her forgiveness. Just a little forgiveness for all he'd done wrong.

"My family was right. Lilah didn't love me. She was a cruel, vindictive creature who wanted nothing more than to control and manipulate."

Jolee considered him for a moment, then she tilted her head, an unconvinced look in her eyes. "Well, plenty of people continue to love terrible people."

"I hate her." And he realized the statement was true. There was not an ounce of love left in him. Even the strange emptiness that he attributed to her being gone no longer niggled at him.

"There is a fine line between love and hate," Jolee said.

"I agree. And I mistook hate for love for too many years. I won't ever do that again."

"Then why?" Jolee gave him a pained look. "Why did you call out her name?"

He'd called out because the sensation of Jolee's release and the feeling of her teeth on his neck at the same time had made him think, for just an instant, that Lilah was back. For two hundred years, he had not experienced one without the other. Release and violence went together, because not only did Lilah like to watch biting, she liked to bite herself. Christian had been her favorite toy to ravage in her lust. Vicious, sadistic bites that made him wonder now how she hadn't killed him.

What had he been thinking? He hadn't. He'd been a mindless puppet, desperate for Lilah's affection—willing to do anything she asked. But how did he explain that to Jolee?

He decided to stick as close to the truth as he could. "Lilah used to bite my neck when she'd orgasm. When I felt your teeth, I panicked. It was like suddenly Lilah was back. I'm sorry."

Her eyes widened at his explanation. She obviously found his words a little odd. Okay, more than a little odd.

"She bit you?"

He nodded.

"Like bit, bit."

He nodded again.

"As in to hurt you?"

She cringed when he nodded.

"Our relationship was not normal," he said.

Jolee raised her eyebrows at his flatly stated words. What else had this woman done to him? The idea that a woman had physically, as well as emotionally, hurt him made her ill. How could someone do that? And no wonder he acted so peculiar at times. That had to be very hard for a man to admit, especially one as strong and proud as Christian.

"Did she . . . take pleasure from hurting you?"

"Yes."

Again, a sick feeling filled her. Her eyes roamed over his chest and arms, looking for signs of this woman's brutality, but his golden skin was perfect. But she didn't doubt his words. She knew that some people did enjoy such things, although she couldn't imagine why. Then again, maybe he enjoyed that sort of thing, too.

No, she decided, looking at his almost angelic face. He'd never been anything but gentle with her. When he'd been making love to her, his touches had been excited, passionate, but always tender.

She still felt she had to ask. "Did you like it?"

He shook his head. "Now, I realize that I didn't. But at the time I was so entranced by her, I would have agreed to anything she wanted. I did agree."

Again, Jolee thought of all the women she'd known who did that very same thing, believing bad situations were acceptable, or could be fixed by love.

Protectiveness surged through her. She stepped closer to him. "I can understand now why you feel like you don't know how to have a relationship."

He stepped closer to her, too.

"I am a little out of practice with anything normal."

"Well, I'm not sure I can really help you with that," she admitted.

He gave her one of his half-smiles, and she wondered how devastatingly handsome he must be when he smiled fully. She hoped to find out one day.

"I think you have a better definition of 'normal' than I do," he said, then almost tentatively reached out to brush a damp strand of hair back from her cheek.

"Well, I'll tell you what. Let's start again. Maybe if we take it slow and work together, we can figure this whole relationship thing out." She smiled at him, suddenly sure that was exactly what she wanted.

Extreme, knee-weakening relief washed through Christian. "I'd like that."

He still didn't know exactly what he could offer her, but he had to be near her. He would think about how to end things when he had to, but until that time he just wanted to glory in her. Thinking about his past with Lilah just made the need all the more powerful. He had to be with this mortal. She made him feel more human than all of his steps, all of his blog entries combined. He needed her goodness to erase Lilah's evilness. His own evilness.

"I know this might seem a little after the fact given you already gave me an orgasm on the hood of your car"—she blushed, her cheeks a rosy pink—"but I think we should go slower. You know, maybe date."

He frowned. Dating? Of course he'd heard of the convention, but he'd never done it. Well, maybe those carriage rides around Hyde Park were sort of dates. But what kind of date did Jolee expect?

"You've never dated?" She widened her eyes, obviously seeing his hesitation.

"No. I don't think so."

She shook her head, tempering her shocked look with a smile. "But you do know what a date is?"

"We go places together, and do things." He tried not to sound too lascivious on that last part.

She smiled, lifting one of her finely arched brows, indicating that he'd failed. "And we get to know each other."

Now, that sounded nice. He wanted to know everything about her. And he did want to take her somewhere special and treat her like the amazing woman she was, like he knew she'd never been treated. Although he didn't know where to take her in the middle of the night in Shady Fork. Now, in New York or London or Paris, there he could take her on a date.

"Would you like to go out on our first official date tomorrow?" she asked. "It's Sunday, so we have the night off."

He noted that not only did he still have Jolee, he still had a job. Something amazingly like happiness swelled in his chest.

He nodded. "What would you like to do?"

He knew what he'd like to do, but he stopped his gaze from wandering down her body, shrouded in his shirt.

"How about dinner?"

"Sure." He couldn't eat, but he'd love to watch her do so.

"Great. Let's meet at seven for a date."

"Let's make it eight. I'm really a lot better at night," he told her. For the briefest moment, guilt diluted the happiness in him. He couldn't be with her like a real man.

Then she laughed, drawing his full attention back to her. "Well, you know I'm a night person, too. Eight, it is."

He knew he shouldn't be ignoring his guilt, but he did.

He wanted this, and he'd make sure things worked out for both of them.

Chapter 17

Jolee glanced at the alarm clock on the box she was using as a makeshift nightstand. It was nearly seven-thirty, and she still didn't know what she was wearing on her date tonight. She searched through her meager wardrobe again. Something to wear to dinner. Something to wear anywhere besides work.

She pulled out a lavender satiny dress with a flounce around the bottom, a scooped neckline, and thin, capped sleeves. She'd worked until closing every night after school and every weekend for nearly a month, bagging groceries to buy the dress for a high school dance. She'd been so excited to go, because it was at a neighboring high school, and she'd hoped the Dugan reputation wouldn't follow her there. Turns out it had, and the boy she went with had only asked her because he heard she was easy. He'd spent the whole night trying to look down the front of this dress and cop a feel.

She grimaced and put the dress back. It was the best thing she had, but she didn't need those memories accompanying her. Not to mention, the dress was a little dated. She wanted to look classy. Not like a prom queen in the early '90s. She chuckled to herself. Like she would have ever been prom queen, even in the '90s.

She pulled out another dress. This one was a simple cotton sundress, blue with white swirling designs around the hemline. She'd had it for years, and the seam on one side was ripped. Plus, now that she thought about it, all she had for shoes were dirty canvas sneakers and flip-flops. Not exactly a good look. Although she smiled imagining Christian's expression if she answered the door in the lavender prom dress with the pink flip-flops. Christian, with his designer wardrobe, would be so impressed.

Christian. She'd lay in bed last night, going over what she'd learned about him. In fact, she'd barely slept a wink, thinking about his relationship with Lilah, and what he'd said about this woman. Jolee suspected that was why he'd told her he needed to get away from his world, because his world included Lilah. But why Shady Fork when he could obviously go anywhere? Maybe because Lilah would never think to look for him in some backwater town.

She also had remembered something else Christian had said. That nothing from his world would affect her. Did that mean Lilah was still out there, looking for him? And dangerous? She'd decided that probably wasn't what he meant. He must have been referring to the fact that he wouldn't let his old life affect his new one. Just like she was hoping to do. Of course, she knew firsthand that ghosts of the past had a way of reappearing. But she wasn't going to worry about this crazy woman. She wanted to focus on Christian, and show him that all women weren't going to hurt him. Funny, they both needed to be shown that. In some ways maybe they weren't that different. Except in their wardrobes. There they were miles and miles apart.

She sighed, finally deciding on a denim skirt. Aside from a small fray at the hemline and the fact that the waistband was a little loose due to lots of working and little food, it looked okay. She could cover the waistband with a nice blousy top in dark red that looked good with her coloring, and the short sleeves covered the still mottled bruise on her shoulder. It didn't cover the bandage on her forearm, but that was okay.

She also found her best panties and bra, a matching set in black cotton, and pulled them on. She didn't plan on having another experience with him like on the car, but the nice underwear did make her feel sexier. And given her rather blah outfit, she needed all the supplementary confidence she could get. Not to mention to make up for the pink flip-flops she'd have to wear.

Finished dressing, she headed to the bathroom to do something with her hair and to put a little makeup on her pale cheeks. She ran a brush through her hair, the long red tresses falling in waves just past her shoulders. As a kid, she'd hated her hair, the brilliant red and the unruly thickness of it making her stand out and drawing attention she didn't want. But now she'd learned to rather like the color and waves. She finished brushing and decided to just wear it down tonight.

She rooted around in the medicine cabinet until she found an old bottle of cherry red nail polish. After a long struggle, she finally got the adhered top off and settled on the cover of the toilet to daub some of the overly thick lacquer on her toenails. She frowned at the results, not sure the polish would really make the flip-flops look any better. Ah well, it would have to do.

Then she returned to the mirror to apply a little dusky rose eyeshadow and a touch of mascara. She decided to forgo the lipstick; she didn't need anything else drawing attention to her mouth. She could give Angelina Jolie a run for her money in the lip department. *Jolie.* She studied herself in the mirror. Would Christian think she was pretty tonight? Would he think she was classy enough to be with him? She certainly didn't feel like it, but she hoped he thought so.

A knock rattled the front door. Giving herself one last appraising look, she decided this was as good as it got, and hurried down the hallway to the kitchen. She opened the door, and Christian stood on the other side, looking . . .

"You look beautiful," he said, stealing her thoughts exactly. Although *he* was beyond beautiful in a black jacket that made his broad shoulders appear even broader and black pants that showed the length of his legs. A deep cobalt blue shirt made his crystal blue eyes even more dramatic, and his hair was mussed in a sexy, straight-out-of-bed way, streaks of pale blond shimmering against dark gold. This man was going on a date with her? He definitely made up for the teenage loser at the prom.

She also noticed she was painfully underdressed compared to him, but she was rather used to that feeling. He worked at the bar in clothes that most people would save for special occasions. What was it her grandmother used to say? "Clothes a fellow was either married in or buried in."

She tugged the loosely knotted, bright red tie at his throat. "You look like a rock star."

He raised an eyebrow at that. "Is that good?"

"I do have a thing for musicians," she told him.

"I'll remember that."

Then he held out his hand, and for the first time she realized he was carrying something.

"What's this?" Jolee said, obviously confused as to why he'd be giving her a gift.

"Well, I think I'm supposed to bring you a token of my esteem when I pick you up for a date." He mentally winced. That sounded more stodgy than rock star-ish.

She grinned, not seeming to notice, and accepted the flat, rectangular package enclosed in a brown paper bag. But if his comment didn't ruin the rock star effect, this gift would.

She unwrapped the box. "Wow, it's a . . . HairDini."

This time he winced outwardly. "I know I'm supposed to bring you flowers or candy, but I didn't have time to go get those."

"But you had a HairDini?"

He shrugged, trying to look cool. "You never know when you might need one."

She grinned at him, those appealing brackets appearing, showcasing her wonderful lips. "This is the nicest gift I've ever received. Thank you."

"If this is the nicest present you've received, I dread to think about the other gifts you've gotten."

Her smile faded just slightly, and he wished he hadn't spoken. Then he realized her smile hadn't faded, it had just changed, growing into a little mischievous grin.

"Well, I have to admit that I mainly like it because you looked so sweet and unsure when you gave it to me."

"Ah, you love to see me humbled, don't you?"

"No, that's not true." She tried to look contrite, but gave up, grinning widely. "Okay, yeah."

He shook his head, amused by her honesty and by how adorable she was. Her dark eyes danced and her little laugh was infectious.

"I will definitely use it, though," she added. "I can never keep all this mess in a bun; it's too thick and unruly."

His gaze drifted to her hair, which was down tonight, brushing her shoulders and neck. The color was fascinating, the deepest red he'd ever seen, threaded with just hints of copper.

He reached out and caught a wavy lock, rubbing the silkiness between his fingers.

"Now that I see your hair down, I think I might have to take my gift back."

He could feel her gaze on him as he savored the texture and the color.

He wanted to kiss her, and from her deepening cinnamon scent, he could tell she wanted the same thing. But he didn't. Tonight was about going slow.

Instead he released the silken strand and caught her fingers. "Ready?"

She nodded, then turned to toss the HairDini on the kitchen counter. "Yes."

He led her outside to his car, and held the door open for her. She attempted to step in, but the material of her skirt, which came down to just above her knees, had little give, making the movement difficult.

He watched as she lifted the hemline up a bit more, exposing the tops of her pale thighs, and slid onto the leather seat. She gave him an embarrassed smile, her cheeks coloring to a light pink. He didn't smile back, his eyes drifting back to her legs, which were properly covered by the thick denim. He swallowed, then closed the door.

As he walked around to his side of the car, he told himself he had to behave. But it was as if now that he'd had a taste of Jolee's passion, he couldn't think about anything else. Not that he'd thought of anything else for days now. He even dreamed about her—and he didn't know that vampires could dream in their dormant state. But he had, today, a vivid dream of her spread across the hood of the car.

He nearly groaned at the memory of the dream and especially the real thing. And her pale thighs, hidden under an easily removed layer of denim. He gripped the door handle and tried to calm himself. This was going to be harder than he imagined. He opened the door and slid in under the steering wheel, his erection making the movement as difficult as Jolee's skirt had for her. Definitely very, very hard.

"So where are we going?"

Christian glanced over at her, taking in her expectant expression.

"It's a surprise."

She grinned, her dark eyes dancing, and instantly her excitement was more important than a little discomfort.

He pulled out of her driveway and headed in the direction of the restaurant. Last night, he'd driven around until nearly dawn, looking for the best place to take Jolee.

He'd found several restaurants, but hadn't been impressed

until he found West Pines Country Club. The club, by his standards, was not that luxurious. But he had liked the restaurant, which was in an old Victorian mansion situated right on the edge of a lake. He realized at night the view wouldn't be that spectacular, but they had a quaint outside seating area, and they would still be able to hear the waves lapping on the shore and see the stars. He hoped for his first attempt at something romantic, this would be a good choice.

"So how does one become obsessed with home shopping?"

He frowned. "Sorry?"

"Home shopping and infomercials?"

He didn't answer for a moment.

"The HairDini," she added with a little smile.

He shrugged. "I just watch a lot of late-night television."

"A sucker for advertising, huh?"

He nodded. Yes, he was. Though nothing he'd bought had given him the happiness the sellers had promised with their wide grins and perky voices. Well, until the HairDini. Giving that to Jolee had made him happy—even if a bit embarrassed.

"We're not going somewhere in Shady Fork?" she asked as he drove past Shady Fork's small downtown toward the highway that would take them to West Pines.

"I didn't think there was any place particularly nice here."

"Oh," she said, and he couldn't tell if she was happy about that or not.

"I think you will like the place I found."

She nodded, but didn't comment.

Jolee's stomach began to sink as Christian continued to drive in the direction of West Pines. She hadn't been there often since she moved to this area, but she knew it was a bigger, nicer town than Shady Fork. She also knew she was probably being silly, that he'd just decided to go there because it was a bigger town than Shady Fork, with more choices of restaurants.

Still, she had a feeling he was going to take her someplace really ritzy. And why hadn't she considered that before? After all, he had money. He dressed like a runway model. He drove a Porsche, for heaven's sake. She should have known his idea of a date and hers would be very different.

She should have been clearer on what she expected. Certainly not a five-star restaurant. She just wanted a place where they could sit and chat.

"Here we are," Christian said, pulling the car up to the front of a huge mansion. The building itself was painted gray with white trim and maroon shutters. A huge wraparound porch encircled the lower level, and two turrets rose on either side of the upper level toward the night sky.

It was gorgeous, and Jolee felt nauseous.

"We can't go here."

"Of course we can."

"Look at me!" She pulled at her top, giving him a pleading look. "I'm not dressed for a place like this."

He scanned her outfit. "You look beautiful."

"I'm wearing a denim skirt!"

"I'm wearing synthetic blend, who cares?"

She stared at him for a moment. If any other man had said that she'd wonder about him, but when Christian said it, it didn't sound strange at all. Christian was just aware of the quality of things. Including his clothes.

Why did he want her? Didn't he see she wasn't of his quality? She didn't fit into the classy world he'd obviously left behind. She looked back at the beautiful restaurant. But she wanted to fit, she realized. Desperately.

Christian caught her hand. "If we go in, and you don't want to stay for any reason, we'll leave. I want this night to be perfect for you."

She felt herself melting right there, into a huge puddle of

mush. She impulsively leaned over and dropped a quick kiss on his lips. She started to pull away to tell him she'd love to go into the restaurant, when he cupped one of his strong hands to the back of her head and drew her back, giving her a deep, thorough kiss that curled her badly painted toes against the worn soles of her pink flip-flops.

When they parted, all she managed was, "Okay."

Christian smiled at her, a quirk of his lips. Then he got out of the car, coming around to open her door. She waited, trying to calm both the delicious aftermath of his kiss and her nerves, both of which made her stomach quiver.

When he opened the door, she managed to ask, "Should I worry that my date actually knows he's wearing synthetic blend?"

Instead of getting the smile or even the feigned insulted look she expected, he frowned, appearing troubled. "Why? Shouldn't I?"

See, it didn't even dawn on him that was unusual.

"Well, let's just say that most men I've known wouldn't know different types of materials from different styles of women's shoes."

"Oh," he said, still sounding a little confused. "Well, I don't know anything about the women's shoes." Then he glanced down at her feet. "But I do like yours, you have lovely feet."

She smiled, finding him very, very sweet. Especially since he didn't comment on her lack of shoes. He caught her hand and led her toward the walkway that led up to the restaurant. At the doors, he stopped.

"Do you want to go inside? I don't want to make you do anything that makes you uncomfortable."

She studied the front door, decorated with beautiful stained glass. She did want to go inside. She wanted to feel like she belonged somewhere this elegant. And with this man at her side.

She nodded. "Yes. I want to."

He nodded back and they entered the foyer.

Chapter 18

Christian watched Jolee's expression closely as she walked through the front hallway that led back to the restaurant proper. Her eyes cast around the place, as if she were trying to take in everything at once. He glanced around, finding the wainscoting and flowered wallpaper to be quaint, but hardly anything exceptional.

"This is beautiful," she murmured, reaching out a hand to touch the ornate molding around one of the windows. She traced the detailing with her fingertip. "Can you imagine living in a place like this?"

She smiled at him. "I bet you have lived in places this nice."

He had lived in places far fancier, but he couldn't even recall any of the larger details about them, much less being fascinated by the intricacies of the molding around the windows.

He nodded absently, lost in her lovely smile, wishing he could share all those places with her. See them through her eyes. Appreciate them with her. Shame filled him. He'd squandered so much, in his life and in his undeath. He'd taken for granted things that Jolee had never even had.

"Can I help you?"

Both of them turned to see a lanky man with thinning brown hair and glasses smiling politely at them.

Christian felt Jolee stiffen at his side as if she fully expected this man to accuse them of trespassing. Then he noticed her fingers went to the seam of her skirt, tugging self-consciously at the material. Christian caught her hand, giving it a squeeze.

"Yes, I have a reservation."

The man nodded. "For two?"

"Yes, under the name Young."

The man nodded again. "Certainly, right this way."

Christian continued to hold her hand, noticing her fingers were cold despite the warmth of the evening. The maître d' stopped by his podium to pick up two menus, then led them through the main dining room toward the French doors, which exited to the outside tables. From the corners of his eyes, he could tell Jolee was still gaping about her, amazed at everything. What amazed him was how simple things like holding her hand and taking her to a restaurant filled him with such contentment. He'd forgotten small pleasures, having existed for nothing but extreme excess.

Once outside, the man led them directly to a table along the railing. He held out the chair, waiting for Jolee to sit. She hesitated, but then smiled at the man, moving to take the offered seat. The man still appeared a little dazed by her lovely smile, even as he told them that the waiter would be right with them and excused himself. He had barely managed that, much less taken notice of her denim skirt. But as soon as he left and it was just the two of them, Jolee seemed to relax, gazing around her with an awed expression.

"This is just absolutely beautiful." She sighed, settling back in her chair.

"I'm glad you like it." He wanted to please this woman as she pleased him.

The waiter arrived, asking if they wanted anything to drink.

Christian scanned the wine menu, finding an acceptable wine on the list.

"Do you drink Domaine Serene?"

Jolee smiled, raising an amused eyebrow. "I don't even know what it is."

"It's a pinot noir."

"Oh. No," she said, then she thought better of it. "But I'd like to try a glass."

He nodded, ordering two glasses. "Do you care for red wines?"

She shook her head, giving him a cute, unsure look. "I don't know. I've never had one." She shrugged. "Since the bar doesn't serve any wine other than wine coolers, I've never tried it. And I don't really drink anyway."

He didn't have the heart to tell her that wine coolers weren't really wine. Plus he was more intrigued by her last comment.

"But you own a bar."

"Kind of ironic, huh?" She laughed. Her laughter seemed to warm the air.

"So why a bar?"

She smiled. "Well, I know how to tend bar. I've been mixing drinks pretty much since I could walk."

He frowned. "Why on earth did you mix drinks as a child?"

She paused, dropping her gaze from his as if she just realized she'd said more than she intended. The table was quiet for a moment, and he was about to change the subject when she spoke.

"Well, when my mother was too drunk to make her own, someone had to." She met his gaze almost as if to challenge him, daring him to look down on her, daring him to feel bad for her.

He did feel bad, but more than that he felt angry at a parent who would do that to a child. But he didn't show her either emotion, afraid she'd stop talking. And he wanted to know everything about her.

"Does it bother you to serve drinks now?"

"I don't serve drinks now. I have this really hot hunk doing that." She nudged his leg under the table with her foot.

His chest swelled at both her description of him and her touch. And that her mood had lifted again. But he didn't allow himself to get distracted from his original question.

"But why a bar?"

Her smile faded, but she didn't look upset by the question. Instead, she appeared thoughtful.

"It's something I can do." She shrugged. "Plus, I made peace with my mother's drinking years ago. She did the best she could, given the hand she was dealt. Besides, I don't necessarily want Leo's because of the bar."

"So what do you want?" But as soon as the question was out, he knew the answer.

"I wanted the karaoke," she said, confirming his own guess. "My mother drank to escape. And I sang. Growing up, I listened to the radio all the time, using music to forget everything else that was happening in my life. I used to imagine I was a famous singer, touring the world."

"So why not go for that?" He could picture her up on a stage, entrancing audiences with her sweet, mellow voice and amazing smile.

She sighed. "Well, first of all, I'm too chicken. And secondly, I know that I'm really not good enough to be a star. I mean, just look at Leo's, every night there are so many talented people up there, singing their hearts out."

"And some not so talented people," he added wryly.

"That's true, too. But I actually like just doing karaoke. It gives me the same escape. And not just me singing, I find the same escape in watching other people sing. Even the bad ones." She grinned. "It's therapeutic."

"And," she added, "I really want to prove to myself that I can be a success at something. That I can run my own business."

"That's really important to you, isn't it?"

She nodded. "Yes."

The waiter returned with the two glasses of pinot noir. He sipped his, watching her over the rim to see what she thought of the dark, richly ripe wine. She took a small sip, her face contorting only slightly at the new taste.

"Not too bad," she told him, but he didn't get the feeling she'd be a devoted red wine fan.

"So what about you?" she asked, setting the glass back on the table. "How did you get so rich that you can work at a bar for free?"

"I inherited, and I invested," he stated flatly, feeling no pride in his money, especially when he saw how hard she worked to keep the bar and herself going.

"That requires savvy."

He raised an eyebrow in acknowledgment, but didn't comment. He didn't want to talk about yet another thing he'd taken totally for granted until he met her. Fortunately the waiter returned to take their order.

"You go first," she said, picking up the menu to quickly peruse the entrees.

Christian ordered the filet mignon, very rare.

She ordered the grilled salmon. And an iced tea.

He smiled at that. She smiled back.

"So what about the rest of your family?" he asked her.

"What about them?" He could tell she was purposely being obtuse.

"Do you have other siblings?"

"Yes," she said, and he could tell she wasn't going to elaborate.

He reached across the table to touch her hand, which toyed with the stem of her wineglass. "I'm not trying to make you uncomfortable. I just want to know more about you."

She stared at him for a moment, then sighed. "I have five brothers and two sisters."

"Big family."

She nodded. "Yes. One big ole dysfunctional family."

Jolee studied Christian's expression. Nothing but interest showed in his eyes. Part of her wanted to just change the subject altogether. She'd been embarrassed enough when she'd thoughtlessly announced her mother was an alcoholic. And he'd met Vance. She didn't want to talk about the rest. But she wanted a real relationship with this man, and she knew she had to be honest with him. He should know who she was and where she came from. She wanted to prove that she was different, not to run away and deny her past. If he couldn't accept her after the truth, then he wasn't the one for her.

"Well," she started slowly. "Vance isn't exception to the rule. All five of my brothers are in and out of trouble with the law on a regular basis. In fact, last I heard, my oldest brother, Rex, was in prison for assault, and one of my other brothers, Harlen, is also in prison for manslaughter. I'm sure it's only a matter of time before Vance, who is my youngest brother, is back in prison for possession. He's already done two stints in the Ashland Correctional Facility. I don't actually know where my other brothers, Rusty and Bobby Jon, are. Knowing the two of them, they're on a tristate crime spree."

She glanced at Christian to check his reaction, but he just watched her with those enigmatic eyes.

"My sister, Libby Ann, has just divorced her third husband and moved herself and her five kids in with her ex-husband's brother. I imagine she'll either be married or pregnant again anytime. And my oldest sister, Fanny, ran away when I was about seven. I heard she'd made it as far as Vegas, and she was working the strip. Although I don't know if that's true or not."

She waited, watching his face, expecting him to be appalled or scandalized, or at the very least disappointed that he was wasting his time on someone who obviously wasn't worth his attention. But he gave her none of those responses; instead he reached across the table and stroked her cheek.

"Jolee, you amaze me more and more."

She was pretty sure her jaw hit the linen tablecloth. He wasn't disgusted in the least by the description of her seriously dysfunctional family. He actually looked . . . proud.

"Are you crazy? I just told you that my family would make most of the Manson family look like pillars of the community."

He nodded, taking a sip of his wine as though she'd told him nothing out of the ordinary.

"All families have a few skeletons," he said.

"Does yours?"

He made a face she didn't understand. "You could say that."

"What are your family skeletons?"

He shook his head as if to tell her he wouldn't answer.

"Wait," she said, "I told you mine."

Christian looked down at his place setting, running a long, tapered finger down the handle of his fork. "Jolee, for all practical purposes, I don't have a family. And I believe if you did talk to my brothers, they'd say I'm the skeleton."

She paused. Because of Lilah. She suddenly felt like such an idiot.

"I'm sorry."

"No, I'm sorry," he said sincerely as he reached for his wine.

She took a sip from hers, too. She was starting to see that maybe they weren't that different after all. They were both recovering from a traumatic past. They were both alone. And they both needed to learn how to trust. She gazed at him over the rim of her glass, a warm, protective feeling stirring deep inside her. They might have started out in very different places, but they were struggling with a lot of the same issues. They needed each other.

She set the drink aside and straightened her posture. Tonight was the most special night of her life. She was in an amazingly romantic restaurant with a gorgeous, wonderful man, and she wasn't going to let this moment be ruined by their pasts.

"Okay, enough talk about heavy stuff," she stated. "Let's think up a new topic."

Christian set his glass aside and relaxed back against his chair. "What's the topic?"

"What's your favorite cartoon character?"

He frowned.

"This is very important stuff," she assured him.

He pondered the question. "I guess . . . Mickey Mouse."

"I knew it," she said as if his answer was very telling.

He raised a curious eyebrow. "And yours?"

"Well, Minnie Mouse, of course."

Despite the pain of thinking about his brothers, Jolee managed to change the atmosphere with her cheerful chatter. She kept her silly questions coming all through dinner, and he easily found himself responding, feeling lighter and more carefree than he could remember. And he'd managed to discover through her silly inquiries that she wanted to travel, she loved the color green, but she didn't like peas.

As much as her funny comments and wacky insights amused him, just being with her created an astonishing sense of contentment, deep inside him, that he couldn't remember ever feeling. His existence had always been about constant questing, constant struggles to feel satisfied. He wasn't sure he'd ever felt true contentment until he'd met Jolee.

He loved to watch how her eyes sparkled when she laughed or the look of amazement when she noticed another detail about their surroundings. Through her eyes, he saw things for the first time. And not just for the first time since he crossed over, maybe for the first time ever.

Jolee finished her salmon with a pleased sigh. "That was absolutely delicious."

Christian smiled, amused at her satisfied expression.

Even watching her eat fascinated him. She ate like she'd never tasted food before and every spice and seasoning was new to her.

But then maybe they were. He knew from the little she'd said about her family that luxuries like restaurants weren't something she'd experienced. And her money was too tight now to treat herself. She might very well have gone without.

He studied her, taking notice of her cheekbones, which would be prominent even if she was thirty pounds heavier. But were they so dramatic now because she wasn't eating? She reached for her iced tea, and he saw the delicate jut of the bones in her wrist, and the slenderness of her arm. He knew her build had probably always been tall and slender, but he now realized that she was almost too thin.

Not that that dampened his desire for her. He eyed her graceful fingers, still holding the glass. He remembered them stroking his hair and face, his shoulders and back. No, she definitely aroused him beyond all reason.

The waiter arrived to clear their plates.

"Are you interested in a dessert menu?" he asked.

"Yes," Christian said automatically.

After the waiter left, Jolee grinned at him.

"What?" he asked, although giving a bemused smile to her.

"You must have a sweet tooth. You barely touched your meal, but you want dessert."

A sweet tooth. There had to be a joke in there somewhere.

"Yes," he told her, even though he'd really requested the menu for her. He wanted her to eat her fill. As far as his own appetite, he'd fed before he left his trailer from pilfered bags from the hospital. So his hunger was fully satisfied. But he'd even managed to eat a couple bites of his filet, suffering only the slightest bout of nausea. Fortunately the steak had been very rare. That helped.

"Well, you should eat more," she said with a worried scowl, like he'd seen her use on Jed. "You don't want to get feeling light-headed."

Warmth heated in the pit of his stomach, radiating up to his chest. Who knew being mothered could be so enjoyable? It was on the tip of his tongue to tell her she needed to eat, as well, but he caught himself. Knowing Jolee, she'd take offense to the comment, assuming he saw a flaw in her. And that certainly wasn't the case. He'd only found perfection.

The waiter returned with the menus, but Jolee didn't even open hers. Instead, she gazed at a lit cobblestone path that led down to the lake.

"Would you prefer to take a walk?"

She smiled, her eyes bright. "Yes. I'd love to."

Christian waved the waiter over to settle the bill.

A few minutes later, they were on the winding path, strolling toward the water. A warm breeze stirred the air and gentle waves lapped the rocks on the shore.

"Oh, look," Jolee exclaimed, pointing out a small gazebo on the edge of the lake, nearly hidden amongst flowering trees, heavy with white and pink blossoms.

She caught Christian's hand and pulled him toward the small building. The gazebo was weathered, but well-built with benches along two of the walls.

She released his hand and walked inside to look out at the water. He followed. The moon and stars reflected and rippled on the dark surface.

"This is so nice," she said, closing her eyes and tilting her head back. The air played with wisps of her hair, and his fingers itched to do the same.

"Happy?" he asked instead.

She blinked over at him, then a broad smile curled her lips. "This is heaven."

Then she hugged him, holding him tight against her slender frame.

"No," he murmured, "this is heaven." He nudged her chin up and captured her lips.

Chapter 19

Jolee clutched Christian's shoulders, leaning into his wonderful kiss. His lips moved over hers, sampling her as if she was some rare delicacy that had to be savored slowly.

She moaned, desire building with each lick, each nibble.

He seemed to sense her rising need, pressing his mouth even more hungrily to hers, deepening the kiss, and sending eddies of need through her veins.

Her hands moved over the hard muscles of his shoulders, down his arms, and then back up again. All through dinner she'd ached for this, for his touch, to touch him. Now that she was here in his arms, it was even more thrilling, more breathtaking than she imagined.

His mouth moved from her lips to brush against her jawline, brushes of heated velvet on her skin. She arched against him, her body desperate for more. He moved to rest his forehead against hers. His breathing was as uneven as hers, and she could also feel his body was as aroused as hers. She had to force herself not to rub wantonly against him.

"Jolee, you make me crazy," he muttered, his voice low as if he were trying very hard to control himself. And she knew he was trying to go slow. For her.

She didn't want that control, she realized with a touch of surprise. She wanted him to give her all the passion he held carefully in check. The realization should have appalled her, she knew. With the few other men she dated, it had been ridiculously easy. But then, she'd never wanted another man like she wanted Christian. She ached for him to touch her again, like he had on the car. And she needed to touch him in return, feeling all that lean strength under her hands. She was surely going crazy, too.

"Jolee?" He frowned down at her, concerned that she hadn't reacted other than to stare up at him.

"Christian . . ." She wanted to tell him that she wanted everything. That she couldn't wait to be with him. But still, in the back of her mind, doubt niggled. They were very much alike in a lot of ways, but they were different, too. Maybe their backgrounds were too different. Maybe he was out of reach.

But he wasn't. He was right here in her arms, and she trusted him. She did, she realized with a small surge of giddiness. And she suddenly felt more confident.

"Christian, I don't want to go slowly. I want to make love with you. Tonight."

Christian was sure that he must be hearing things. He had to be. Hadn't they decided their relationship had to go slow? Hadn't they both admitted that they didn't really know what they were doing in a relationship? He certainly didn't. He didn't have a clue. All of this was totally new to him. But at the same time, he did know that he only felt right when he was holding her.

"Are you sure?" What if this was just an impulsive decision brought on by passion?

She stared at him and nodded. "I've never been more certain."

"But it's rather fast."

She nodded, but the desire in her eyes didn't wane.

"I don't want you to think you made a mistake later." He

truly didn't want that. He couldn't bear for her to pull away again. He couldn't bear it if he did something again that caused her to pull away.

She laughed, the sound soft and a little breathless. "The fact that you are trying to talk me out of it only makes me more sure."

He blinked at that. "That's all I had to do to convince you?"

She laughed again. "Apparently. Now please just kiss me."

He didn't have to be asked twice. He caught her mouth, nudging her soft lips open so he could taste her and feel her raspy little tongue against his.

A pleased moan vibrated low in her throat and straight into him, creating a violent shiver throughout his whole body. He tightened his hold on her, pressing her fully against him. Their chests, their stomachs, their hips aligned perfectly with only the thin barrier of clothing to separate them. The barrier that had to disappear. He needed to feel her bare skin all around him.

She seemed to feel the same way, rubbing against him. Even through their clothes, he could feel her swollen nipples begging for his touch. A memory of how sweet and ripe those taut little points had tasted caused him to groan. Before he thought better of it, he reached for the hem of her top. Pushing it up, his mouth found the distended nub, sucking it through the cotton of her bra.

She gasped, and her knees threatened to give out from under her. He caught her easily and lifted his head to be sure she was all right. She watched him with heavy-lidded, passion-filled eyes.

He knew he should stop this now. He should steer her to his car, take her home, and make love to her there. But he couldn't seem to let her go even that long. He wanted to satisfy her now. He needed to feel her convulsing release under his hand, and in the air around him.

He balanced her against him so she was draped back in

one of his arms, while his other hand moved to her breast. He stroked the rounded flesh, swirling around her nipple again and again until she wiggled, silently begging him for more.

He responded, sliding his hand downward over her bare stomach and the soft denim of her skirt until he reached the hem. He caught it and pushed the material upward until the black cotton of her panties was exposed.

He looked at her as much as their angle would allow, amazed at how beautiful she was. Her breasts rose up and down with her deep, uneven breaths. Her legs were long, lithe, her mound plump under her panties.

He touched her there, through the material. She gasped loudly, bucking against his hand. He stroked her with more pressure, and another whimper escaped her, the sound low and husky. He pressed his lips to hers, in an attempt to hush her little noises, not because he didn't love them. He did. But he could sense others nearby. Not close enough that they could see them in their secluded spot, but certainly close enough to hear.

She responded to his kiss wildly, stroking him with her lips, writhing frantically against his hand. He nudged the crotch of the panties aside, finding her clitoris hidden in the silky, moist folds of her sex. She gasped, and he swallowed the noise into his mouth, savoring it.

Lifting against his finger, she demanded that he touch her harder. He obeyed, swirling his thumb firmly against the tiny nub while he sank a finger inside her, savoring the wet, suctioning heat.

His thumb only made a few more swirls around her aroused flesh, and he felt her vagina convulse around his finger, squeezing him as her violent release scented the air, hot honey and spicy cinnamon.

His own release threatened at the combination of her beautiful body limp under his hand and her heady scent. His erection strained against his zipper, but he forced himself to ignore his need. He wanted her satisfaction far more than his own.

She raised her head, smiling. "Wow . . . that was . . . wow."

He smiled down at her, affection laced with his need, making his desire almost unbearably intense. They had to get back to their trailers. He didn't care which one. He just had to make love to her.

But he kissed her again as he removed his hand from her panties, only to cup her through the cotton, molding his fingers to her moist heat. He couldn't bring himself to stop touching her.

"Oh!" a female voice gasped from behind them. Christian immediately dropped his hand from Jolee and smoothed her skirt. Then he broke the kiss to glance over his shoulder at the speaker. Two women stood at the entrance of the gazebo, their open mouths and bulging eyes making them look like croaking toads.

The taller of the two women spoke first. "Sorry. We didn't realize anyone was in here."

The shorter blonde nodded, her mouth still hanging open.

Neither woman moved. They continued to stare. The tall woman even rose up slightly trying to get a glimpse of Jolee.

Christian shifted, using his shoulders to shield Jolee more.

"Good night, then," he finally said, not really caring if he sounded brusque.

Jolee stood stock-still; he even thought she was holding her breath. And he could tell she was mortified. The sooner these two busybodies left the better.

"Good night," he repeated, and the two women suddenly seemed to take the hint. Both of them started, then gave their apologies and bustled away.

Christian started to hold Jolee away from him to see if she was okay, when one of the women said, "Can you believe that? And in a public place, no less."

"Did you see how she was dressed?" the other woman hissed.

"They will let anyone anywhere these days," the first woman agreed dolefully.

"Well, it's clear what he was hoping to get when he brought her here. And he didn't even have to wait long after dinner to get what he paid for."

Both women moved away on a cloud of catty laughter.

Christian felt Jolee, who'd begun to relax a little, stiffen against him. Rage rose up in his chest, his first thought to follow the meddling, hateful women and confront them. But that would only serve to embarrass Jolee more.

"I'd like to go," she said flatly.

"Jolee."

"Please," she said, her even tone breaking just a little at the end.

He nodded, taking her hand. Just once he'd like to give this woman an orgasm without everything falling apart directly afterward.

Jolee allowed Christian to lead her to the car, not seeing the beauty of her surroundings any longer. All she could focus on was her humiliation and her disgust. Both with those women and herself.

She'd only gotten a quick peek of them over Christian's shoulder, but she recognized them immediately. Or at least, she recognized their type. They were immaculately dressed, manicured, coiffed, and they were the same types who'd looked down on her family her whole life. But what bothered her more than them was herself.

She had been kissing Christian like she wanted to swallow him whole, and him with his hand on her . . . In a public place!

Once in the car, she closed her eyes. She was so disgusted with herself. Her entire life she claimed over and over that she'd never act like her family. A family that existed on gratifying their impulses, no matter how base. Yet she'd been let-

ting Christian finger her at a fancy restaurant, right there in a
gazebo overlooking the lake, where anyone could walk by.
Where they were supposed to walk by.

She cringed at her own description of what they'd been
doing, but it was the truth. He had been. And she'd been loving it. Not even thinking about her surroundings or how she
must appear. How she even appeared to him.

"They didn't see anything," Christian said.

She nodded, too embarrassed to talk. They'd obviously
seen enough. And they'd certainly said enough.

Neither spoke as he pulled out of the restaurant's parking
lot and headed back toward Shady Fork. Back to the dumpy
trailer park where she belonged.

She wanted to look over at him, see his expression, but
she was too much of a wimp. Chicken that she was, she
couldn't bear to look over and see his dismay—or worse, his
disgust.

The silence continued for several miles, until Christian
downshifted and she heard the quiet clicking of the blinker.
He pulled over into the breakdown lane and put the car into
neutral. For an instant, she wondered if he was going to kick
her out off the car. No, Christian was too classy for that.

"Jolee, look at me," he said, his voice low, the words
clipped.

She obeyed, to find him turned in his seat as much as the
steering wheel would allow.

"What's going on?" His eyes roamed her face, but she
couldn't tell what he was thinking. Big surprise.

She looked away again, staring out her window at the
darkness. She didn't want to talk about this right now. Embarrassment and shame were too vivid at the moment.

A vague, shadowy memory like the sway of the trees outside appeared in her mind. An image of her sister, Libby
Ann, sprawled against the side of Chubby's Diner on Route
8 in Sawyersville. A local boy, a kid who'd never talked to
the likes of a Dugan, stood with his pants down around his

knees, pumping into her. Right there, near the smelly old dumpster out back.

Even now that memory made Jolee feel ill. And she'd just been doing something not too terribly different. The only difference being that she'd been near a beautiful lake rather than a stinky metal dumpster.

She still couldn't bring herself to look over at Christian. A man who also wouldn't have given a Dugan the time of day if strange circumstances that she still didn't understand hadn't brought them together. And like that kid—Jolee didn't remember his name now, but she did remember his contemptuous laugh as he and his buddies left Libby Ann against that back wall—would Christian leave?

"Can we just go home?" she said, so disgusted with herself.

Christian didn't move for a minute, then she heard the leather seat creak, and he shifted the car into gear.

Jolee just needed to get back to her trailer. And rethink what she was doing.

Chapter 20

Irritation continued to eat at Christian, although he wouldn't show that to Jolee. He knew she'd perceive it as annoyance with her, which wasn't the case in the least. Even though he was a little disheartened that she had withdrawn from him. But she had a lot of pride and those women's words had stung her.

More than that, he hated that those women had implied that he and Jolee were using each other in some way. That she was with him for money, which was ridiculous if they knew Jolee. Just her reaction at the hospital had been enough to show how much she hated to take anyone's help. Much less money.

But what about himself? He was using her. Using her to make him feel human. Human in a way that his "plan" hadn't even begun to achieve. He found peace in her smiles. Redemption in her touches. Normalcy in her affection. And even though those things could only be short-lived—he'd have to leave her eventually—he had to take them. Selfishly, he had. That wasn't fair to her.

But even as he called himself every kind of greedy bastard, he knew he couldn't walk away from her. Not yet. And he'd make absolutely sure he never hurt her. Never.

He pressed the accelerator down, wanting to be back at his trailer or hers, wherever he could hold her, and hopefully chase away the anguished look in her eyes. He pulled into their road, slowing down between their trailers.

"Do you want to go home?"

She nodded, and he pulled into the weedy patch near her old, broken-down car. He shut off the engine and got out to open her door, but she was already out of the car when he reached her side.

"Thank you for dinner," she said, not meeting his eyes.

"No. Thank you."

She nodded, still not looking at him. Then she moved to step around him. "Good night."

He caught her hand, stopping her. She looked up at him, pain and uncertainty still vivid in the dark, bottomless brown of her eyes.

"We're not saying good night yet. Not like this."

She hesitated, but then nodded. She continued to her door, but didn't let go of his hand. Some relief filled him, seeing that as a positive sign. Although he wouldn't be totally relaxed until he held her again. Once inside, she released his fingers immediately.

She crossed her tiny kitchen to her counter. "Would you like some tea? I think I have some. I don't have any coffee. I hope you're not a coffee drinker. I don't even have a coffee pot."

"Jolee," he said, to stop her agitated rambling. "Come here."

She glanced over her shoulder at him. Then she turned to face him and walked slowly over. He caught her around the waist, tugging her to him. He kissed her lips, coaxing her into responding. She did, her arms coming up around his neck, hugging her tightly in return. They tasted each other for a few sweet moments, then he gently broke the kiss.

"Now tell me, are you embarrassed by those ladies seeing us? Or are you ashamed of what we did?"

She stiffened, but he didn't release her. Instead he stroked his fingers down her back, trying to soothe her.

Finally she did relax a little and admitted, "Both."

The response didn't surprise him. "Why?"

She nibbled the inside of her lower lip, obviously trying to decide if she could tell him.

"Jolee, you can trust me."

But she didn't answer him. Instead she asked, "Why do you want to be with me? We aren't in the same league. What could you possibly see in me, when it is so clear you could have any woman in the world? Christian, you are classy and cultured. And I'm . . ." She looked down at herself, shaking her head. "I'm trailer trash, born and bred."

He frowned. "You aren't . . . trailer trash."

"Yes, I am. You take me out for an elegant, romantic dinner, and I'm wearing an old denim skirt and flip-flops. And as if that isn't bad enough I embarrass you outside the restaurant by getting . . . amorous."

He raised an eyebrow. "You think I was embarrassed?"

"Well, you should have been." Her cheeks stained a deep rose.

He shook his head, amazed that she was trying to take the blame. "Well, first of all, I'd like to think you were acting amorous because of me. And I certainly wasn't embarrassed. I was rather enjoying myself. A lot."

She smiled slightly at that, although the pink in her cheeks darkened even more.

"And I also believe I'm the one who should take the whole blame anyway. I believe I kissed you first."

"But I'm the one who propositioned you," she reminded him.

"Hmm . . ." He pretended to consider that. "You're right, you did. Do you intend to take that back now?"

She laughed at his worried expression. But she sobered again. "Christian, I don't know. Those women's words really bothered me. Do you really want to be with someone who is so completely different than you?"

He didn't have to hesitate in the slightest. "Yes," he stated, pulling her to him.

Yes, he wanted to be with her for that exact reason. She was different, and she made him forget. And she made him feel whole, in a way nothing and no one had in centuries.

Relief and delight rippled through her at his emphatically stated yes. There was no doubt there. No embarrassment or shame or pity in his eyes. Just warmth and passion.

"Although," he added, "I am going to give you a bad reputation if we keep making love in public places."

"Yes, maybe we should try to curb that habit," she agreed, although she smiled.

"Should we start now?" He glanced around her rundown trailer. "We are in private."

Her smiled widened at his eager expression. "Yes, I think so."

Despite the lightness of their exchange, as soon as their lips met they both seemed to explode into flames. They consumed each other, tasting, nipping, neither able to get enough of the other.

Her hands explored the hard muscles of his back and his shoulders, wanting to touch all of him. She pulled at his jacket, trying to get the garment out of the way so she could get closer to his skin, only to encounter the crisp warm cotton of his shirt underneath.

She groaned in frustration against his mouth. In return, she felt him smile.

"Can . . . I . . . help . . . you?" he asked between kisses down her jawline and neck.

She let her head fall back, lost for a moment in the feeling of his velvety lips brushing over her sensitive skin. But she wanted too desperately to touch him not to refocus on her task.

"Yes," she murmured. "Lose the shirt and jacket."

He lifted his head and grinned at her. Then he shrugged out of the jacket, letting it fall to the floor. His hands loosened the red tie, pulling it off over his head only to loop it around hers. She grinned, straightening it against her top. Then his fingers went to the buttons of his shirt, and her smile faded, replaced by pure admiration as with each flick a little more golden skin appeared. He peeled the shirt off, too. It landed on the jacket.

She drank in the sight of him, his broad shoulders and chest corded with lean muscles, narrowing down to a rock-hard abdomen. Tentatively she touched his shoulder, feeling the heat of his skin and sinew underneath. Her fingers stroked down over his chest, lower to his stomach, unhurriedly exploring him. His muscles rippled under her fingers, holding her captivated.

Slowly, her hand still discovering him, she circled him. Tracing the muscles that defined his ribs, around to his back, caressing the indentation of his spine, up to his broad, powerfully muscled shoulders.

"You are beautiful," she whispered, lost in the textures of his body. She pressed an openmouthed kiss to his shoulder blade, feeling him tense under the touch.

She paused, afraid that she'd done something he didn't like, or worse, something that reminded him of Lilah.

"Don't stop," he told her, his voice low.

She smiled and began to kiss the length of his spine, resisting the urge to nibble him, just in case it brought back unwanted reminders of Lilah. She slipped her hands around his waist, stroking the rise and fall of the muscles that lined his belly. Her fingers brushed the waistband of his pants, then downward. She pressed her cheek to his back, stretching an arm down to cup her hand over the hardness under his zipper.

"Oh," she breathed, feeling the hard, full length of him against her palm. Her breath caught then. He was huge!

He growled low in his throat, then revolved to face her. He caught his tie, still around her neck, and slowly walked backward, tugging her with him.

"Where—where are we going?" she managed, still far too amazed and aroused by his incredible body to think straight.

"I need you in a bed. Now." He led her down the dark hallway.

She nodded adamantly, even though he couldn't see her.

Once in her small room, he flipped on the light and then kissed her, the pressure of his lips insistent, a little wild. She responded in kind, so on fire she was surprised her clothing wasn't singed.

But she didn't get too long to be surprised. Christian ended the kiss, only to tug her top off over her head. Quickly followed by her skirt, which dropped down around her ankles. She stepped out of it and reached for the button of Christian's pants. But he caught her wrists, spreading her arms wide, his eyes roaming down her body slowly, admiration in his pale eyes.

Her body reacted as if he were touching her. Her nipples strained against her black bra. Need moistened her already damp panties. She shivered, desire making her nerve endings go haywire.

"I've never seen anyone as beautiful as you," he murmured.

She didn't know if that was true or not, but she was pretty sure he'd probably never been with a woman in black underwear wearing a red tie and pink flip-flops. She probably looked rather silly, but she felt beautiful under his intense gaze. She wanted to be his.

"Touch me," she pleaded.

He released her arms; his large, perfectly formed hands slid up her sides to pull her against him. He kissed her on the lips, then on the neck, slipping the tie up over her head and casting it aside. His lips found a sensitive spot right at the base of her throat. She whimpered as yearning seemed to shoot directly from that point to between her thighs. God, she wanted this man.

He continued down across her chest to the swell of her breasts above the top of her bra. His lips caressed the pale skin, while his hands shaped the curve of her bottom, pulling her hips tight to his.

The thick hardness of his erection pressed to her mound, and she cried out. She was almost frantic to have all of that delicious length deep inside her.

"Christian, you're killing me!" She squirmed in his arms, trying to get free to lead him to the bed, but he didn't let go.

He smiled, a slow, sexy smile. "That isn't my intent."

She felt his hands working at her back, and her bra sprang free. He nudged the scrap of cotton out of the way and took one of her nipples into his mouth. She cried out as he sucked on the sensitive flesh, abrading it gently with the edge of his teeth.

"Yes, it is," she said almost petulantly. "Death by desire."

His lips stilled on her nipple, but before she could ask him what was wrong, he changed breasts, lavishing her with little nips and sucks. She moaned, any other coherent thought gone.

She couldn't take much more of this torture. She needed him inside her. Deep.

"Christian, please," she pleaded, rubbing him again.

"Please what?" he asked against her breast, ending the question with a flick of his tongue against her aching nipple. Her knees threatened to buckle, but he held her weight easily.

"Please make love to me."

"Patience. It's been a long time. And I want to take my time. I want to enjoy every inch of you." As if to prove it, he moved back to the other nipple.

Briefly, she wondered how long it had been for him, but

she couldn't concentrate on anything other than his lips at her breast. She gasped, her hips automatically grinding against him.

After several more suckling nibbles, his mouth left her breast to burn a trail of wet, lingering kisses on her stomach. His tongue delved into her belly button, and she wiggled at the ticklish and erotic sensation.

He smiled up at her indulgently, then caught her hips, holding them immobile. His lips brushed the edge of her panties, his tongue tracing the edge from the top of her thigh to where the thin strip of material disappeared between her legs.

He released her hips and slid the material down her hips, over her thighs to her ankles. She balanced herself on his shoulders as he lifted each of her feet to cast the flip-flops and then panties aside. He remained kneeling as he looked up at her. She panted at the sight of him, his eyes blazing like blue fire, his perfectly sculpted mouth just inches from the curls at the apex of her thighs. The image was so exciting, so erotic that she whimpered. Her whole body hummed with eager heat.

He smiled at her reaction, leaning forward to slowly place a kiss to her curls, never breaking eye contact with her. She gasped, again her legs shaking. He stood then, scooping her easily to his bare chest. He placed her in the center of the bed. He didn't follow her. Instead he remained at the edge, his hands going to the button on his pants.

She watched with fascination as he flicked the button free, then pushed down the zipper. He shoved the waistband past his narrow hips, letting the pants drop to the floor. Her eyes dropped to the part of his body that she'd only felt, but never seen. His penis rose up, magnificently thick and long, from a nest of dark gold curls.

She sat up, wanting to hold him, to feel his width and heat in her hands. To explore him. He crawled on the bed before she could reach for him. Then he moved over her, his mouth finding hers, the weight of his body pressing on hers, wonderfully hard and powerful, his skin smooth like golden velvet over tempered steel. She gave herself over to his touch, gasping as he started down her body, raining dozens of nibbling kisses over her.

"This is agony," she said, wiggling under him, her body burning up. Burning for him and for release.

"No, this is ecstasy."

He was right. Who knew they could be one in the same? Who knew she could want a man so badly her body threatened to ignite?

His lips brushed the curls between her thighs. Her hips rose at the slight touch. He smiled up at her, his grin sinfully sexy.

"I wonder what you taste like? All hot and sweet like warmed honey?"

He trailed a finger down the slit of her sex, just a teasing graze of his fingertip.

"Maybe I shouldn't taste you, though, since this is agony."

She glared at him as best she could, although it was hard to concentrate on the action as his finger made another grazing pass. Then he spread her legs apart and situated himself fully between them. With his thumbs he spread the folds of her sex, looking at her, his eyes hungry.

She dug her hands into the comforter, another broken whimper escaping her parted lips.

"You do look luscious."

He was evil. Deliciously, wonderfully evil.

"Maybe just a little taste." He looked up at her, then brought his mouth to her, licking his tongue along the full length of her labia. Again he didn't break eye contact; he watched her reaction, making it all the more intense.

She lifted her hips, crying out, the comforter knotted in her clenched fists. His tongue found her clitoris, swirling around and around the small nub, in tight, raspy little circles, only leaving to dip deeper into her.

His mouth *was* ecstasy, his lips, his tongue making love to her, his blond head moving between her spread thighs. And all the time he watched her as if every nuance of her arousal was important to him. It was the most thrilling, most mind-bogglingly erotic thing she'd ever experienced.

His tongue began to speed up, moving in rapid, steady flicks, building the fire inside her, until she tensed under him. Her orgasm burst through her like fire touched to the head of a match, sizzling alive, hot and fast.

Jolee cried out, and Christian felt her convulse under his mouth. Sweetness washed over his tongue, her release tasting like honey, just as he knew it would. The small noises she made. The quiver of her body. Her sweet taste and spicy scent all fired his own arousal, but he didn't leave her. He lapped her, savoring her taste and the gradually slowing ripples of her orgasm until her body calmed, and she sprawled limply on the bed. He kissed her damp curls, then slid up beside her.

She smiled at him, the slow curl of her lips languid and satisfied. "Holy cow."

He smiled back. "Is that good?"

"Mmm-hmm." She curled against him like a content cat.

Then he tensed, waiting.

She lifted her head. "What's wrong?"

"I'm waiting for something or someone to ruin this moment."

She frowned, then laughed. "I think we broke the curse."

He paused, slightly wondering if her words were really true, and not about their previously interrupted escapades. He still hadn't felt the hunger. Only his arousal. How could that be?

She snuggled against him and he suddenly didn't much care. He was too filled with smug pride, and also just a hint of surprise at how easily he was remembering where and how to touch a woman. He hadn't done this in nearly two hundred years. He wondered now how he'd believed human mating was base and distasteful. Touching Jolee, hearing her pleasured sounds and feeling her body react, was anything but distasteful. It was absolutely awe-inspiring. He loved every reaction she gave him, reveling in it. Of course, with Jolee there was something just naturally right, something innate about being with her. He simply knew how to touch her. How to please her.

He wanted to continue making love to her, to hear those delightful little noises she made, but he restrained himself, letting her relax after her intense release. Lazily, he ran his hand up and down her narrow back. He loved the feeling of her silky skin against his. He was content just to touch her. Content. He liked that word. He liked the feeling even more.

Desire still pulsed throughout his body, but his own gratification didn't matter at this moment. His mental contentment was as gratifying and had been out of his reach for . . . forever. He nuzzled his cheek against the top of her head, smelling the fresh herbal scent of her hair.

"I love the feeling of your body against mine," she sighed, running a leg up the length of his.

Arousal shot through him at the delicious friction.

"I love your body, period," he murmured, his hand gliding down to explore the soft roundness of her bottom. He felt her smile against his chest.

"What did you mean when you said you haven't done this in a long time?" she asked.

He lifted his head slightly to look at her, although from his angle he could only see the top of her head and her dark auburn hair cascading across his chest. He considered what to tell her. He could hardly tell her the truth. He couldn't even recall the last female mortal he'd been with. Probably some lightskirt he picked up in White Chapel. The exchange of a few silver pieces, a quick tumble in his carriage, then she was back to the street for another man with too much money and too much drink to take his turn. Perhaps that was why it had been so easy for Lilah to convince him that mortal sex was so vile. He hadn't had many truly beautiful moments. But that had been his choices, not the act itself.

He stroked his hand back up Jolee's spine. If he'd found Jolee first would he have even been tempted by Lilah? He didn't think so. Even with her vampire powers, Lilah couldn't compare to this slender mortal curled around him.

God, why couldn't he have found Jolee first? Rhys flashed into his mind. His face anguished, unbearable pain darkening his eyes. And rage. Rage at Christian for what he'd done. Done to Jane. His mortal. His love.

Jolee lifted her head to look at him, concern in her dark eyes. "Are you all right?"

He didn't deserve her concern. She wouldn't give it if she knew the truth. Then she touched her slender fingers to his cheek and smiled, and damn him, he couldn't end this need for her. Even though he didn't deserve one moment of this kind of heaven. He pulled her up so he could taste the lushness and warmth of that smile.

When they parted, Jolee regarded him with solemn eyes. "I haven't been with a man in over two years. I want you to know that I don't just go to bed with men on a whim. You . . . you are special."

He smiled, running his fingers along her cheekbone. "I haven't been with a woman longer than that." Much longer.

"Really?" Her eyes widened. "But when did you leave Lilah?"

"About six months ago."

She frowned. "You didn't . . . with Lilah?"

He shook his head. "She didn't like to have conventional sex."

Her frown deepened, the puzzled look in her eyes almost comical. "What did she like?" Then she blushed. "I shouldn't have asked that."

Her words were his out; he could just not talk about it. But he needed to. He wanted her to understand that the gentle warmth, her uninhibited response, her affection, it was all so special to him, too.

"She preferred violence, as I said. The only gentleness she showed was to manipulate. She was very good at manipulation and control. She enjoyed finding her own release through that violence. My gratification was only to be derived from satisfying her."

"Was it?"

"Not often."

"You poor thing," she murmured, pressing a lingering kiss to his jaw. "But it seems to me I'm not doing much better. I haven't hurt you, but I haven't satisfied you either."

His cock throbbed at her softly accented words. "Yes, you have. More than you know."

"Well, I want to give you more," she said. Her hand, which lay in the middle of his chest, glided down his torso, fingering the line of hair beneath his navel to the thatch of curls surrounding his sex. Her fingertips grazed the coarse hair. His cock pulsed eagerly at the teasing touch.

She rose up to press a kiss to his chest.

"Is it my turn to play with you?" she asked, flicking her small pink tongue against his nipple.

"Do you want to play?"

She nodded, her dark eyes no longer drowsy, but sparkling, eager, and a little naughty. She traced her finger up the sensitive underside of his cock, and he groaned.

"You're so hot," she murmured as she ran her finger up the length again. Sitting up, she gazed at him, her lips parted just slightly, her breathing uneven as if touching him was as arousing for her as for him.

"And you are so big," she said, her voice breathy. Her fingers curled as far around his girth as she could. She squeezed gently, then worked her tightened fingers up the shaft, then back down him.

He closed his eyes. God, she felt good. He couldn't even

imagine what if would feel like to be buried deep inside her body.

"How could she not want to touch you?"

It took him a few moments to figure out who "she" was. Two hundred years of obsession, and with the touch of Jolee's fingers, it was all gone.

She leaned over him, her hair falling forward, tickling his skin. Pressing openmouthed kisses to his chest and stomach, she continued to stroke his cock, tapered little fingers milking his hardened flesh. Sheer willpower kept him from throwing her down on the bed and sinking deep inside her. Her mouth moved to the jut of his hipbone, then over to the line of hair leading to his groin. She kissed downward, her wide, impossibly full lips getting closer to his erection.

He groaned again.

She lifted her head. "Does that feel good?"

He nodded, meeting her gaze. "Yes."

He continued to watch her in awe as she lowered her head, her pink tongue darting out to lick the head of his cock. His hips rose in reaction to the fleeting touch.

"And that? Do you like that?"

"God, yes."

She smiled, then moved to lick him again. This time she twirled her tongue around the top like she was eating ice cream. She moaned as if it was just as tasty.

He couldn't keep his hands still any longer. He stroked her back, her shoulders, coming around the front of her to cup one of her breasts. She looked up at him from where she was still lapping him, then she opened her mouth and slowly took the swollen erection between her lips.

Christian growled. Nothing had ever been so arousing, so totally erotic as Jolee's gorgeous lush lips wrapped around him, sucking, licking. Her mouth moved up and down him, hot and wet. Her hands stroked the rest of the length that she could not take into her mouth. Each synchronized stroke propelling him close to a soul-shattering release.

He closed his eyes and gritted his teeth, not wanting the intense pleasure to stop, but not wanting to orgasm this way. He had to be inside her. That was where he wanted his first orgasm with her. Joined. One.

He groaned again, trying to control his desire. She moaned in response, the noise vibrating in her mouth and over his cock. That one additional sensation was almost too much. He caught her under the arms, careful of her sore shoulder. With ease, he set her over him so her legs straddled his hips. His cock nestled between her damp folds, wanting entrance. But he couldn't enter her until she invited him inside her. A male vampire could not enter a female mortal without invitation. The translation of old folklore had really messed up that one.

"Jolee, invite me in," he rasped, his breathing uneven. He rubbed his cock along her sex. She gasped and nodded.

"Say it, baby," he urged, noting the desperation in his voice.

"Christian, please come inside me."

He growled greedily and positioned himself to enter her when she cried, "Wait!"

He stared at her. *God, please don't let her have second thoughts now.* He didn't think he could bear being this close to making love to her and lose the chance.

"Do you have a condom?"

He frowned, confused. "No. Should I?"

She nodded, then groaned with her own frustration. "I don't either. And I'm not on anything."

On anything? She was on him. And he wanted her all the way on him.

"Christian, I can't have sex without protection. I know we are both safe. But I can't risk pregnancy." She groaned again. "This is awful."

He started to tell her that he couldn't conceive a child anyway. Nor could he distribute or contract any type of disease. But that wouldn't make any sense to her. And she'd probably think the "no pregnancy" thing was just a line. Plus, after hearing about her family, and particularly her sister, he didn't think she'd take any chances. She was too responsible to be reckless, at least about this.

"That's okay," he managed to say, his voice even sounding calm. Inside his desire ripped through him, urging him to enter her. She'd invited him. He could.

"God, this is such a stupid thing to have forgotten," she said, looking as pained as he was.

"Don't worry. We can still satisfy each other." He began moving his hips, sliding his cock along her wet labia. She gasped, her hips automatically moving with his. He pushed her knees farther apart, so she was forced more directly along his hard length.

She leaned forward, her hands linking with his, moving them up over his head, pinning him there as she glided over him with exquisite pressure. The tips of her breasts grazed his chest, his cock sandwiched in her hot, wet mound.

Her movements gradually became more frantic on top of him as they glided toward release. Then she rose up, pressing down tightly on him, crying out. His cock pulsed in response, ready to explode at the wanton sight of her above him. Dark red hair clung to her neck and cheeks, her breasts still puckered and rosy, and her legs spread over him, dark auburn curls hugged over golden brown curls. And the absolute pleasure he could see on her face. Beautiful.

His cock throbbed again, release right there. But he tensed himself, determined to control it. He couldn't settle for less than being inside her. He'd waited a long time for her—and he wouldn't accept less than all of her.

Chapter 21

Christian eased Jolee off his chest where she'd sprawled after her last orgasm. She had fallen asleep almost immediately, but he'd held her for a while. Even though her body against his was silken torture, he hadn't moved. He liked feeling her heart beat against his silent chest, and her even breaths on his skin. But he had to get up and draw her curtains and make sure the sunlight wouldn't sneak around the edges in a couple hours. He might have lost his ability to bite, but he didn't believe he was that changed. He was still a vampire.

He pulled the flimsy rolled blinds over the windows. They would not keep out enough light, but fortunately she had curtains, too. The combination would be safe. Not to mention the back of her trailer was shaded by trees.

To be absolutely safe, he should go back to his trailer, but he wanted to stay with her. In her tiny bedroom, amongst her strawberry and cartoon character bedding. He grinned at the whimsical comforter as he covered her; somehow it suited her. Then he walked out into her trailer, feeling the need to look around, see personal things about her. What she liked.

He entered her bathroom first, looking in her medicine

cabinet, finding her toothbrush and a nearly empty tube of toothpaste, whitening with baking soda. He picked up a bottle of nail polish, the color she had on her toes. The bottle looked ancient, the lacquer gumming up the top. He put it back. He also found some cosmetics, a hairbrush and deodorant, which he opened and sniffed. A flowery scent that he recognized, although it was usually lost under her natural spicy scent.

Her shower only contained a bar of soap and a nearly empty bottle of shampoo. No bottles of lotions and scented soaps. No perfume. No other toiletries. Not that she needed them, but he did know enough about women to know they liked to occasionally pamper themselves. Mortal women and vampiresses weren't different on that count.

He moved on to the kitchen to look in her cupboards. Aside from a box of something called "Tastee O's," several boxes of macaroni and cheese, a few cans of soup, and some teabags, her shelves were as empty as his. He turned to the refrigerator to discover she had just as little in there. No wonder she was so thin. She made him feel like a glutton—and he lived on a liquid diet. He fully intended to buy her some things, which he knew would be a fight because Jolee was determined to make her own way in life. But she was going to have to accept his help. He wanted to take care of her.

And she needed some furniture, he decided. Making a mental list of what she needed, he headed back to her room. She still lay in the same position in which he'd left her. He watched her for a moment, fascinated by the peacefulness of her features and the curl of her hair on the pillow. Then he glanced around, taking in the room. He noticed nothing personal. Just an old radio on the dresser and a lamp and alarm clock on the box that served as her nightstand.

Materially, he'd once had everything that he could have possibly wanted. A life of luxury—and it had never been as perfect as this barren little room. All he needed was Jolee, but he wanted to give her everything.

Jolee woke, her limbs still feeling boneless and languid. She rolled over, feeling for Christian in the dim light. He was sprawled on his back in much the same pose she'd seen him in when she'd peeked in his bedroom. One arm rested above his head, the other on his bare chest. One corner of the Strawberry Shortcake comforter covered his hips, the little cartoon girl grinning widely.

Jolee smiled at the sight. Slowly she stroked her hand down his muscled belly and under the cover. His penis was soft against his thigh, but still large even in its unaroused state. Everything about this man was extraordinary.

She continued to touch him, and although he remained soundly asleep, his penis began to enlarge under her exploring fingertips. She shivered, a ripple of desire shimmying down her spine. She couldn't wait to feel him inside her. She'd thought she'd die last night when she realized they had no contraceptives. But because Christian was truly remarkable, he just accepted her misgivings and satisfied them without penetrating her. And it had been wonderful.

She hoped it had been for him, too. Although she intended to make up for it tonight. Maybe even now. She lifted the cover to admire his full, heavy erection. The shaft extended up to his belly button and the width couldn't be circled by her long fingers. She'd never seem a man so . . . enormous. And absolutely beautiful.

She ran a fingertip up his sensitive underside, but still he didn't rouse. She should just let the poor man rest. She leaned down and pressed a kiss to the bulbous top, loving the velvety squishiness of it under her lips, a direct contradiction to the steely shaft below.

He stirred, his hand slipping into her hair.

"Jolee?" His voice was almost slurred with his exhaustion.

"Sorry to wake you. I couldn't resist touching."

"Mmm . . . like it," he mumbled, and she wasn't sure if it was his response to her touch, or a question.

She smiled fondly. How could someone so strong and powerful be so cute?

"I need to sleep," he slurred with regret.

"I know." She kissed his lips. "Sleep in."

"Take my car to work," he said, somehow making the mumbled words sound like an order.

"Okay," she said, even though she didn't intend to. Then she decided maybe she would to go to the drugstore to get condoms. She glanced over her shoulder at the alarm clock.

"Oh crap," she said, scrambling off the bed. It was already after four P.M. She'd slept the whole day away. She didn't have time to get condoms, and she was going to have to take Christian's car to make it to the bar on time.

She opened her drawers to grab underwear, jeans, and a T-shirt. She cast one last admiring glance toward Christian, then rushed to the bathroom for a quick shower.

"What's got you smiling like the cat that caught the canary?" Jed said as he watched her fix a tray of drinks.

"What do you mean?" she asked, even though she knew exactly what he meant. She'd been grinning like a fool since she got here. But she just felt so . . . happy. Absolutely, positively happy. She caught herself as she nearly laughed out loud with the joy of it all.

Jed raised a bushy eyebrow at her, his blue eyes knowing. "I think I have a fairly good idea who's got you all giddy. Where *is* pretty boy?"

In her bed! But she didn't say that, instead just grinning even wider. "He'll be here."

She left Jed to deliver the beers. For a Monday night, the bar was relatively busy. As usual, a group played pool and several of the tables were occupied. It wouldn't be a great night, but she couldn't bring herself to worry. She was simply too happy. She could worry later after the novelty of being with Christian wore off. Yeah, like that was ever going to happen. The bar was doomed. She giggled.

She finished serving the drinks, returning to another table where customers had already left. She tucked a nice tip into her apron, then began to load the dirty glasses onto her empty tray. As she worked, she heard the front door open and close. A few seconds later, she sensed someone standing behind her.

She spun, grinning broadly, assuming the person was Christian. Instead it was Vance.

He looked better than he had the other night, but he still wasn't the picture of health. His skin was pale, and the purplish circles under his eyes made his features look more drawn and skeletal. But his gaze didn't appear quite so wild.

How had she ever believed Christian was an addict?

"Hi, sis." He always used "sis" when he was feeling contrite. At least she wouldn't have to worry about another attack. She dropped a quick look down to his hands, which hung limply at his sides. No, he didn't seem to have a weapon tonight.

"Listen," he said. "I'm real sorry about the other night."

She nodded, but then returned to clearing the table. While she was glad to see he wasn't in the throes of withdrawal, she didn't really want to hear his hollow apology. She'd heard them one too many times to believe he meant them.

"I was in a bad way."

She nodded again, lifting the tray and bringing it to the bar. She set it down, then turned to face him.

"Vance, I don't have any money."

Her brother looked around. "You look like you're doing okay."

She sighed. "I wouldn't give you any money even if I had it. You need to get help."

His dark eyes narrowed. Vance had once been a hand-some kid. Now he was dirty and thin. Despite herself, her heart did go out to him. Even after all the times he'd been awful to her. She just wished he'd get his act together. She wished any one of her siblings would. She cared about them, but also it would somehow validate that she could change, too.

"I ran into Mark," Vance said. "He said he stopped by for a visit."

Jolee snorted at that. "Is that what he told you?" A visit sounded altogether too congenial for what it had really been like.

"Mark said you got a new boyfriend. Said the guy looked loaded."

Mark could tell that in the tiny amount of time between when he saw Christian, and Christian knocked him uncon-scious? She didn't say anything.

"You gotta help me out," Vance insisted. He stepped closer. "Give me a couple hundred and I leave you alone for good."

She didn't have a couple hundred. Not that she'd give it to him if she did.

"No," she insisted.

"Your new man can spare it."

So that was his plan. "No."

Over Vance's shoulder, Jolee saw Christian enter the bar. He spotted her right away, and from the protective look on his face he recognized Vance immediately. He strode in their direction.

Vance saw him. "Your boyfriend is that guy from the other night?" He didn't seem too pleased by the realization, and Jolee realized he'd probably hoped that her boyfriend would be someone easier to bully.

She didn't think anyone could bully Christian. And he'd protect her. Her chest swelled. Or rather her heart.

"Is everything okay?" Christian said, coming to stand next to her. Vance stepped back.

"Yes," she told him. "Vance was just leaving."

Vance hesitated, then strolled toward the door. But not before he shot both of them a look of pure hatred. The rage she saw there startled her. Sadness filled her, because she really knew that she'd never have a real brother in Vance. He was too consumed by his problems.

"Are you sure you're okay?" Christian asked, studying her.

She nodded, glancing at the door as Vance stepped outside.

"I just need to realize that I'll never have a real family." She sighed. But then she slipped her arms around his waist. "But I'm so glad I have you."

Christian closed his eyes, guilt rushing through him, her words painful.

He squeezed her tight in return. "Damned right."

She grinned up at him, and pride filled him at the happiness he saw glittering in her eyes.

"Did you get condoms?" she asked.

He grinned. "You had my car."

"Oh, yeah," she remembered, then winced. "I only ground the gears twice."

"You can destroy the clutch for all I care. But I'm going to be the one who drives to get the condoms tonight."

"Why?"

"Because I can drive faster."

She laughed and kissed him lingeringly. If one of the customers hadn't waved for another drink, Christian would have continued to kiss her. Instead, he pulled away and turned her in the direction of the thirsty patron.

"Get to work."

She frowned at him over her shoulder. "Hey, who's the boss here?"

"You are," he said obediently.

She swayed away, her step light and flirty.

He groaned. Oh, she so was the boss.

He headed to the bar, only to catch Jed's knowing look.

"Okay, you were right," he admitted to the old man on the way by.

Jed chuckled merrily, then brought his ever-present cigarette to his mouth.

Chapter 22

"Where are we going?" Jolee asked later, watching the all-night pharmacy pass them by.

"I have to go to Super Biggie Bargain Mart."

She frowned, trying to imagine Christian shopping at the discount retail chain.

"What do you need there?" She'd be willing to bet he wouldn't even buy his underwear there. If he wore underwear. She glanced at his lap. "I thought we were just getting condoms."

"I also need some food . . . and other things," he said, sounding rather evasive.

Food and other things? And here she was only thinking about tasting *him*—and other things. Disappointment tugged at her insides. At work, she could have sworn they were both desperate to get each other alone. Both of them had found excuses to touch one another, a brush of arms as they made drinks. A hand on a back as they passed. Twice he'd even pinned her against the shelves along the back of the bar as he reached over her for a bottle of liquor. Liquors she didn't even think he actually used.

And now he wanted to shop.

She made a frustrated sound low in her throat.

"What's wrong?"

"Nothing." She knew she didn't sound very convincing, but darn it, she was hot and bothered!

The store's parking lot was surprisingly crowded given the time of night. Christian pulled into a space and shut off the engine.

"Are you sure you're okay?"

She nodded. She'd been better than okay all night. In fact, the whole night had been great, which was surprising given the visit from Vance. She was amazed how easily Christian had made things better.

She supposed she could wait a little longer to make love with this man. She was being impatient and greedy. After all, she knew he had less food in his house than she did. He did need to shop.

"Yes," she assured him. "I'm just anxious to get you alone."

He smiled, a sexy little curl of his lips. "I'm anxious, too. This will be quick."

She hoped so.

When they got into the store, they headed right to the food section. They wandered the aisles, Christian stopping here and there to pick up some food item and frown as though he'd never seen it before in his life.

"Have you had these? Pop-Tarts?" He gave her a questioning look as if they were something completely new to him.

"Sure," she said.

Who hadn't had Pop-Tarts? Of course she was talking about someone who probably had caviar for breakfast before he moved here. She picked up a box of cereal bars, scanning the box dispassionately, then putting it back. She strolled a little farther down the aisle, and she noticed Christian grabbed the box she'd been looking at and tossed it in his cart. He hesitated, then grabbed another and tossed that in, too.

"Is there anything you'd like?" he asked finally. He looked miserable, as though shopping was just too much for him. She understood that feeling.

"Condoms," she stated.

He smiled, shaking his head. "You have a one-track mind."

Didn't she know it.

After an eternity in the food aisles and a cart loaded high with every sort of fare, they finally made it to the pharmacy aisles.

But instead of going straight to the contraceptives, he turned down the shampoo and soap aisle. She crossed her arms and watched as he lifted practically every bottle, reading the description, then debating. Finally, he chose a pink shampoo with flowers on the bottle. He also added some pink conditioner and a bottle of lavender-colored body wash. He also added some peach-colored lotion.

What on earth? But she didn't question his peculiar choices in toiletries, because he'd finally turned to the aisle with the condoms. He frowned at the row of boxes hanging from metal hooks. Apparently he was as confused by the condoms as he had been by prepackaged food. Of course, the condom confusion made a bit more sense. He'd said he hadn't had sex for a long time.

"Do you have a favorite?" he finally asked.

"No," she said, then smiled slightly. "But even if I did, it wouldn't matter, because you've only got one choice, big boy."

She pulled a box labeled "Maximum" off the hook and handed it to him.

"A superior size for the superior man." He raised an eyebrow, looking extremely arrogant.

God, even his smugness made her hot.

He grabbed a few more boxes, adding them to the growing pile of stuff.

Jolee took two of them. "I'll buy these."

"No," he said, attempting to take them back.

She held them over her head, acting as if he couldn't reach them. Rather ridiculous given he was several inches taller than she was. But he didn't grab them. Instead he crossed his arms over his chest, regarding her with an amused grin.

"It's only fair," she said. "I'm using them, too."

Finally he nodded. "Okay, but only because I know you will argue until you're breathless. And I have better plans to make you breathless."

"Thank God, because I'm pretty much ready to jump you right here in aisle eleven."

Christian appeared a bit surprised by her announcement, but then another smug smile turned up his lips. "Well, you only have to wait a little longer, then you may jump me as much as you like."

Her knees trembled like jelly at that promise. Lord, she wanted him.

But she had to get her legs under control as Mr. Super Shopper now headed over to the furniture department to look at nightstands. She lingered behind, wondering if he was really as attracted as she was. Because frankly, any furniture outside of a bed held no interest for her.

She strolled around the store until she ended up in the women's clothing department. A red polka dot skirt caught her attention, and she pulled it off the rack to admire the satiny material. Putting it back, she flipped through the other garments. She stopped here and there to take something off the rack to look at it closer. A blue flowered skirt with a swishy hemline. A lavender one with little white and gray geometric shapes. She even found several tops that would look great with them.

"Find anything you like?"

She looked up from the sundress she was holding. She held the simply cut, black with multicolored polka dot dress against herself, striking her version of a fashion pose. She laughed.

"One day." She sighed. "Once the bar takes off."

He nodded, and she joined him as they approached the checkout.

"Damn it," he muttered, feeling the pockets of his dark gray pants. "I forgot my wallet in my car. I think it's in my glove box."

"Do you want me to go look?" she asked when he just stood there looking confounded.

"Would you mind?"

"Of course not." Although she had no idea when he would have put his wallet in the glove box. She'd driven his car to work, and had the keys, so the vehicle was locked when he got to the restaurant. And she hadn't seen him put it in there after they left the restaurant last night. But he seemed pretty sure.

Maybe he had put it in there when he got to the bar. He must have a second set of keys.

She started toward the exit when Christian called to her. She turned, giving him a questioning look. He pointed at the boxes of condoms still in her hand.

She handed them to him, and he tossed them into the cart.

"I'm paying for those," she reminded him.

"I know," he assured her. "Oh, maybe look for my wallet under the seat. I know it's in the car somewhere."

She strode to the automatic doors at the front of the store. He seemed awfully confused tonight. She'd have to make sure he ate some of his massive quantities of food once they got back to the trailer. His blood sugar must be out of whack.

Christian watched Jolee leave, then hurried back to the women's clothing. He quickly found each item she'd looked at, her cinnamon scent stronger on the ones she touched the longest. He didn't understand the sizing, but he could guess which ones would fit her. He piled them on the cart, and headed to the checkout farthest away from where she'd reenter the store. Fortunately, he got a cashier who didn't have much to say and scanned quickly. He threw the four boxes of condoms on top of the clothes.

By the time Jolee returned, the clothes and condoms were bagged and placed under some of the other items.

"I couldn't find it," she told him, flashing an embarrassed look between the cashier and the already bagged items in the cart.

"Oh," he said, trying not to smile at his own lame lie. "I found it."

She frowned. "Where?"

"It was in my pocket. I don't know how I missed it."

She gave him a worried look, but didn't comment. After following him around the store, watching him stare bewilderedly at everything, she probably thought he was a lunatic. But it was in part her fault. She hadn't given him any help. She didn't comment that any food was her favorite.

And he didn't even know what one did with cuisine like Hot Pockets and Sugar Smacks. They sounded like mildly offensive endearments rather than food. And the toiletries. He was clueless what a woman would want. If he were in Paris or Milan, he would go to one of the exclusive shops and feel confident he was buying her something nice.

The cashier scanned the pink shampoo. But with a name like "Salon Simulators," which promised to reproduce the results of the most expensive European salon, on any hair type, well, he had his doubts.

But he also knew that Jolee wouldn't be comfortable with expensive gifts. Not yet. One day maybe, but she was too proud, too determined to survive on her own to take anything too expensive from him.

"Your total is $476.86," the woman said, a slightly raised eyebrow the only indication that the total surprised her.

He handed her a credit card.

"When you decide to shop, you really shop," Jolee murmured.

"All necessary," he told her.

Jolee nodded, although she watched his card go through with a rather bemused expression. He signed his name, took his receipt, and pushed the mounded cart toward the exit. Now the tricky part, convincing Jolee to accept the gifts.

"Shouldn't we bring all this stuff to your place?" Jolee said as he parked in front of her trailer.

"Well, I thought I'd keep some of the groceries over here. If that's okay."

She smiled broadly as though she was very pleased by the idea. Maybe it wouldn't be too hard to get her to accept the items after all. They began to carry in the many bags, placing them in a cluster on her kitchen floor.

"What do you want to leave here?" she asked, picking up two of the bags and setting them on the sideboard. Christian didn't answer. Instead he came up behind her, bracing his hands on either side of her, pinning her between himself and the counter. He nuzzled her neck, pressing kisses down her nape toward her shoulder.

She tilted her head forward, giving him better access.

"I've been dying to do that all night," he said, licking the delicate skin just below her ear.

She shivered. "You could have fooled me, Mr. Shop-aholic."

He nipped the crook of her shoulder playfully. "Feeling neglected?"

"Maybe a little."

"Well, we can't have that."

He slipped his hands under her T-shirt, caressing her stomach on the way up to her breasts. Her nipples were already distended, poking greedily against his palms. He caught them between his thumbs and forefingers, gently squeezing them through the satiny material of her bra.

She whimpered, turning in his arms. Her mouth found

his, and they kissed with all the passion they'd kept restrained for so many long hours. Her hands knotted in his hair as he kissed down over her neck and chest. His fingers found the button of her jeans, then the zipper. He kissed her bared belly just above her panties.

She whimpered, wriggling under his touch. He could smell the spiciness of her arousal and couldn't stop himself from leaning in to breathe deeply. Peeling down both her jeans and panties, he bared her from the waist down. His mouth watered at the sight of her dark auburn curls against her pale thighs. Again he was amazed at how his desire for this woman was even stronger than the hunger. And definitely more uncontrollable.

Even as he told himself to slow down, he spread her legs apart. Her sex parted, too, as if offering him invitation inside. He groaned, his cock pulsating at the sight. But he remained focused, covering her with his mouth, his tongue delving inside her heated folds.

She cried out, clutching the counter for support. He seized her hips, holding her steady as he tasted her. Nothing had ever been so delicious, so pleasing. Not even quenching his hunger. The hunger no longer controlled him. Only his passion for Jolee mattered. Only his arousal demanded to be satisfied.

He licked her clitoris, the tight little nubbin quivering under his tongue. He continued massaging her with slow sweeps, each one nudging her closer to release. Her small little moans grew louder, more frantic. Then he tasted her release. Honey on his tongue. So satisfying. So humbling.

After the last ripple of her climax, he rose, smiling at what a gorgeous sight she made. Her legs were still spread as she leaned heavily on the counter. He'd like to take her just like that. Hard, up against the cupboards. But not this time, this time he wanted to watch her face as he entered her. He wanted to focus on every nuance of her body wrapped around him.

His cock jerked, urging him to do just that.

Chapter 23

"Good golly," Jolee breathed, trying to regain control of her pleasure-weakened body. "How do you do that?"

"Do what?"

She would have smiled at his innocent tone if she'd had the strength. "How do you have me satisfied before I even have a chance to get you out of one piece of clothing?"

"I'm just good."

"Yes, you are," she agreed heartily. She straightened and started to reach for him, but he caught her fingers, holding them to his chest.

"Let's go to your room. I'll even let you take off a few pieces of my clothing." He started to pull her to the hallway. She followed gladly until she recalled the condoms. She did not want to forget those. She couldn't stop again. She had to make love with this man, fully. Her satisfied body started to tingle again with renewed desire. She was insatiable for him.

"Wait." She tugged free and returned to the pile of groceries. She bent down to open the first bag, finding the condoms right away.

"Here they . . ." She noticed something beneath the

boxes. Black material with multicolored polka dots. She pulled out the sundress she'd been admiring. "What's this?"

He answered her obvious question with the obvious answer. "The dress you were looking at."

She picked up the bag, digging through the rest of the contents, disbelief building more and more as she discovered each article of clothing she'd looked at. She didn't know what to think.

"Christian, you shouldn't have done this."

"I wanted to." He shrugged as if the purchase wasn't any big deal.

Not a big deal to him, but definitely a big deal to her. He'd spent a ton of money. "But I can't accept them."

"You know, the fact that you are standing in your kitchen, naked from the waist down, arguing with me, should be rather entertaining, but I'm not amused. In fact, I'm a little annoyed, because I'd much rather be making love to you at this moment. You can take the clothes, and you will."

Her frown deepened even more at his officious tone—and at the fact that she was actually a little aroused by his bossiness.

"This is too much." She gestured to the bag. "I don't want you to spend this kind of money on me."

He stared at her for a moment, then he sighed. "I know you don't. But I wanted to. I want to take care of you. I want to give you things that will make you happy. I knew you'd argue, because you want to prove you don't need help. But this wasn't help. It's a gift."

A gift. Guilt curled in her belly. He wanted to do something nice, and she hadn't even said thank you. And all because every gift in her life had come with strings. But she knew he'd done this only for the reasons he'd said, and no other. She looked back down at the bag.

"Thank you," she said almost sheepishly. "I love them." And she loved him. Her breath caught. Oh my God, she loved him. It was just a fact—a true, unchangeable fact.

"It was too much, though," she murmured. Just like the feelings overwhelming her. Everything about this man was too much. Too perfect. Too wonderful. And she didn't want it to ever end. And that was too scary.

Then he gave her one of his cute little smiles and she knew it was also too late to worry. She loved him.

He shook his head, forbearance clear in his eyes. "The clothes are not nearly enough for what you've given me."

"What have I given you?"

He looked down for a moment, then he took a deep breath. Finally he met her eyes again, and simply said, "Peace."

She didn't quite know what that meant, but her heart skipped at the admission. She knew it was somehow a difficult one, and a very important one. Poor Christian. What had Lilah done to him?

"Now come here," he ordered sternly and crooked his finger.

She set down the bag and walked into his arms. She really did love it when he was a little domineering. Especially when she knew she was really going to like what he was ordering her to do.

She kissed him gently. "I love the clothes. They are beautiful."

"You will make them more beautiful," he murmured against her hair. Then the hand on her back slid down to cup a cheek of her bottom. "Although it will be hard to beat this look."

She laughed. "You're finding this amusing, aren't you?"

"No, I'm finding it immensely arousing."

She could feel that, as his erection prodded her belly. She made a small noise in the back of her throat. "Me, too."

She shifted out of his arms, and this time she led him down the hallway. Once they reached her room, she stopped at the foot of the bed. She tossed the box of condoms on the mattress, then she reached for him, tugging the hem of his shirt from the waistband of his pants. Her fingers moved the small buttons, working one after the other free, revealing a tempting trail of golden skin, right down the center of his chest and stomach.

She slipped her hands under the opened material, molding her hands to his torso, her fingers shaping to each swell and each groove of his lean muscles.

"You"—she leaned into kiss the alluring curve of his collarbone—"have an amazing chest."

Slowly her hands traced over him. "It's like you were carved out of marble. Ageless and perfect."

His body tensed; his already hard muscles seemed to actually turn into the stone she had described. She lifted her head to see his expression, to see what suddenly made him freeze, but he just watched her with unfathomable pale eyes.

She didn't want that expression. She wanted those incredible eyes filled with passion. She wanted him to feel what she did when he touched her. Gliding her hands upward, she found his nipples, circling them. They pebbled under her touch, smaller imitations of her own already puckered nipples.

She teased him with sweeps of her thumb until she felt him moving just slightly under her touch, pressing against her fingers.

His arms came around her to pull her against him, but she wiggled away.

"Uh-uh," she warned, giving him a disapproving look. "No touching me until you are totally nude. I know your tricks. If I let you touch me now, you'll have me on the bed panting before you even lose the unbuttoned shirt."

Christian grinned, raising an eyebrow. "I wouldn't think there'd be a real problem with that."

"Well, there isn't," she admitted, but when he reached for her again, she added, "Except I want to look at, and touch, you."

Well, only a fool would argue with her about that. He quickly slipped his shirt off, and reached for his pants. Just as swiftly he had those off, too.

He stood in front of her, painfully aroused as her gaze wandered down his body.

"I didn't know there were men like you," she stated. "And I can't believe you are mine."

Her words both thrilled him and displeased him. He was pleased that she considered him hers, but even if he could, he wouldn't tell her that there weren't many men like him. That in fact he wasn't even a man. Would she want him anymore if she did know? Not his Jolee who came from a rough background, who likely just wanted to be with a nice, normal guy.

Jolee walked closer to him, her eyes again scanning the length of his body. They stopped at his rigid length. His cock twitched under her scrutiny. She smiled slightly, her eyes meeting his just briefly before she touched her fingers to him, her hand curling around him.

He made a growling noise deep in his throat. His eyes closed as she stroked him. Her fingers explored his length, the head, the shaft, and his testicles below.

"I want to feel you inside me," she murmured as she pressed her mouth to his chest, her tongue darting over his skin, her hand still holding him, fondling him.

"I want all of you." She stroked upward to emphasize *all*.

He growled again, this time the sound loud and feral.

He picked her up, placing her in the center of the bed. He followed her down, pinning her under his weight. She spread her legs, positioning him in the cradle of her thighs. The springy curls at the apex of her legs teased his erection, spurring him on, inviting him to enter the slick heat just beyond.

"I can't wait this time," he told her. "I can't wait any longer to feel you."

She shook her head, gasping slightly as his cock skimmed between her damp lips, rubbing her engorged clitoris. "I—oh—I can't wait either."

He rolled away from her to find the box of condoms,

which had fallen to the floor when both of them had dropped onto the bed. He ripped the flaps, and pulled out a link of several condoms. Tearing one off, he dropped the others on the makeshift nightstand.

When he turned back to Jolee, he found her watching him with eagerness glittering in her dark eyes. He also noted that she was still half-dressed. He wanted nothing between them. He didn't even want the condom, but he wouldn't argue that, for her sake. The shirt and bra, however, had to go.

Dropping the condom on the pillow next to him, he reached for her shirt, pulling it over her head and tossing it to the floor. Then he looped his arms around her, finding the clasp of the white bra. She kissed his shoulder and his arm as he worked the hook and eye free. Not an easy task with Jolee's amazing lips moving over his skin.

Finally he flung the scrap away and gazed at her. Creamy skin, with pouty, rose-colored nipples beckoning him.

"Amazing," he murmured, brushing a thumb across one of her lovely breasts. His hand left her only to pat around for the foil packet, but his eyes remained fastened on her, awed by the perfection of her. With more force than necessary, he tore the plastic square open.

His gaze left her as he frowned at the sheer circle surrounded by a ring. How the hell did he tie this on? French letters tied on, didn't they?

"Can I?" she asked.

He gladly handed her the item. He'd never seen a condom, much less used one. At the time when he'd had cause to use one, he hadn't had the sense.

"Lie back," she said, nudging him against the mattress. She turned to face him, looking like a kneeling fairy. Her dark red hair brushed the swell of her breasts. Her legs were folded under her, knees tight together, hiding the dark auburn curls that matched her hair.

He started as she slipped a hand under his cock. Then with her other hand, she placed the rolled condom on the sensitive head. He watched with intent interest as she pinched the top of the latex, and then in short, repetitive, and very arousing strokes, she unrolled the snug sheath until it encased him.

For a brief moment, he wondered at how many other condoms she'd put on other men, but he disregarded the thought. He'd be the last. She'd never make love with another man except him. He didn't know how he could make that happen, and he didn't have time to think about it, because she leaned down and placed a kiss on his hipbone. He couldn't remain passive any longer. Between the squeeze of the condom and her nibbling kisses, he couldn't hold back. He caught her under the arms and dragged her up on top of him, relishing the velvety smoothness of her skin moving over his.

She laughed at his sudden action. Her eyes gleamed with a mixture of joy and desire. A very, very sexy combination.

He kissed her, the touch of their lips seeming to ignite them both. She moaned, opening her lips to him, her tongue caressing his, her fingers sinking into his hair. He tangled his fingers in her silky hair and deepened the kiss even more.

She moaned again, nipping his lip greedily. Hungrily, he rolled her under him. Again she opened for him, this time cradling him between her legs. An eager invitation for him to enter her.

"Baby, I can't wait," he muttered roughly.

"No," she agreed, her voice husky with need.

He rose up on his arms to position himself, the head of his cock opening her. Slowly, he eased into her body, her tight wet vagina stretching to accept him.

"Are you all right?" he asked.

She nodded, her eyes closed, her lips parted. "Oh God, yes."

He leaned down and nipped her full bottom lip. He pushed— another inch, another contraction of moist heat all around him, then a bit more of himself, then more taut, stroking heat.

"Damn," he muttered, "you feel so good. So tight, so hot." Nothing had ever felt this good.

She groaned, arching against him, taking him deeper into her. She rose again, and he was buried in her heat to the hilt.

The muscles in his arms strained as he tried to remain composed. He wanted this to go slow, he wanted to absorb every detail. Her arousal cocooning them in cinnamon and slick desire. The tiny pulses that stroked his rigid length. The way he was so deep he couldn't feel anything but her. The way she gasped as he shifted, moving ever so slightly inside her. The peace that mingled with his desire, giving him more joy than he ever believed possible.

He leaned forward and kissed her, trying to keep the action unhurried, tasting the warmth of her soft lips, the sweet tang of her tongue. Jolee moaned and caught his head in her hands, intensifying the kiss. She squirmed under him, her hips rising up as much as they could to stroke him. Her long, gorgeous legs curled around his hips, holding him against her like her vagina held his cock.

He groaned, and all control was lost. He had to move. To feel the stroke of Jolee's responsive body and remember. Remember what it was like to be a man. What it was like to love. And what it was like to be loved in return.

He thrust deeper, his movements a little frenzied, a little desperate, but his lack of control didn't seem to distress her. She continued to cling to him with her entire body. Her heels anchored to his back. Her fingers clutched his shoulders. She lifted to meet him, accepting him with just as much wildness.

"Christian," she cried, her voice as frantic as he felt. "Oh my God!" She writhed under him, her head twisting back and forth on the pillow, red hair clinging to the pillow, to her flushed face.

"Is it good?" He impaled her completely.

"Yes! Yes!" She bucked against him, her release right there. Right on the verge.

He braced himself on one arm and slid a hand between them to her mound. She was spread wide to accommodate him, her clitoris nearly bared for his touch. He brushed his thumb over the swollen bud.

She rose up again with a ragged cry. Christian gritted his teeth, focusing on the upsurge of her arousal in the air around him. Another deep thrust, another rub of his thumb, and another rush of arousal crackled the air.

Jolee screamed, driving him deep inside her, and she came. Her release poured down over them like a sudden cloudburst. Christian shouted, too, his own orgasm joining hers, flooding them both with rapture. Nothing had been so perfect. So close to heaven. The only heaven he'd know.

"I didn't know it could be like that," Jolee said, lazily running her fingers over Christian's chest.

"Nor did I." He pulled her tighter against him, and she had the impression that he was as overwhelmed as she. Their several intimate moments before tonight had been wonderful and intensely satisfying—the best Jolee had ever experienced—but they didn't even begin to compare with having this man inside her. As soon as he'd entered her, she felt like she was one with him. She knew what he wanted, and he knew what she needed. It was . . .

"Perfect." He sighed.

Yes, that was the only word. She lifted her head, resting it on her hand. "I've never experienced anything like that."

He rolled over to face her, mimicking her pose. "How much experience do you have?"

The question startled her, and immediately old wariness uncurled in her chest. Then she saw the jealousy clouding his eyes. And a little insecurity, too. She relaxed and reached out to caress his cheek.

"Not much. I've been with three men. Two I was with for a while. One was a stupid mistake, before I decided that I didn't want to be like my sister."

"Were you with Mark?"

She shook her head. "No. That could also be why he's so bitter. Given my sister's reputation, I'm sure he thought I was a sure thing, too."

Christian gazed at her as she traced her fingers over the sharp cut of his jawline, dipping a finger into the small dimple in his chin.

"Did any of the men treat you the way you deserve?" he asked.

She met his eyes, amazed to see concern warring with jealousy. Her heart ballooned. That was one reason she was falling so hard for this man—even when he was hurting, he was more worried about her. She kissed him. He tilted his head readily to deepen the kiss.

"None of them treated me like you do," she said when she pulled away. "Like I'm something special."

"You are something special. The most extraordinary woman I've ever met."

"Even more extraordinary than you thought Lilah was?" She closed her eyes just briefly, angry with herself for asking him. For reminding him of her.

But he didn't hesitate. "Yes." He reached out to brush her hair from her cheek, the touch tender. "You are generous, sweet, smart, funny. And very sexy."

She grinned saucily.

This time, he leaned in to steal a kiss. But despite his incredible description of her, Jolee felt she had to ask, "What was Lilah like—I mean, when you met her?"

He fingered a lock of her hair. Finally he said, "She was beautiful. A beauty that was beyond compare."

Jolee's heart sank. What had she expected? She knew that this woman must have been stunning to capture Christian's heart the way she had.

"She had long, pale blond hair and equally pale blue eyes."

"Like yours?"

He frowned as if he'd never even noticed his eye color. "Yes. I guess."

"Was she tall or short?"

"Very petite."

Of course. She shifted her own too long and too thin legs under the Strawberry Shortcake comforter.

"And quite voluptuous."

She tried not to glance down at her own small breasts, which were thankfully hidden under the covers, too.

"She knew she was lovely, and she used that to her advantage. She controlled men with a bat of her eyelashes. I didn't allow myself to see that, believing she was devoted to me in the same way I was devoted to her."

Jolee frowned, disliking this woman more and more. Beautiful and manipulative and cruel.

"Did she just like to prove she could have other men? Or did she really . . . have them?"

Christian smiled, the gesture not the cute curl of his lips that she was used to, but more of a sneer. "Oh, she had them."

Disgust filled her. How could Lilah have wanted other men when she had Christian devoted to her, as he said? Jolee just couldn't fathom it.

"She even had my own brother."

Jolee immediately stopped pondering this woman's stupidity and gaped at him. "Your brother?"

He seemed to realize he'd said more than he intended, his gaze leaving her to study the bows and strawberries on her comforter.

"Christian?" She tilted her head, trying to get him to look at her. "Is that why you don't see your family?"

He shook his head. He fingered the edge of the comforter, playing with a loose thread. "It was, but not now. I realize now that all Rhys was trying to do was prove to me the kind of woman Lilah really was."

"Rhys? Is that your brother's name?"

"Yes. I have two brothers. Rhys and Sebastian. My only family." He still didn't meet her gaze, but she didn't need to see his face to hear the pain in his voice. He loved his brothers. Missed them. She understood that pain, although her family had never been close.

"Are they older than you?"

"Rhys is older and Sebastian is younger."

"Where are they now?"

"They are both in New York City."

"Do they know you are no longer with Lilah?"

"Yes."

"Then can't you just forgive each other?"

He laughed at that, a cold bitter sound that only mocked real laughter. "No. I don't think they could ever forgive me."

"Why not?" His brothers surely missed Christian as much as he obviously missed them.

He shook his head again, then caught her and pulled her tight against his muscled body. "I don't want to talk about this. I just want to hold you." He leaned forward and kissed her, his lips aggressive and devouring, and instantly arousing. Her body tingled everywhere.

Christian's hand slid down her body to slip between her thighs. Very quickly Lilah and his brothers didn't matter. All she could think about was this beautiful, wonderful man making love to her.

Chapter 24

Christian gazed at Jolee as she curled against him, her eyes closed, her breathing even. Soon dawn would arrive and force him to sleep, but for right now, he could simply watch her.

She slept peacefully, contentment clear on her face even in slumber. That gave him a modicum of consolation, but not much. How could he feel any solace when she was oblivious to the fact that she was cuddled up to a monster? Of course, he'd even allowed himself to forget that fact until she'd asked about his brothers. Then all his past deeds returned to him in full detail.

How had he allowed himself to forget? How was he finding peace when Rhys was suffering? Despite his self-serving decision to help this mortal, and his grand plan to be human, he was still nothing but a monster. Egocentric, self-satisfying, and heartless.

No, maybe not totally heartless. After all, he finally understood the horrendous thing he'd done to Rhys. He comprehended fully the terrible, never-ending ache that must be crippling his brother now.

He'd once believed he already understood that pain. He'd

believed that Rhys had caused him that kind of pain by being with Lilah. He'd held the anger tight to him for nearly two centuries. But it had only taken one bite, one bite with which he'd intended to kill, for him to realize his anger had been totally unjustified. He'd tasted the love in Jane's blood when he killed her. Love for Rhys, and he'd finally understood. What he'd believed was love for Lilah was nothing more than obsession. An all-encompassing obsession that had distorted all his beliefs and destroyed all his chances at happiness. And now destroyed his brother's chances, too.

But even that bite and the horrible realization that had accompanied it hadn't made the magnitude of Rhys's loss totally clear. That had taken the sweet mortal sleeping against him. Jolee had made him truly understand.

He studied her again, taking inventory of her luscious lips, parted slightly, the faint smattering of freckles over the bridge of her nose, her arched eyebrows. A mortal. The very creature he'd once disdained. She'd shown him all the things he couldn't see himself, couldn't remember, powerful vampire that he'd been.

She'd shown him friendship, and generosity and passion and love. He could sense her love warm on his skin like the cheery heat of a fire, like the tender embrace of arms holding him, protecting him.

Jolee was perfection. Real perfection, not the false, affected perfection he'd once worshipped in Lilah. Jolee was everything Lilah hadn't been. And he didn't deserve to be here with her. She was far too good for him. Tightness clenched his chest.

No, he wasn't heartless. He had feelings, deep, overwhelming feelings for this woman. This mortal. This creature that he never believed he could love. But the feelings didn't warm him. Instead they made him feel more disgusted with himself. Disgusted with what he was. Because he now understood what his brother must have felt for his mortal. For Jane.

How could he have this woman, when his brother had lost his? He couldn't. He didn't deserve Jolee. Even though every fiber of his being told him he needed to be with her, he knew he had to let her go.

More pain filled him. Oh yes, he had a heart.

Jolee stretched, then snuggled closer to Christian. She hated to get out of bed. She wanted to stay curled against him, but she had to get ready for work. She had a delivery coming this afternoon, and she had to be at the bar. Her crotchety beer delivery man would be even more irritable if she was late.

She leaned over to kiss Christian's cheek, but then she slipped out of bed. It wouldn't do to let herself admire him too long. Otherwise she would stay in bed and touch him and she'd definitely be late. Besides, Christian hadn't even moved when she kissed him. He slept like the dead.

She carefully pulled open one of the drawers to her dresser, the ancient thing only sticking once. She grabbed underwear, then started to go to her closet to grab the rest of her clothing. She paused just as she reached for her usual jeans. She had new clothes. The bags were still in the center of the floor where they'd left them.

"Oh, no, the groceries," she cried, ignoring the bag with her clothes and heading to the many food-filled bags. She began rooting through them, looking for the items that should have been refrigerated. A few things like some hotdogs, sandwich meat, and a container of potato salad gave her a little concern so she threw them out. But for the most part, everything was salvageable. She put the cans and dried goods in her cupboards and the fresh fruit and veggies in her fridge. The old Frigidaire was definitely the fullest she'd ever seen it.

She turned back to grab the last bag outside of the one containing her clothes. Christian's odd assortment of toiletries. She started to leave them in the white plastic bag on the counter then paused, pulling out the bottles to examine them one at a time.

"He bought these for me," she murmured. She opened the bottle of shampoo, sniffing in the clean, floral scent. She glanced back at her cupboard and then to the closed fridge.

"You are such a sneak," she said with a shake of her head, referring to Christian. "You bought all this for me."

Which explained why he kept asking her if she liked this and that. And why he'd seemed so overwhelmed. He'd been shopping for her. She shook her head again, but love expanded her chest. She picked up the toiletries and the bag of clothes and headed down the hallway. She paused in her bedroom doorway to watch him sleep, her chest swelling with so much love it was almost painful.

"I love you," she whispered, then headed to the bathroom with her new treasures. She loved him. She was absolutely head over heels in love with her battered knight. He might be battered, but she knew she could heal him. She could make him whole again.

Sometimes the best ideas came from the simplest things. Jolee stared at the old black phone mounted on the wall near her office door. The ancient, rotary-style device had just rung moments earlier, a woman asking if Leo's was going to have karaoke tonight. And if a tall blond guy was going to be bartending tonight.

Jolee said yes to both questions, not feeling the least bit irritated with the woman's query about Christian. She could hardly blame her female patrons for looking. He was gorgeous. And as long as they only looked, more power to them.

But her female clientele's interest in her lover wasn't what triggered her brilliant idea. It had been that old phone itself.

She stared at the black relic for a moment, debating if the

idea was truly brilliant or incredibly bad. Sometimes it was hard to tell.

She nibbled her bottom lip, then lifted the receiver. The idea was worth a shot, and the likelihood it would even work was pretty low. She poked her finger into the correct holes, twirling the plastic circle, then she waited. An automated voice asked her for city and state.

She guessed. "Manhattan, New York."

"Name please."

What was the name? She frowned, almost ready to hang up when the name came to her.

"Rhys Young."

The line went dead for a moment.

Then the automated voice said in clear, monotone enunciation, "I'm sorry there is no number under that listing."

Damn. She hung up and dialed information again. This time she tried Sebastian.

The line was quiet for several moments and she decided her idea was foiled. Then the computerized voice said, "Please hold for that number."

She scrambled to find a pen near the cash register. She ripped off a scrap of receipt paper from the credit card machine and scribbled down the numbers as the monotone voice repeated the number for the second time.

She stared at the digits as the voice on the receiver told her they could dial the number for her for an additional seventy-five cents. She pushed down the receiver, still staring at the paper. She could talk to Christian's brothers. She could tell them that he was sorry for the rift. She knew he was. She'd seen the pain in his eyes when he talked about them. Maybe she could help them end this fight. Or maybe she'd just make things worse.

She nibbled her lip again, then picked up the handset. She slowly dialed the numbers and waited as the phone rang. Maybe no one was home. Just as she was about to hang up, an answering machine picked up, the voice on the other end in complete opposition to the computerized voice of the phone company.

"Hello there. You've reached Carfax Abbey. Please leave a message and I will get back to you as soon as possible."

Christian's brother. Even though Jolee couldn't see the speaker, and he hadn't given his name, she could almost hear the relationship in his voice. The same amazingly sexy richness to his tone, and a hint of the same unusual accent.

The machine beeped, prompting her to leave a message, and this time she didn't hesitate.

"Hi, my name is Jolee Dugan, and I'm trying to reach Rhys and/or Sebastian Young. I know your brother Christian, and I just wanted to let you know that he's fine. And that he really wants to talk with you." She paused, wondering what else she should add. "He's working at my bar in Shady Fork, West Virginia. And my number at the bar is 304-555-7678. I look forward to hearing from you."

She carefully hung up the receiver, keeping a hand on the phone for a moment. Maybe this had been a mistake. She was meddling, and it wasn't her right. She and Christian had only been together for a little while. A very little while.

"No, Christian needs to talk to his family," she said determinedly to herself, picking up the piece of paper with the number and slipping it under the register.

She turned back to the empty bar, feeling oddly deflated after the build-up of courage. But she busied herself with prepping the bar to open. Jed would be here soon to chat and then Christian would come. She'd done the right thing. And even if she hadn't, Christian would realize she'd only done it to be helpful and forgive her. She hoped.

Christian had debated not showing up at the bar tonight. Even though he knew he had to end things with Jolee, he couldn't bring himself to leave her in a lurch. And it was a good thing he didn't, he noted as he entered the barroom. Leo's was hopping.

Jolee, who hustled around the filled tables with a tray balanced on one hand, didn't see him right away. She talked to the guy who'd been admiring her the other night. He was admiring her still. And who wouldn't? She was wearing the red polka dot skirt and red knit top he'd bought her, and even though most of the outfit was covered with a white bar apron, he and the admirer could see a good length of her lovely legs.

Christian immediately started in their direction, but stopped. He could hardly act like the jealous beau when he was planning to walk away. He planned to leave Shady Fork tonight. His departure would hurt and confuse Jolee, but it was for the best.

"Hi." Jolee's voice snapped him out of his painful reverie.

He hadn't even realized she'd approached him. Strange, since her scent was so strong around him. But her scent seemed to stay with him always. He wondered if it would after he was gone, hundreds of miles away. He stared at her wide, beautiful smile, but couldn't speak. Pain choked him. How could he leave this woman?

Her wonderful smile faded into a frown. "Christian? What is wrong?"

He shook his head, still unable to speak. Hell wasn't self-imposed squalor. It wasn't living like a pauper. It wasn't even tending bar in a run-down dive. Hell was never seeing this woman again. He'd found his ultimate punishment.

"You need to eat, don't you?" she said, giving him one of her reprimanding looks. Then she caught his hand and tugged him toward the bar.

"Come on, I brought you an orange and a yogurt, because I knew you wouldn't remember to eat. You really need to be more careful."

She released his hand once she reached her tote bag stowed under the bar. She squatted down to rummage through the old, battered tote. He'd meant to buy her another one. He forgot. She stood, holding out the promised snack. He accepted them, his chest tightening unbearably at her indulgent smile.

"Don't you take a single drink order until you've eaten those. I can't have my man feeling ill." She winked at him, then turned to leave, but he caught her wrist. When she gave him a questioning look, he pulled her against him and kissed her, desperation making him a little rough. How was he going to survive without her?

After they parted, she grinned up at him. "Wow, remind me to provide you with a snack more often."

She kissed him again quickly before skipping off to the karaoke booth, red and white polka dots dancing around her long, gorgeous legs.

"Woo-wee," Jed said from his usual perch. "You two got it bad."

Christian considered denying it, letting the man know what a jerk he was, but he couldn't.

"Yeah, I got it bad."

"Well, that's good. You two are good for each other. I can tell these things."

Christian approached him, considering the old man's words. "How can you tell?"

"Hell, you don't get to be my age without learning a thing or two. I even had a grand love of my own once. Gertie." Jed winked. "A fine woman."

Christian studied the old man, a man that was probably over a hundred years younger than himself. Wrinkles scored his leathery cheeks, and there was no hint of what his original hair color had once been. Now it was only a wild shock of white. But his blue eyes were not clouded by age or by hard living. They were bright and shrewd. The eyes of a wise man hidden in a derelict body.

Christian marveled at that. That he'd lived far longer than Jed. He'd experienced far more, yet this old mortal was far more insightful. For the first time, Christian longed for his

immortality to truly disappear, not because of his past behavior as a vampire, but because he wanted the knowledge
and understanding that maybe only came from aging. Truly
aging.

He glanced at Jolee as she put out the songbooks and
chatted with the patrons. He wanted to grow old with this
woman. The realization startled him. Just like the notion of
loving a mortal, the idea of aging, of turning into the stiff,
stooped man across the bar from him, had once repulsed
him. He'd found nothing admirable in the process of the
body winding down after a too short life. But now, he couldn't
imagine any more worthy purpose than growing old in the
arms of the woman he loved. In sharing life with her. A real
life. And all his love.

He was nothing more than a perfect shell, existing on the
fringe of life. Jed had lived. Jed had experienced life. And
he'd learned from it. So had Jolee. Christian was suddenly
humbled by that. Christian had only started to learn. And it
was far too late.

"It's damned overwhelming, ain't it?" Jed said, drawing
Christian's attention back to him.

"What?"

"That kind of love. The real kind."

Again surprise shook Christian. It was as though Jed was
somehow picking up his feelings, using some sort of preternatural sense. But the old man wasn't. He just knew. He'd
lived through what Christian was only experiencing for the
first time.

"Yes, it is very overwhelming," Christian admitted. Then
he added, "I don't deserve her."

Jed nodded, again as if he knew that exact feeling.

Then Jolee's softly accented voice rang out over the microphone. "Thank you for coming to Leo's tonight. I'm
going to get the karaoke started with a song I dedicate to my
sweetheart."

Jolee smiled across the room at him, her dark eyes glittering with happiness and desire. Once more, Christian was practically brought to his knees by a rush of humility. Humbled that this amazing, beautiful, compassionate woman cared about him. She started to sing, her sweet, slightly husky voice filling the room, telling him that he alone gave her the sweetest taboo. That she didn't quite feel worthy of him, either.

He took a deep breath, and told himself that he did have to leave. He did. Leaving would be the only noble thing he'd ever done.

Chapter 25

The remainder of the night was very busy. Jolee was kept tied up at the karaoke booth for most of the evening, and Christian was occupied with drink orders. The majority of the patrons tonight were female, she couldn't help noticing. Many of the women repeatedly approached the bar to talk with Christian, but tonight their attempts to flirt didn't bother her—much. Christian showed no interest in them. He appeared to be polite but distant.

And just as many times as women talked to him, Jolee saw him looking in her direction, yearning in his pale eyes. Even now, as she moved around the room to wipe down the empty tables, the memory of that look sent shivers throughout her body.

She glanced over to where Christian washed up the glasses. He wasn't looking at her now, and in fact he'd said very little since the bar closed, but she still sensed his hunger. Or maybe it was her own.

She picked up her tray, loaded with ashtrays, and headed behind the bar.

She set the tray down near him, grimacing at clear ashtrays now heaped with ash and cigarette butts. "These alone show what a busy night we had."

Christian glanced at the tray, then at her. "*You* had a great night."

She frowned slightly. She couldn't be certain but she thought he'd emphasized *you*. But she decided she was probably being overly sensitive.

Christian finished rinsing the mug he'd just washed and set it upside down on a towel on the bar. He wiped his hands on his apron. "I'm going to go mop the bathrooms."

Again she wondered at his dismissal, but again decided she must be reading more into his behavior than was really there.

"It was very nice of you to offer to do the mopping. Jed looked like his arthritis was bothering him tonight."

Christian nodded without comment and left the bar.

Okay, maybe she wasn't being overly sensitive. Maybe something was wrong. She turned to the register, hitting the cash-out key and the register drawer jangled as it popped open.

She started to take out the stacks of money when she paused. She set down the ones and fives on the counter next to her and slid a hand under the register. The scrap of paper was still there with Christian's brother's number on it. Had he seen it? Was he upset at her meddling?

She didn't think they'd called. The bar had been too loud for her to hear the telephone from her vantage point near the stage, but she hadn't seen Christian answer the phone. And she didn't think he'd remain silent if he'd actually talked to his brothers. But that number, hidden under the register, that might cause him to act distant.

She looked over at the bathrooms, debating whether to approach him, but she hesitated. Chicken.

Instead, she finished collecting the money and went to her office to do the accounting. Once she was nearly done, she heard Christian back at the bar, washing the ashtrays. Jolee decided she couldn't put off talking to him any longer. And even if he hadn't discovered the number, she had to tell him.

She wandered out to the bar, leaning against it, watching him wash. He glanced at her, but then returned his attention to his task.

She watched him a little longer before she worked up the nerve to ask, "Christian, what's wrong?"

His hands hesitated in the sudsy water, then started scrubbing again with renewed vigor.

"Did I do something wrong?" Lord, she was such a chicken. She should just ask him outright about the number.

He stopped washing to look at her, his eyes unreadable. Damn, she hated that look.

"No," he finally said. "You didn't do a thing wrong."

"Then why are you acting so aloof?"

She saw the indecision in his eyes. The discernable emotion was better than the blankness, although not much. Despite his hungry stares all night, she had the feeling his uncertainty was a bad sign.

"Did you not like me dedicating that song to you tonight?" She had wondered after she'd done it, if she had the right to place a public claim on him like she had. Maybe that was overstepping her bounds.

But he shook his head. "Your song was beautiful. It meant more to me than you can ever know."

Relief caused her to release a pent-up breath. "Good. I meant it. Every moment with you"—she grinned—"even the sort of strange moments, has made me feel more alive than I have in years. And I don't know what I did to deserve you, but I'm so happy you are with me."

Christian stared at her. How could she say this to him? He was the one who didn't know what he'd done to deserve her. He hadn't done anything. He'd done nothing but horrible deeds for the last two hundred years. How could he deserve this perfect woman?

He started to reach for her, but stopped. He was supposed

to be telling her he had to go, not comforting her. He had to leave. All night he'd watched her, telling himself he would go, even as he wanted to do nothing more than to hold her.

"Jolee." He took a deep breath, then began again. "Jolee, I have never been as happy as I've been with you."

She smiled and reached out to touch his jawline. "I'm glad."

"But—"

Her smile disappeared and her hand dropped from his face. She shook her head just slightly as if to say she refused to hear the rest of his words. Then she turned to the few still dirty ashtrays. She began emptying them into the trash can.

"It really was a good night," she said, too cheerfully as she cleaned.

He moved closer, his intent to make her look at him. His hand caught hers to stop her almost frantic tidying. But she still didn't look at him; she stared down at the tray.

His hand slid up her bare arm, memorizing the silky texture of her skin. Then he stepped closer behind her, his other hand going to her other arm, rubbing up and down its length.

"But Jolee," he murmured, "you have it all wrong. I don't deserve you. I don't."

She leaned back against his chest, her hands crisscrossing over her front to capture his hands as they stroked her skin.

He pulled her tighter to him, burying his nose in the disheveled knot at the back of her head, breathing in the floral scent of shampoo. The pink shampoo. It didn't smell nearly as good as Jolee herself. He nuzzled her neck, breathing in her unique spiciness. The scent brought his simmering desire to an instant boil. He pressed his lips to her neck.

"I told myself all night this wouldn't happen."

"What?" she breathed, tilting her head to give his roaming mouth better access.

"That I wouldn't touch you."

She laughed with disbelief. "Why ever not?"

"I don't know." And at this moment, it was true. Why did he think he could walk away from her? He couldn't. God help him, he just couldn't. He'd pay for his sins later, he promised, but not yet. Not now.

He slipped his hands under her arms to her stomach. Her rounded bottom fit perfectly against his groin. She wiggled slightly, working even closer to him.

He groaned against the fragile skin of her neck. She wiggled again, and he nipped her.

"Are you teasing me?" he muttered roughly against her ear.

She released a hitched breath, then asked, "Is it still teasing if I fully intend to give you whatever you want?"

He moaned deep in his throat. "I didn't do anything to deserve you. I wasn't a good person before I met you." His hands nudged up her shirt, finding the warm satiny skin of her stomach. His fingers skimmed upward to her breasts, cupping them.

"I'm no better than any of the men you've dated before," he told her, nipping her earlobe. His fingers found the front clasp of her bra, unfastening it. Her breasts spilled free, her hard little nipples prodding his palms. He squeezed them, plucking them until she cried out and wriggled more.

"I'm actually far worse," he admitted in a low, feral tone, one of his hands leaving her breasts to inch beneath her skirt until he found her panties. He stroked her through the cotton, her lips down there already damp and slick.

"I'm selfish and greedy, and I can't bring myself to leave you. Or this." He slid his hand under the waistband of her panties, parting her, plunging his finger inside her tight passage. Wet fire stroked him in return.

She braced her hands on the bar's nicked top to steady herself as he entered her over and over, experiencing the textures of her flesh, the tightness of her muscles.

Her head fell back against his chest, locks of her hair tickling his chin. She panted as he stroked, his thumb swirling around her clitoris as his finger filled her over and over.

"Can you be happy with me, knowing that I've done awful things?"

She nodded, an almost mindless bob of her head as she strained toward release. Did she even know what she was agreeing to? Was that why he was asking her now? To assure the answer he wanted?

His hand stilled, his thumb pressed firmly to the tiny bud at the top of her sex, his finger deep inside her pulsing fire.

"How can you want me?" he asked, aching to be worthy of her passionate response, of her love.

"You only did what Lilah wanted you to do," she whispered, her eyes closed, her head still heavy against his chest. But she didn't move under his pinning touch. "You did it because you thought she loved you—and you loved her. And you aren't that person anymore. You have real love now. My love."

His chest tightened, and he couldn't force a breath into his seized lungs. He sensed she loved him—he'd felt the emotion in the air around her as they'd made love. He saw it in her eyes when she looked at him, but he hadn't let himself believe it. But now she'd told him. She loved him. She wanted nothing more than to make him feel whole again.

He had to be inside her, to be one with her. To feel her heartbeat as his, to feel her breath and her life. To be whole like she promised.

She whimpered as he removed the pressure of his fingers, but he didn't pause. He hooked his finger over the waistband of her panties and pushed them down. She didn't stop him; in fact, she wiggled to make it easier to get them down. They fell to the floor and she readily kicked the small white scrap aside.

He returned his hand to her, this time shaping the rounded swell of her bottom, teasing a finger down the enticing crevice until she parted her legs and allowed him to enter her tight vagina from behind. She fell forward again, supporting herself on the bar. Her breathing was loud and ragged in the silent bar.

"I want to take you now," he told her, entering her again with his long finger, the other fingers cupping her plump mound.

She nodded, whimpering. "Yes."

He leaned over her, caging her body against the bar, his chest to her back.

"A good man, a decent man wouldn't take you like this. Especially after you've admitted that you love him."

She gasped, his finger stroking deep. "I—oh—I think you are good. God, so good."

He smiled at that, even though that wasn't exactly the good he was talking about. He kissed the back of her neck, nipping her skin.

"Damn, I want to just bury myself deep inside you right now." He nipped her again.

"Yes. Oh God, yes." She lifted her hips, nudging her bottom against him, urging him to do just that.

He groaned. With an invitation like that he didn't know how he was going to stop. But he would. This couldn't continue—not here.

"Jolee, love?" He stilled his hand to gain her attention. She whimpered.

"I don't have a condom."

"In my bag," she murmured breathlessly. She lifted a hand from the bar to gesture vaguely at the floor.

He glanced down at the tote from which she'd gotten his snack earlier.

"Snacks and condoms. Is there nothing you don't have in there?"

"What can I say? I'm a regular Mary Poppins."

Christian didn't get the reference, but it didn't really matter to him. All that mattered was Jolee and the desire snapping in the air around them. Desire made more powerful with love.

He released her to kneel down and dig through the bag. Sure enough, she'd packed a strip of four condoms.

"How did you know we'd need these?"

"I didn't. I just hoped. Now get back here." She glanced down at him, need clear in her dark eyes.

"Impatient little thing, aren't you?"

She nodded. "Just trying to show you that I can be selfish and greedy, too. Now, drop trou . . ."

He frowned, not understanding what she wanted.

"Pants. Off. Now."

"Ah." He nodded with understanding. He stood and came back behind her, but he didn't undress right away. First he lifted her skirt, admiring her raised bottom. He slowly stroked her again.

She moaned, lifting herself even higher. "Please, Christian."

He quickly undid his pants and donned the condom. Positioning himself, he entered her, his cock filling her in one smooth stroke.

She cried out, gripping the counter. "Yes!" She bucked back against him.

Her wanton movements, the silent demands of her body urged him on as he filled her over and over. With each thrust, he felt their oneness. His arousal rocketed with hers, rising higher and higher. Even penetration pushing both of them farther until nothing existed but them. Their bodies, their desire, their love.

Jolee screamed, the sound muffled against her arm as she burst around him in an explosion of white hot flames. He followed her orgasm, his own as violent, as all-consuming.

They fell forward on the bar, his body creating a cover over her, his arms wrapped tight around her waist, his cock still deep inside her.

"God, I love you," he muttered against her ear. "I don't deserve you, but I love you."

She turned her head, and kissed the corner of his mouth, his cheek, his jaw. "That's all that matters to me."

* * *

Jolee slipped out of bed. Even after very little sleep—she and Christian had both been insatiable—she still felt light and giddy, as though she was moving with no gravity to hold her down. Christian loved her! The idea was still so unbelievable. So amazing that she could hardly believe it.

She turned back to look at him, sprawled on her bed, unconscious and unaware of the thrilling sight he made, naked and utterly beautiful. She hummed low in her throat. The things that body could do to her.

She lingered just a moment longer, then forced herself to leave him. She knew there was no point trying to wake him. After he'd made love to her for the third time last night, slow and leisurely sex that still made her melt and her toes curl, just in memory, he'd fallen into a deep sleep. A well deserved sleep.

She headed to the kitchen, ravenous. She'd eat and then head to the bar. Again, she'd managed to sleep most of the day away. Although her sleep was well deserved, too. A girl had to have stamina to keep up with Christian.

She leaned against the kitchen counter, eating a yogurt and then a cereal bar. She finished a second cereal bar, then headed to the bathroom, humming. Her life was really changing. Her bar was definitely doing well. She'd found an amazing guy. Things were just getting better and better.

She turned on the shower, then stripped off her T-shirt and undies. The water felt lovely on her tired muscles. Muscles that were tired from something wonderful, rather than hard, fruitless work.

And all this had happened because he'd nearly hit her with his car. Wasn't fate crazy? It was as crazy as lucky, but good luck had finally found her, and she was absolutely euphoric with her changed life. Finally she was really leaving the old Jolee Dugan behind.

Chapter 26

"I'm sorry, Jolee." Jed shook his head, looking around the ransacked bar just two hours later. "I didn't even hear a thing. Damned ears. Playing out on me."

Jolee shook her head. "Don't apologize. I'm glad you didn't hear anything. Knowing you, you would have come up here and gotten hurt—or killed."

She stepped gingerly into the center of the barroom. Glasses and bottles of liquor were broken everywhere. The ancient jukebox had been hit with something, likely one of the over-turned chairs scattering the floor. The glass was cracked, but the old machine still remained lit up. She couldn't say the same for her karaoke sound system. It was destroyed.

She wandered over to the booth and stared at the smashed CD players and CDs. Then she simply turned away, going outside to wait for the police to arrive. She collapsed onto the low concrete step, staring blankly at the road. The sun was starting to sink down in the sky, brushing the tops of the trees in a warm yellow glow. It had to be long past five. Time to open the bar. But she wouldn't open tonight.

Jed's scuffed boots appeared beside her as he leaned

against the post that supported the overhang. She smelled the acrid scent of smoke as he lit a cigarette.

"We'll get it cleaned up," he said, his voice gruff and determined.

She nodded. Rage choked her and she couldn't speak. Tears choked her, too, but again, she didn't allow herself to succumb to them. She wouldn't cry. Tears never, *never* did any good.

She gritted her teeth, determination starting to replace her anger and grief. She hated to think it, but she had no doubt who did this. Vance. He'd ruined her bar, stolen her money, she knew it.

She didn't have any proof, but she didn't doubt it was him. The timing was a little too convenient and the look in his eyes . . . She should have guessed he'd do something. It hurt her. Hurt her that her own brother would do such a thing. But she had no doubt. And she would tell the police to investigate him. She was done trying to give him a chance. He'd messed with her future. With her chance at success. And she wasn't going to be dragged back down by her family.

She'd get Leo's cleaned up and opened again. This wouldn't destroy her dream.

As Christian pulled up to the bar, his first indication that things were not right was the lack of cars in the parking lot. He pulled his car to a stop near the back door, but walked around to the front entrance. A hand-written paper sign taped to the door read, "Closed temporarily for renovations."

He frowned. Renovations?

He reached for the doorknob, but the door was locked. He could hear the strains of music through the open window, and a clinking like someone was picking up glass. He peeked in the window but didn't see anyone. He thought to simply turn to shadow and enter. But he couldn't if he wanted to. The hospital showed him that power was iffy at best. If it wasn't totally gone now.

"Jolee?" he called, suddenly more worried about her than his disappearing abilities. What was going on?

The clinking stopped, and she appeared from behind the bar. She looked around until she located him in the window, then she walked carefully over to the door, unlocking it.

"What's going on," he asked as he stepped inside. His concern didn't lessen as he took in her drawn features and her disheveled hair. He could feel her despair swirling around them. Then he smelled the intense scent of alcohol.

"What happened?"

She sighed, looking down at her hands, damp with liquor. She wiped them on her apron. "The bar was broken into last night."

He glanced at the bar, realizing that most of the bottles were gone from the back shelves. Broken, obviously, from the smell of liquor and the clinks he'd heard.

"Are you all right?" he asked, knowing she couldn't be. Jolee had worked too hard to have a devastating setback like this.

But she nodded. "The police just left a little while ago, and I was beginning to clean up." She glanced down at her hands again. Her shoulders sagged. This was the first time he'd seen her look like everything, her hard work, her struggles, were just too much for her.

He pulled her into his arms, hugging her tight.

"It was Vance."

Her words took a second to penetrate. Then he realized she was referring to who'd done this. And she was right. He could smell his scent, smarminess in the air.

He moved away from her. "Did you tell the police?"

She nodded. "They said they'd question him. But they probably won't find him. I'm sure he went back to Sawyersville or wherever."

"He did it." Of course, he couldn't help her with the police. He doubted an officer would accept his verification that it was Vance just because he could smell him.

Just then Jed came out of the bathroom, carrying his mop and bucket. Christian left Jolee's side to take the cleaning paraphernalia from the old man.

"I'll help her."

Jed started to argue like he had the night before, when he'd stepped in to help him with the mopping.

"Just have a seat."

But instead of following Christian's order, Jed began to pick up the overturned chairs, muttering about Christian thinking he could tell him what to do just because he was dating the boss lady.

"Damned right," Christian informed him. Then he turned back to Jolee. "Okay, boss lady, let's get this place renovated."

Jolee glanced over at Christian as he mopped the floor. She'd felt a thousand times better after he arrived. He was a steady strength beside her, just as he'd been that night Vance had broken into her trailer. He worked efficiently, helping her clean up all the glass and debris. Then he swept up all the tiny shards of glass and now he mopped. She stood at the karaoke booth, sorting through the CDs, trying to salvage what she could. The rest she tossed in the trash can.

All of this was going to cost her a ton of money. Replacing the liquor and the barware. But the karaoke was going to be impossible to replace for a while. That made her heartsick. Not to mention all the money from her great night was gone. The safe had been cracked open, the ancient hinges proving too little for Vance's purpose.

She sighed. She wouldn't give up. Then she glanced at Christian. She wasn't alone anymore. Christian was here to stand by her. Then she looked at Jed, frowning at another cracked ashtray, which he then tossed in the trash. She wasn't alone.

The front door opened and Jolee started toward it.

"Sorry," she called. "The bar is closed."

A petite woman with short-cropped, messily styled hair stepped into the room. She glanced around, her gaze stopping on Christian. Jolee frowned, her own eyes going to him. Did this woman know him?

Christian stood stock-still, the mop stopped in midswish. His usually golden skin was as pale as paste, his eyes wide as if he were staring at a ghost.

Jolee frowned back at the woman. Was this Lilah? But she immediately disregarded the idea. While this woman was petite as Christian had described, he'd also said Lilah was beautiful, with long blond hair and pale eyes. This woman was more adorable than beautiful. She looked like a pixie with wide eyes and a pert nose. There was an almost otherworldly look to her elfin features.

"Holy shit! I never thought I'd see the day when Christian Young was pushing a mop. This is brilliant."

Jolee's eyes moved from the small woman to the two men now standing behind her. The one who'd spoken grinned widely in Christian's direction. The other man didn't smile. Instead he watched Christian with a concerned, almost grim expression on his handsome face.

For a moment, no one spoke. Then the grinning man broke the silence. He came forward to extend his hand toward her.

"Hi. I'm Chris's baby brother, Sebastian."

Shocked, she accepted his handshake. She didn't know why she was so shocked; he looked like Christian with the same full, sculpted lips and tousled dark blond hair, although there was an openness to this man that Christian didn't show as readily.

"I'm Jolee."

Sebastian nodded as though he'd already deduced that. He left her to go over to Christian. He pulled him into an embrace, clapping a hand on the middle of Christian's back. Christian remained stiff, mop still in one hand, his gaze still on the tiny brunette and the other man who Jolee assumed was Rhys.

Sebastian released him, then stepped back to follow his gaze. Christian absently handed the mop to Sebastian and then took a step toward the woman.

"Jane?" Christian shook his head as though he couldn't quite believe what he was seeing.

A swell of jealousy pooled in Jolee's stomach. Who was she? Why was Christian so stunned to see her?

The brunette nodded. "Yes, Christian. I'm fine." She then grinned up at the tall man behind her.

For the first time, Jolee realized the man had his hands on Jane's shoulders. They both wore wedding bands. A measure of relief filled her, although she was still confused by Christian's strange reaction.

"You were dead," he murmured, coming to stand in front of her.

"Dying," the man behind her corrected. "But she returned to me. She's fine now. We're fine."

Christian looked at the other man, still obviously dazed. "Rhys."

The man then smiled, a curve of his sculpted mouth, the gesture so similar to Christian's little grins. "It's good to see you, Chris. You look good doing a little honest labor."

He released Jane and stepped forward to also clasp Christian in a brotherly embrace. Jolee smiled, even though she didn't fully understand what she was witnessing.

"How did you find me?" Christian asked, glancing back and forth between his brothers.

Jolee's stomach sank. Things seemed to be going well, but she was still worried that Christian would think she'd stepped in where she shouldn't have.

But instead of letting his brothers reveal her involvement, she stepped toward him and admitted, "I called them."

Christian turned to her. "You?"

She nodded. "I knew you were miserable without your family, so I called." She winced slightly. She couldn't tell if he was upset or not. Then he strode over to her, pulling her against him. He hugged her tightly to his chest.

"Thank you," he murmured against her hair.

Her heart soared. "You're welcome."

"Well, shit," Jed suddenly announced from behind the bar. "A reunion like this calls for a drink."

He lifted a full plastic beer pitcher into the air, then took a large gulp directly from the pitcher. He exhaled in satisfaction when he was done, using his shirtsleeve to wipe foam from his moustache. Then he held out the pitcher. No one moved.

"What? You pretty boys don't know how to celebrate?" Jed rasped.

"Oh, I like this guy," Sebastian stated, walking over to take the offered beer. He took a long swallow. He turned and handed it to Christian. "You heard the man, pretty boy. Celebrate!"

Christian smiled, and Jolee was thrilled to see a full-fledged smile on his lips as he raised the pitcher to his lips. He looked directly at her as he took his drink, and she could see the happiness and the love in his eyes. Suddenly the break-in, the mess, the karaoke system, none of it seemed so bad. Not bad at all.

Jolee rested her chin in her hand as she leaned on the bar, watching the three brothers and Jed, seated around a table, talking animatedly. Several more times, Christian had smiled. And several more times those amazing smiles had been directed at her. She sighed.

"It's a remarkable sight, isn't it?" Jane said, shifting on her bar stool to glance from the men to Jolee.

Jolee knew exactly what she meant. "Yes. It's almost scary that brothers can be that beautiful."

Jane smiled. "I'm shocked on a daily basis." She turned fully on her stool. "So how did you meet Christian?"

Jolee raised an eyebrow at that. How to tell that story without scaring this woman to death?

"He rescued me from my drugged out, knife-toting brother. Then he nearly ran me down with his car. Somehow things progressed from there."

Jane nodded as if she totally understood. "I think meeting the Young brothers is always an odd experience. Rhys saved my life, then very shortly after that started insisting we marry."

"Fast mover."

Jane laughed. "You have no idea." But she looked down fondly at the plain gold band on her finger.

Jolee studied the simple ring on Jane's finger. Would she and Christian ever marry? The idea thrilled her beyond words. She glanced over at him; another real smile curved his lips at something Sebastian said. She had been right, he was even more staggeringly beautiful with a real smile on his lips.

"Thank you for calling," Jane said, drawing Jolee's attention back to her. She gazed at the table, too, although Jolee was certain her attention was on Rhys. He looked very happy, too.

"I knew I had to. Christian was suffering."

"Rhys and Sebastian were, too."

Jolee nodded; she could tell. The brothers all seemed very happy to be together again. But as far as she could tell, no mention of Lilah had been made. Christian's most stunned reaction had been to Jane.

"Christian was really shocked to see you."

"Yes. I guess he truly believed I died. Poor guy. I kept telling Rhys that we should try to find him, although I don't think we ever would have looked here."

Jane's eyes widened, then she added, "Not *here,* here, but—well, I meant . . ."

Jolee laughed at the woman's agitation. "You don't need to apologize. Believe me, I know that Christian is as out of his element here as I'd be in some hoity-toity mansion."

She continued to smile, but her admission caused her joy to dissipate just a little. She didn't fit with Christian, not really. She glanced over at his brothers with their expensive clothes and perfect looks. Jane also looked perfect with smooth, creamy skin, funky hair, and a cute flippy little skirt and silky top. Then Jolee looked down at herself in her liquor-stained apron. Her heavy hair was falling from its knot at the back of her head. Strands clung to her neck, which was sticky from the humid night air. She knew her cheeks must be flushed from all the cleaning she'd done tonight.

She crossed her arms over her chest, feeling like the ugly duckling of the group. Even Jed appeared less mussed.

"You'd fit in anywhere," Jane said with a reassuring smile as if she knew exactly what Jolee was thinking. "I grew up in a ramshackle Victorian house in a small town in Maine. Half of the house was a funeral parlor my father owned. What did I know about living in a big city like New York? Nothing, but I figured it out. It's amazing where you can feel comfortable if you are with the people you love."

She shot another adoring glance toward Rhys, then she added, "It's also amazing who you can become."

Jolee followed her gaze, except she watched Christian. He talked with Jed. The old man reached over and clapped him on his back with almost fatherly affection.

"What was Christian like?" she asked suddenly. "I mean, when you knew him?"

Jane gave a little laugh that didn't quite sound like amusement. But then she sobered. "The Christian I knew was pretty scary. He was angry and bitter."

Jolee wasn't surprised by her description. That was the Christian she'd first met, too.

"But that was the Christian that Lilah created." Jane winced slightly as if she thought maybe she said too much.

"I know about Lilah," Jolee assured her.

"You do?" Jane seemed surprised.

"Well, I know a little."

Jane nodded.

"Did you know her?"

Jane shook her head. "No, thank God. All I know about her is she was a very bad, very selfish vam—" Her big eyes widened again, then she added quickly, "Vain. Very vain."

Jolee frowned slightly, wondering what Jane was about to say, but Jane's next admission pushed that question right out of her mind.

"I think it's a good thing for all of us that she is dead."

"Lilah is dead?"

Jane nodded, another pained look creasing her elfin features. "Christian didn't tell you?"

Jolee shook her head. "No. How did she die?"

Jane glanced over her shoulder almost guiltily, then she leaned forward on the bar. "She killed herself."

Killed herself? "Why?"

Jane shook her head. "I don't know. Rhys said she was crazy. Maybe she did just go mad and kill herself."

Jolee looked over to Christian. Did he blame himself for Lilah's death in some way? Was that why he'd been so strange in the beginning? And was he truly over the woman? If she hadn't killed herself, would he still be with her? Taking her insane abuse?

Jolee couldn't think about that. It did't matter anyway. Lilah was dead, and she loved Christian now.

"I've upset you," Jane said.

"No. I wanted to know about her."

Jane nodded.

"Jane, how did she kill herself?"

"She walked out—she walked into a fire."

Jolee stared at her. Walked into a fire? Who killed themselves that way? Someone who was crazy, obviously. And as cruel as it was of her, all Jolee could feel was relief over Lilah's demise. She had destroyed, or nearly destroyed, a family and Christian. She couldn't have any sympathy for the cruel woman.

Then Christian stood, grabbed the handles of the four beer pitchers that they were using as mugs. The plastic had mostly survived Vance's pillaging. Christian came to the bar, but rather than hand the pitchers to Jolee, he walked to the tap and began filling them. He grinned at Jolee, and she noticed that he was still a little uncomfortable looking at Jane.

Once the pitchers were filled again, he leaned over and pressed a kiss to Jolee's lips.

"Thank you," he said against her lips. She smiled and kissed him again.

Then he scooped up the pitchers and went back to the table to serve them. Jolee sighed as she watched him go. God, she loved him.

"Well, I don't think you have to worry about fitting into Christian's world," Jane said with a small knowing smile. "I think he's doing fine fitting in right here."

Jolee smiled, and then laughed as his brothers began to razz him about his bartending abilities. Christian didn't look offended by the teasing; in fact, he looked quite happy with himself. And he did know how to serve a drink with flare.

Suddenly she didn't worry about fitting in. It was true. If Christian had managed to be comfortable here, she could manage to fit in with him.

Chapter 27

"Jolee's hot," Sebastian observed. Then he took a sip of his beer, watching her over the wide rim of the beer pitcher.

Possessiveness flashed through Christian, but then disappeared like a quick jolt of lightning. This was Sebastian, and he was just making a comment. He had always just said whatever came into his head. Christian smiled. It was good to know some things hadn't changed.

"So are you going to cross her over?" Sebastian asked.

Christian shook his head. *Always* saying whatever he thought. At least he waited for Jed to call it a night before he asked.

"Sebastian, I think his love life is his own business," Rhys said.

"Yeah, well, you'd do well to remember those words." Sebastian leaned closer to Christian. "Thanks to Rhys and Jane, there is just way too much PDA in our house."

Rhys frowned. "PDA?"

"Public displays of affection," Sebastian stated.

Rhys snorted, but Christian noticed he didn't deny their baby brother's accusation.

"So are you going to bite her?" Sebastian asked again.

Christian gave him a sharp look, then glanced over to Jolee. She was deep in a conversation with Jane and hadn't heard them. But instead of looking away to answer Sebastian, he studied her.

He hadn't allowed himself to really, truly imagine an eternity with her. He'd always intended to let her go. He didn't know how, but he knew he'd have to. But now, now that he knew he hadn't killed Jane, now that he saw Rhys had found happiness with a mortal, and that Jane had accepted vampirism with no hesitation or regret, maybe he could be with Jolee forever. He wanted that. God, he wanted that. But even if Jolee could accept the truth about his real nature, he had another problem.

"I can't bite her," he admitted lowly.

"Oh, please, don't tell me you are going to be as big a dolt about this as Rhys was about Jane." Sebastian sighed.

Rhys frowned at him.

"It's so obvious that you and Jolee are in love," Sebastian said. "If the air was any thicker with your emotions, we'd have to call the paramedics for oxygen. Between you and Rhys it's like being on Planet Love, and I need a spacesuit to protect me from the treacherous atmosphere."

Christian stared at his brother. "You are weirder than I remember."

"No, he's the same," Rhys said flatly. "You've just managed to forget."

Sebastian ignored them. "So are you going to bite her?"

"I can't bite," Christian repeated.

"What?" Sebastian asked as if he must have misheard.

"I can't bite."

"What?" Sebastian repeated, but this time Christian knew that he'd heard, he just couldn't wrap his mind around the information. He stared at Christian in appalled disbelief. Even Rhys looked a little stunned.

"After I bit Jane"—he glanced regretfully toward Rhys— "I stopped feeding from humans. Well, I did drink human blood, from the blood bank, but I rationed it, only drinking as much as absolutely necessary to survive." He hesitated to tell them about the twelve-step program. It seemed rather silly now.

"Great, another one turning to the bag," Sebastian muttered, shaking his head. Christian gave him a questioning look, but Rhys spoke before he could ask what he meant.

"That shouldn't affect your fangs."

"I also stopped using my preternatural abilities. And gradually they seem to have disappeared," Christian said.

"Wait," Sebastian said. "You can't do anything vampy? And absolutely no fangage, even when you're getting jiggy?" Sebastian asked.

Christian shook his head.

Sebastian looked as if he might expire at the very thought. But finally he managed to say, "Wow, that sucks. Or doesn't suck, as the case may be."

"But you haven't tried to bite her since you discovered that Jane is fine. Maybe you could now. Maybe it's guilt-induced or something," Rhys suggested.

Christian shrugged, but he had a feeling Jane's existence wouldn't help. Even now, as he longed to bring Jolee over to him, he didn't feel the hunger. It was as if the urge to feed had gone dormant inside him.

"I could bite her for you," Sebastian said, looking quite eager at the prospect.

Christian glared at him. He wouldn't share her, much less let another vampire, even his brother, cross her over.

"No," Rhys stated flatly for him. "According to Dr. Fowler—"

"Oh, God," Sebastian groaned. "Here we go."

Christian looked confusedly between his brothers, but waited for Rhys to continue.

"According to Dr. Fowler, if a vampire truly intends to take a mortal to mate, then only he or she should perform the bite. It is the only way to create an unbreakable bond."

"Who the hell is Dr. Fowler?" The name sort of rang a bell with Christian, but he couldn't quite place where he'd seen or heard it.

"He's pretty much the Reverend Moon of the vampire world," Sebastian said, not hiding his disgust.

Rhys frowned at Sebastian. "No, he isn't. He's a scientist who has researched preternatural creatures and has learned a great deal about them. About us, in particular. For example, did you know that more and more research proves vampirism is actually a virus?"

"A virus," Sebastian scoffed. "That's so appealing. Give me the good old curse explanation anytime. Thanks."

Christian ignored him and turned to Rhys. "So you really believe in this guy's work?"

"I do."

"Maybe there is a scientific reason for what's happening with my hunger," Christian pondered, half to himself.

"I wouldn't doubt it," Rhys said.

"You two are whacked. I'm taking my pitcher and drinking with the ladies." Sebastian headed over to the bar, slipping onto a bar stool beside Jane.

"Why is Sebastian so opposed to this guy?" Christian asked.

"Because Dr. Fowler is on a campaign to stop vampires from using mortals as a food source. He believes that is the primary reason why vampires have never been accepted into society."

Christian nodded, but he still didn't follow.

"Sebastian is the most promiscuous biter I know. And he has no intentions of stopping. He doesn't even want to consider the idea. Hell, he's created a nightclub that caters just to vampires' obsession with feeding, and mortals' fascination with being bitten. He doesn't want that to end."

"Well, if this Fowler doesn't promote biting then he wouldn't help me. He'd probably be quite pleased that I can't."

Rhys shook his head. "No. He's actually a big advocate of integrated mating. He believes that if vampires and mortals are soul mates they should bond. He believes this shows the human population that vampires are actually capable of love and true commitment."

"No wonder Sebastian hates the guy."

"Yes, Sebastian is only committed to his own pleasure," Rhys said, but smiled fondly toward their hedonistic little brother.

"I was the same way," Christian pointed out regretfully.

Rhys shook his head. "No, you had great commitment skills. You just picked the wrong female." Rhys looked over at Jolee talking happily to his wife and their brother. "I think you might just do better with this woman."

But Christian didn't return his brother's smile. "I'm so sorry. About Lilah. About what I did to our family. About Elizabeth."

"Lilah destroyed our family, and she killed Elizabeth."

"But I brought her into your lives."

"Christian, I can't feel anger about the past anymore. I still miss Elizabeth and love her. But if things hadn't happened the way they did, I never would have found Jane. So I can't stay bitter."

Christian could see the sincerity in Rhys's eyes. Rhys had found his soul mate in Jane.

"How did you know Jane was your mate?" he asked.

"My body knew long before my mind, seeing as I was a little messed up when I met her."

Christian gave him a pained look. "Sorry."

"Not your fault either." Then he added with a wry grin, "Well, maybe a little, but it doesn't matter now. But to answer your question, I just knew—and so did Jane."

"But I thought I knew once before." He'd followed Lilah blindly through two centuries.

Rhys nodded. "How do you feel about Jolee?"

Christian watched her as she talked with his family. The family she'd returned to him.

"I love her," he answered simply.

"How did you feel about Lilah?"

Christian considered that. "Wanted her. I would have done anything to have her."

Rhys nodded.

But Christian's own words sank in, defining in his mind. "But with Jolee, if she didn't want me, if she couldn't accept me, I'd let her go. I'd love her forever, but I couldn't force her to be with me. I love her too much to ever hurt her."

"Well, there you go," Rhys said.

And Christian knew his brother's blandly stated words said it all. He looked back to Jolee. *There you go—there's your true mate.* He was humbled by the emotion coursing through him. Love. Family love. True love. It was all so overwhelming and something he hoped he got the chance to never take for granted again.

"Thanks for coming," he said, knowing the words were too inadequate for the feelings inside him. But he couldn't seem to manage more.

"I'm glad you are back to being the Christian I remember."

Christian was, too. And he had Jolee to thank for that. He looked over at her. He only hoped she could accept the truth. That she would still want him.

Jolee waved to Christian's family as they disappeared into his trailer. Christian remained with her.

"Are you sure you don't want to go with them?" she asked, not wanting him to feel obligated to stay with her. He'd spent years separated from his brothers; he must want to spend as much time with them as he could.

"Trying to get rid of me?" he teased, pulling her into his arms.

She smiled. "Not a chance."

He kissed her possessively.

She sighed as he broke the kiss. "How do you do that?"

"What?"

"Make me totally desperate for you with just a kiss."

He caught her hand and started toward her trailer. "Believe me, love, you do the same thing to me."

He barely had her inside the trailer before she was back in his arms, and he was kissing her senseless.

He walked her backward down the hallway, his lips pressed to hers, his hands busily working their clothing off. By the time they reached her bedroom, they were both nude and he'd only broken his kiss twice, once to remove her shirt and once because he tripped on his pantleg.

"You're pretty darn good at this," she said, collapsing onto the bed, pulling him with her.

"You, too."

She grinned, and then she moaned as he began to touch her.

His lovemaking was slow and leisurely. He worshipped her with his mouth. With his hands. With his whole body. And once he was buried deep inside her, he just remained still, looking down at her, caressing her face and her hair.

"Jolee?"

She nodded, gazing into his pale eyes, reveling in the feeling of his weight on top of her, his thick length inside her.

"Thank you."

She smiled and stroked his cheek. "I want you to be happy."

"I am."

His words made her heart flip. "I know how you feel." When she was with Christian, she simply knew everything would be all right. She'd never known that feeling. Never really felt safe until she'd met him.

"Jolee, I want to give you forever."

Jolee's heart stopped mid-flip. Was he saying what she thought he was?

"Do you want that? Me? Forever?"

She nodded immediately. "Yes." She threw her arms around him. "God, yes!"

He began to move inside her until they came together, and Jolee had never believed that such ecstasy could be hers.

"Can you contact Dr. Fowler?" Christian asked Rhys as he poured a beer.

Rhys stopped watching Sebastian and Jolee as they fiddled with the new karaoke system that Christian had insisted on buying for Jolee. He knew she still didn't feel comfortable when he spent money on her, but he'd brought up the fact that they were going to be together forever, and she needed to get used to his help. She'd relented.

Now, he just hoped they had forever.

"Sure," Rhys nodded. He got out his cell phone. "I can make some calls and try to find him." He gave Jane a quick kiss, then headed outside to make some calls.

Christian watched him leave, hoping Dr. Fowler would have an answer. Christian hadn't partaken of a blood bank repast in two days, and while he could feel the hunger building within him, he knew he couldn't feed from Jolee. His fangs hadn't appeared—not once.

He glanced at where Jolee watched Sebastian connect some of the wires. She asked questions, and Christian knew that was because she wanted to know every detail. If anything happened to this sound system, Jolee would know how to handle it. She was determined. And she was strong.

But was she strong enough to accept the truth about him? Even if Dr. Fowler could help, his aid might be a moot point. If she couldn't accept him, then he would let her go. It would kill him, but he would. Given her family and background, she craved to be normal. No black clouds hanging over her. Vampirism was a big black cloud; it certainly didn't make a person normal. And it didn't lend itself to an average life.

Then he looked at Jane, sitting talking to Jed. The old man glowed under her attention. For all practical purposes, Jane looked like a normal human. She was kind and sweet. Vampirism hadn't seemed to change her. Maybe if he used Jane as an example . . .

He looked back to Jolee. She and Sebastian now beamed at each other. He assumed the karaoke installation was going well. Then Sebastian strode across the room, smiling at a number of the female customers.

"You know," he said in a quiet voice once he reached the bar, "you went from being one of the evilest vampires in the world to a sideshow for horny women. I admire that."

Christian shook his head. Sebastian would admire that.

He gestured to the box on the floor behind Christian. "I need that cable."

Christian handed the black cord to him.

"Oh," he added before he headed back to Jolee. "I was looking for a towel in your bathroom, and I found something called a Popiel Pocket Fisherman and a Thigh Master. Should I be worried?"

Christian shook his head again. Sebastian should have been worried, but now Christian was fine. Or he would be.

"And I'm not even going to ask about the Being Human list on your fridge." Sebastian raised an eyebrow at that. "Bro, you are one odd dude."

Christian smiled as Sebastian left to return to Jolee. Imagine if he knew about the blog.

A few moments later, Jolee announced, "Karaoke is now open."

The patrons cheered, but Christian suspected many of the women at the tables nearest the stage were really cheering for Sebastian rather than the karaoke. Several ladies had been watching him quite avidly all night.

The bar was crowded, and none of the patrons seemed to mind that all they could serve was draft beer. The new liquor supplies would be delivered tomorrow. If Vance had intended to bring Leo's to a screeching halt—although it had almost seemed that way—his burglary had only created a minor delay.

Sebastian, ever the ham, picked up the mic and announced he'd be the first singer of the evening. The women cheered. Then he started singing "Pour Some Sugar On Me" by Def Leppard, and the women started waving their arms and hooting, and looked ready to pounce.

"He's crazy," Jane stated, watching him with amused amazement. Christian laughed, thoroughly amused, too.

"Some of those women are going to attack him if he isn't careful," Jolee said as she joined Christian behind the bar.

"If anyone can handle himself with the ladies, it's Sebastian," Jane said.

"I have no doubt." Jolee laughed. She left to call up the next singer. Sebastian was immediately surrounded by admirers as he stepped away from the stage.

Jolee returned to the bar once Hitch was at the microphone screaming "Carrie Ann" by the Hollies. Rhys also returned from outside, although Jolee's presence didn't allow him to do more than give Christian a nod, which he assumed meant that Rhys had located Dr. Fowler.

"Poor Hitch," Jolee said, watching the women circling Sebastian.

"Why? Because he's obviously in such pain?" Rhys asked as he slid onto his bar stool.

"Be nice," Jane warned, elbowing him. He slipped his arm around her under the guise of avoiding being nudged again.

"No," Jolee said with a smile. "Even his screaming can't get any attention tonight."

"Sebastian has that effect," Christian said as he filled another mug of beer.

"Not just Sebastian," Jolee said, jerking her head to a group of ladies watching him.

As if on cue, the she-clown, who'd pinched his ass that first night, approached the bar. She openly admired him—and Rhys—as she ordered her drink.

As she walked away, she stopped to say to Jolee, "I like the new renovations. They are very, very nice." She gave another significant look to both brothers.

Jolee and Jane both began to laugh after the woman returned to her table.

"Easy for you to laugh," Christian said, "she's never grabbed your ass."

Jolee and Jane laughed harder. Even Jed chuckled around his cigarette. Sebastian joined them at the bar.

He sighed contentedly. "I like it here. I even like that guy singing." He sighed again. "I think I might stay here forever."

"Well, you would be great for business," Jolee said, laughing again as more women wandered past the bar to admire the view.

As Hitch's song neared its screeching finish, Jolee excused herself to go change the music, but Sebastian shot up.

"Can I do it?" he asked eagerly.

Jolee laughed. "Sure. As long as you can keep your fan club at bay."

"Oh, I can handle it." He walked toward the stage, a swagger in his step until the she-clown got him, pinching him right on the left cheek.

"I think you've lost your admirer to another," Jolee laughed, nudging Christian.

"As long as I don't lose you." He pulled her against his side, kissing her.

Christian was still worrying about just that as they lay in bed later that night. Jolee snuggled against his side, her leg flung over his, her hand on his chest. He'd made love to her twice since they got back from the bar, and after the second time she'd fallen right to sleep, exhausted.

She'd had a busy night at the bar, and he knew he shouldn't have been so demanding, but he couldn't seem to help himself. Where his hunger might be dormant, his libido wasn't. Even now, just stroking the smooth skin of her back, feeling the warm stir of her breath on his skin, he wanted her. His cock pulsed greedily, but he ignored its demand.

He had to tell her the truth. He had to tell her even before he talked to Dr. Fowler. Jolee needed to make the choice whether she could handle what he had to tell her. Tomorrow, he'd have Rhys contact Dr. Fowler again and tell him to wait. Then if Jolee wanted to be with him forever, they'd talk to the doctor together.

Jolee stirred, stretching, then opening her eyes to smile sleepily at him. "Hey, you're still awake?"

He nodded.

"Sorry to fall asleep on you."

"You're tired." He kissed her forehead, intense love filling him.

"Mmm," she agreed, letting her eyes drift shut again.

He thought she slept, but then she said lazily, "I love your family. Your brothers are wonderful, and Jane is the nicest person I've ever met."

He considered mentioning that Jane wasn't quite a person but couldn't do it. He couldn't see revulsion in Jolee's eyes. He couldn't bear for her to pull away, frightened of him. Or nearly as bad, think that he was insane.

She opened her eyes and smiled at him. "I'm so glad I will finally have a real family. A family who loves and cares about each other."

He nodded. A real family. A real undead family. Did the fact that they were nice trump the death factor?

She reached up and touched his cheek. "What is it? You look worried."

He hesitated, then asked, "Remember we talked about all families having skeletons?"

She nodded, her eyes becoming less sleepy.

"Jolee . . ."

She levered herself up on her elbow to look at him more closely.

He couldn't do it. He couldn't tell her.

"It's nothing," he said, picking up her hand, which gently brushed his chest. He pressed a kiss to the palm, then simply held her fingers.

"Are you sure?"

He nodded. "I'm just being . . . silly."

She frowned but accepted his explanation. He knew she realized there was more that needed to be said, but she didn't pressure him. Maybe she didn't want to hear the truth any more than he wanted to say it.

Chapter 28

As Jolee worked around the bar that next afternoon, putting away the large shipment of liquor, she thought about the previous night. What had Christian wanted to tell her?

He wasn't exactly back to the hot/cold guy she'd first met, but he was acting . . . strange. Last night at the bar, he'd seemed almost edgy. Then they'd gotten back to her trailer and he'd made love to her with so much passion that she sighed just thinking about it. Then she sighed again, her body tingling at the memory. But underneath all the passion, she had the feeling he was holding something back.

In bed, he'd started to talk about his family, and she thought he was finally going to share what was bothering him. But he stopped. And he made love to her again, and while it was wonderful, she had the feeling it was just another diversion from what was troubling him.

He'd told her earlier that he wasn't a good person. That he was just as bad as any of her past boyfriends. She didn't believe that, refused to believe that. But . . . but what if it was true? What if . . .

No, she just didn't believe that about him. Or about his brothers and Jane. But he had mentioned the skeletons in his family's closet. From what she'd seen, his brothers and Jane made her family look even more like the Mansons.

Rhys reminded her of the quintessential oldest brother, a little serious, but very caring. Sebastian was the carefree, charming baby brother. Jane was simply the nicest woman she'd ever met. She really liked Jane, and felt a kinship to her right away. The new friendship with Jane was as novel as having Christian's love. She knew Jane could be a true friend.

She didn't want to lose that. And she couldn't lose Christian. She loved him. Madly. And she was petrified that he was going to end things with her. She didn't know why, exactly. After all, he'd proposed.

She paused from cutting open a box of beer. At least she thought he'd proposed. That was all that "giving her forever" could mean, right? But now, she just wasn't sure. He hadn't said anything to his brothers about proposing. He hadn't even said anything more to her.

She turned to start putting the beers into one of the coolers. She was so confused. Did Christian regret the suggestion? Was that what he wanted to tell her? She didn't think so, but she didn't know.

A noise pulled her from her fixating, and she looked up from her task to see a man in the doorway. He appeared to be in his sixties, wearing a brown tweed jacket despite the warmth of the day. He also wore a tweed golf cap and small wire-rimmed glasses. If he'd been smoking a pipe, he'd have made the perfect stereotypical professor.

"Hello," he said, his voice deep. "Are you open?"

She wasn't, but she didn't really feel like being alone with her swirling, unanswerable thoughts.

"Sure. What can I get you?"

"Could I have a scotch, neat?"

"Is Johnnie Walker all right?"

He nodded, sitting down on a stool across from her.

She searched through her boxes to find the newly delivered liquor. She cracked the seal and poured his drink in one of the new highball glasses that Christian had insisted on paying for. She placed it in front of the man.

"Thank you." He took a sip, then nodded as if to acknowledge the liquor was acceptable.

"Do you know where Shady Fork Mobile Estates is?" he asked after his second sip.

The question surprised her. He looked as likely to be going to her trailer park as . . . well, Christian living there. Shady Fork Mobile Estates was obviously a surprising place.

"Sure. You make a left on the road, and it's the first right. About a half mile."

He nodded.

"Are you visiting someone there?"

"More business, really," he said.

She nodded, wondering what kind of business he could have there, but she didn't think it was polite to ask. She returned to stocking the beer cooler.

"I'm a scientist," he said, and she stopped to look at him.

"Really? What do you study?" And what would he be studying at the trailer park?

He took another sip of his scotch, then said, very matter-of-factly, "I'm here to meet with a vampire."

She laughed, but quickly realized he wasn't sharing her amusement. "A vampire?"

"Yes, he lives in Shady Fork Mobile Estates."

"Oh." It was all she could think to say.

"I'm well aware of the fact that you probably think I'm mad. Many do. But vampires, werewolves, fairies, they all live amongst us."

She nodded slowly, but didn't speak. Maybe she should ask him to leave, but decided it wasn't wise to irritate the man. He could be dangerous.

"This particular vampire has a problem in that he cannot bite. Not humans, anyway."

"But that's a good thing, right?" She couldn't believe she was encouraging this conversation.

"Not in this case. He wants to mate with a mortal woman, which requires him to be able to bite. So I've come to see if I can find any cause for his inability. It's the first time I've encountered such a case. It's very exciting." His deep tone didn't change to show his enthusiasm.

Jolee watched nervously as he reached for the cuff of his sleeve, and she wondered if he had a knife or some other weapon hidden under the innocuous brown tweed. A stake maybe. What if he thought she was a vampire? She backed a little farther down the bar. But he simply checked his silver wristwatch.

"It will be about three more hours before he rises."

Jolee hoped that didn't mean he intended to stay here for that amount of time. He lifted his glass, draining the rest of the liquor.

"Well, perhaps I shall do a little sightseeing," he said, and set the glass down on the bar. "It's lovely country here."

She nodded, just wanting him to go.

He pulled out his wallet and held out a ten to her. She hesitated, then took the bill. She only half turned away from him as she rang up the drink. The cash drawer dinged, the small sound loud and unnerving in her ears. She quickly gave him his change.

"Thank you for the drink," he said, placing a tip on the bar. "And for the directions."

She nodded. After the door closed behind him, she rushed over to twist the lock. Then she crept to the window, watching until his car, a silver sedan, left the parking lot.

You just couldn't ever tell about people. She shook her head and went back to work.

Jolee greeted Christian as soon as he entered the bar. "I have to tell you about the guy who came in here today while I was putting away stock."

"Okay." Even though she didn't seem particularly upset,

he worried that "the guy" was somehow connected to Vance or her hometown, and he hated that he couldn't be with her when she came into work early. Maybe he could convince her to hire someone to open the bar. If Dr. Fowler could help him, she'd soon have to anyway.

"Okay," she said as if she was preparing for a big story. "This man came into the bar—"

"If I wasn't concerned with the fact that you are telling me that the door was unlocked while you working here alone, I'd think you were setting up a joke."

"Well, it had to be some sort of joke. Even though he seemed awfully serious. He was a harmless enough guy, except he was in town to go to, of all places, Shady Fork Mobile Estates, to meet, get this . . ."

Christian's stomach sank before she even finished the sentence.

"A vampire." She waited as though she expected him to burst out laughing or at least frown in worried dismay. But he couldn't do either. Oh, he was dismayed, but mainly because this Fowler character had already arrived and announced that there was a vampire living in Shady Fork Mobile Estates. He had asked Rhys to contact the doctor again and tell him they didn't need his help yet. He hardly expected the man to show up so soon. And going around town telling people there were vampires in their midst? Christian was starting to side with Sebastian on the legitimacy of this supposed doctor.

"Christian?" she finally questioned when he didn't react. "Isn't that the craziest thing?"

He nodded vaguely.

She frowned. "What's wrong? You look pale."

"It . . . it just scares me that you could have been hurt."

She smiled. "No, he was harmless. I think."

Just then, Rhys, Jane, and Sebastian strode into the bar. Rhys and Jane both looked concerned, and Sebastian wore a general look of disgust. Christian groaned silently. He didn't think their expressions were a good sign.

"Christian, can I talk to you for a moment?" Rhys asked, forcing an easy smile at Jolee. Christian didn't think she bought the look, but she smiled back.

"Sure. I'll be right back," Christian told Jolee. He could tell she wanted to ask what was going on, but she just nodded.

Jane stayed at the bar, but Sebastian followed them.

"Dr. Fowler is here," Rhys said as soon as they were outside in the parking lot.

"And he's a loon," Sebastian added.

Rhys frowned at him.

"Well, he is," Sebastian said.

"I know he's here," Christian said. "Would you believe he showed up at the bar for a drink and told Jolee he was here to see a vampire?"

"What?" Rhys said.

"See." Sebastian shook his head. "Loon. Total loon."

"I'm starting to agree," Christian stated, "but at the moment I'm a little more concerned with Jolee. She thought the man was a nut, but now I don't know what to do. It was going to be hard enough to tell her about me—us—without Fowler breaking the news first."

"Are you going to tell her?" Rhys asked.

"I don't know." Christian knew he had to do something. But he didn't know how. If he'd been able to break the news slowly, maybe he could have eased her into the idea. Oh, who was he kidding? There was no easing anyone into the idea of vampirism. But Fowler really hadn't helped the situation.

"You should tell her," Sebastian said with a definitive nod. "She'll accept you. I can tell."

Both Christian and Rhys gave him a dubious look.

"What?" Sebastian said defensively. "If there is one thing I know, it's women, and she loves you, man. She'll understand. Just go slow. And be sincere."

"Like you know about sincere," Rhys said flatly.

Sebastian sneered.

Christian ignored his brothers, trying to decide what to do. Fowler had sort of thrown the information out on the table, but he was the one who had to tell her. And he did have to. If he wanted a future with her, he had to. She deserved the truth. And if she couldn't accept him, he'd let her go. It was the honorable thing to do. And he wanted to be honorable, for her.

"Okay, I'm going to do it."

"Good," Sebastian said.

Rhys nodded.

They entered the bar, and Christian strode directly to the bar and to Jolee.

"Jolee, I need to talk to you."

She hesitated as if she didn't want to talk. As if she was afraid of what he was going to tell her. Did she guess?

"Okay." She nodded. "Do you want to talk in my office?"

"Could we go somewhere a little more private?"

"Well, I can't leave the bar," she pointed out.

"Sure you can." Sebastian stepped forward. "Rhys and I run a nightclub. We can handle the bar for a while."

She looked at his brothers apprehensively.

"It's okay," Jane assured her. "We'll do a good job."

Jane's promise seemed to pacify Jolee, and she nodded. "Okay."

Christian waited while she walked down the length of the bar and joined him. He could feel her anxiety as she fell into step beside him; it was an oppressive feeling on his skin. He wanted to take the emotion away, but he knew it was going to get worse before it got better.

Chapter 29

Jolee sat in Christian's car, unable to calm her racing heart or relax back against the seat. What was he going to tell her? She kept chanting to calm down, but her body wouldn't listen. She simply had too much bad news and negative experiences in her life to let herself believe this would be any different.

She managed to throw a quick glance over at Christian, but he was focused on the road, his jaw set, his expression grim.

Dread filled her. This wasn't good.

He parked the car in front of her trailer, and came around to open the door for her, but she couldn't wait for him. She was too nervous.

He stood back and waited for her to close the door, then he let her lead him into the trailer. Once inside, they both just stood there.

Finally the tension was simply too much.

"What is going on, Christian?" she demanded.

He didn't answer right away. Instead, he stared down at the floor as if the worn beige linoleum was suddenly fascinating.

"Please," she said, "tell me. You're scaring me."

He looked up then. "That's why I don't want to tell you. I never, never wanted to frighten you."

Her chest tightened and she found it hard to breathe. He was frightening her, very much. But now they couldn't not go forward. She knew he had something awful to tell her, and as much as she'd like to just go back and pretend there was no problem, there was.

"Is it about your family? Or you?"

"All of us."

She couldn't imagine what it could be. They were a great family. They hadn't even hesitated to forgive Christian for Lilah. They hadn't hesitated to take her in and make her feel a part of them.

"Are . . . are you in the mafia?" She knew it was a lame suggestion but one of the only ones she could think of.

He frowned. "No."

"A cult?" she added almost jokingly.

He paused at that.

Oh God, they were in a cult. Although she hadn't noticed Christian having any odd religious beliefs. She didn't notice that with any of them. And what cult would let its members own a nightclub? That didn't seem to add up.

But Christian said slowly, "I guess you could say, we are in a cult of sorts."

She frowned now, waiting for him to continue.

Instead of giving a description of their beliefs and strange rituals, he said, "You know the man who came in today?"

She nodded. Was he a member, too?

"He was here to see me."

This was the big news? She stared at him, confused. That the odd man in the tweed coat was here to see . . . Her eyes widened.

He nodded at the realization in her eyes. "I'm the vampire."

Jolee gaped at him. Was he serious? He sure looked serious. Dead serious. She laughed slightly at her pun. This was crazy.

He still just watched her, no amusement on his perfect features.

"You are kidding, right? Sebastian set you up to this, didn't he? I can tell he's a joker."

He shook his head. "I was born in 1795. In England. That makes me two hundred and ten years old."

She stared at him again, then shook her head. "There is no such thing as vampires."

"Yes, there are. I'm one. My brothers. Jane."

Jane? Jane, the girl next door, sweet and friendly?

"This is ridiculous," she stated, getting irritated. Why was he telling her this? What was the point? It wasn't funny. It was creepy.

"Why are you telling me this?" she demanded out loud.

"Jolee," he said almost coaxingly. "I didn't want to, but I had to. You deserve to know."

"Deserve to know you are insane?" She stepped back from him.

"I know it does sound insane. I know. But it's the truth. Lilah was a vampire. She made me a vampire, and she made my brothers vampires, as well."

She couldn't even think what to say. He wasn't relenting on this. He didn't think this was a joke, he believed it. She could see his conviction in his pale eyes.

Rage filled her. She loved this man. She trusted him, and he was telling her something stupid like this. She suddenly didn't know who this guy was.

"Lilah was a vampire?" she asked slowly.

"Yes."

"And you're a vampire?"

"Yes."

"Show me," she said suddenly. "Show me you're a vampire."

He stared at her for a moment, but then looked away. Finally he admitted, "I can't."

"Why not?" she almost taunted, her anger making her rude. "If you are a vampire, shouldn't you have fangs and turn into a bat and all that good stuff?"

"Yes," he said. "But I can't. Since I've been here I've stopped using my abilities, and now it's like my vampirism has gone dormant. That was why I wanted to meet Dr. Fowler. I had hoped he could help me."

Dr. Fowler? Oh yes, the crazy in the tweed.

"Help you bite?"

"Yes."

This was just nuts. Then she recalled something the man had said. "He was here to help you bite so you could mate."

He nodded. "Yes."

"With me?"

"Yes."

"Oh my God!" She covered her face with her hands. "Oh my God."

"Jolee, I know this is a lot to absorb."

"Absorb? I don't intend to absorb this. You are crazy."

He started to step toward her to speak again, but she put up a hand to stop him.

"No. I don't want to hear any more."

"Jolee, I love you."

She laughed bitterly. "Well, this is an interesting way of showing it."

Her emotions were strangling her, rage, fear, hurt, disappointment. "You know what? You need to go."

When he didn't move, she pointed at the door. "Now."

He hesitated, then nodded. Without another word, he left, leaving her in the kitchen to stare at the closed door.

She remained in the kitchen, staring blankly for . . . she had no idea how long. Then she finally crossed to turn the lock and barricade the door with one of her folding chairs.

What had just happened? She didn't even know. She couldn't believe any of it. Christian, the man she'd made love with, worked with, trusted more than anyone in her life, the man she loved, had just told her he was a vampire. It was so crazy she couldn't wrap her mind around it. She couldn't believe it.

He'd said he was as bad as the men she'd dated in the past. But he was wrong. He was worse. Because he'd made her love him, and then he'd revealed that he was insane.

She closed her eyes and tried to pull in a calming breath. But a ragged, frantic laugh escaped instead. Why? God, why was this happening? She'd loved him. She'd thought she'd found the perfect man. Finally.

How had he acted so normal? Okay, he was never normal. He was always far different from anyone she'd ever met. But he hadn't acted insane. She paced her living room, trying to understand how a person could just suddenly say what he had. It didn't make sense.

She paused, looking out her window at his darkened trailer. He did stay up all night. But she'd woken him up many times during the day. Shouldn't he be dead or something during the day?

"Why are you even questioning this?" she asked herself. "He's crazy. You have just made the mistake of falling for another loser. Again."

Except she knew that wasn't true. She'd never fallen for any other man. Not like she had for Christian. And that was why this hurt. It hurt so much she could barcly breathe.

A vampire? Why a vampire? Because he was nuts. There didn't have to be any reasoning behind his choice.

He did get pale a lot.

"So he's sick. He probably needs medication."

He was very strong.

"So he's physically fit."

Why was she trying to find things that supported his delusion? Was she that desperate for a man? No, she was just that desperate for him.

Then she remembered the list on his fridge. His twelve steps to being human. He had that because he believed he

was a vampire. Nausea filled her. All the time they'd been together he'd believed he was a vampire. Although it wasn't
like it mattered *when* he believed it. He did believe it.

She collapsed onto one of her folding chairs and dropped
her face into her hands. She wasn't going to cry. But she'd
never wanted to more.

Her heart was broken. And she'd left her bar in the hands
of a family of wanna-be vampires.

"How did it go?" Rhys asked as soon as Christian entered
the bar.

"Great. She's pissed, and she thinks I'm a lunatic."

"She'll come around," Sebastian assured him.

Yeah, she'd come around and realize she was insane herself to have feelings for him. And who could blame her?
Jolee just wanted someone normal. She wanted a man to
stand by her side and love her. Even if she ever did believe
him, she wouldn't want his lifestyle. She'd been on the outside looking in for her whole life. Why would she become an
even bigger outcast than her last name had made her? She
wouldn't. And Christian knew it had been just another selfish act on his part to expect that of her.

Christian kept the bar going the remainder of the night
along with his brothers and Jane. He'd closed up, putting all
the money in a zippered bank bag that Jolee had in her desk.
He'd bring it home with him since she didn't have a new safe
yet—one oversight when he was replacing items.

He wrote her a note, telling her he had the money and
he'd drop it off tomorrow. He didn't add that that would be
the last time he'd see her. He imagined that was implied.

"Was Jolee not feeling well tonight?" Jed asked as he slid
off his stool and headed toward the back door.

"No," Christian said.

Jed nodded. "You don't look too well yourself."

He shrugged. He didn't care about himself, only Jolee. Was she okay? He hoped so. He hoped she would go on and forget about him. She deserved to be happy, and if he couldn't give her that, then he prayed she found happiness with another. The idea made him ache, made him want to shout out in pain, but he had to let her go.

"You two had a fight, eh?"

He blinked at Jed. A fight? He wished. He could apologize for a fight. He could make amends. He couldn't make amends for who he was, aside from just leaving her alone.

"A bit more than a fight, Jed. I don't think you will be seeing me around much anymore."

"Why? What happened?"

"Let's just say we're too different." He assumed the old man would think he was saying that he didn't fit in with her and her life. After all, when he started here, he didn't. Now, this stupid, run-down bar was exactly where he wanted to be. But he should have known better about this shrewd old man.

"Give her time. It takes us mortals a little time to wrap our minds around beings like you."

Christian stared at him. "Mortals? Beings like me?"

Jed shrugged with nonchalance. "You don't live behind a bar for thirty years and not see a few things."

Jed's blue gaze actually unnerved Christian. How could this man be so wise, so blasé about what he was saying? He didn't consider insulting the old man's intelligence.

"How did you know?"

"It was that face of yours. Prettier than any man should be. And your brothers, too."

That surprised Christian. Most humans didn't notice that. They just responded to the beauty. They didn't question it.

"And," Jed added, "I have been watching you tend bar for quite a few nights now. While those bottles were blocking the mirror, I didn't see. But the other night, I noticed something a little strange about your reflection. You're a little see-through, son."

The mirror. He hadn't even thought about that the other night. But apparently no one else had noticed. Vampires weren't invisible, as folklore portrayed them. They were more just . . . blurry. And a little see-through. But someone would have to be looking for it to really notice.

Then he realized that was one thing he could have used to prove to Jolee he was telling the truth. He couldn't show his fangs or transform to shadow, but his odd reflection would have been there. Now it was too late. And for the best, too. She needed a normal life. A real life. He knew that now.

Still he stared at Jed, then shook his head. "You're something. Why didn't you say something earlier?"

Jed grinned. "I didn't see any point. I can tell you are a good sort, no matter what you are. Another thing you learn from living behind a bar. And I know you love our Jolee girl. She'll come around."

She wouldn't, but Christian didn't tell the man that. He'd only argue and there would be no point.

"Good night," Jed said, thumping him on the back with almost fatherly affection. The gesture caused Christian's chest to tighten. He'd come to care about this old mortal, and he would miss him.

"Good night, Jed."

Jed disappeared outside, and Christian finished locking up. He didn't have a key, but fortunately Sebastian's powers weren't shot. He locked the door from the inside and slipped under the door in the form of mist. He was a terrible show-off.

"So what do we do now?" Sebastian asked when they got back to the trailer park. Christian glanced at Jolee's trailer. All the lights were off. Not even her radio played.

"I'm going to bed." Christian trudged up his front steps, actually feeling his 210 years of existence.

"You really are a complete dolt, you do know that," Sebastian stated as he followed him into the trailer. "Jolee is your mate. You spend nearly two hundred years worshipping a lunatic, then you finally find your real mate. She is wonderful and loving and crazy about you, and you plan to just let her go."

Christian turned to his brother, irritated. "I don't want to let her go, but I can't make her accept me. You know that. Look what Lilah did, trying to make Rhys accept. She practically destroyed us all. I won't hurt her!"

He took a breath, calming himself. "Besides, she deserves better than me."

With that he left his brothers and Jane in the living room. He needed to be alone. He went into the second bedroom, which was bare except for an old mattress on the floor. He collapsed on it, dropping his arm over his eyes. He just wanted to forget. He just wanted to feel no pain.

Jolee looked at her clock. It was 8:30 A.M. and she hadn't managed to sleep a wink. But how had she really thought she was going to? Not every day did the man she love tell her he was a vampire. That merited a night of insomnia.

She sighed and pushed out of bed, padding to the kitchen. She supposed she should walk to the bar and make sure that everything was all right. For some reason, she believed the place was fine, which was strange as she thought Christian had to be certifiable. And the rest of his family was questionable at best.

She wandered to the fridge and got out a pitcher of orange juice. She carried it to the counter and started to reach for a glass. Her hand paused as she noticed the items on the countertop. She set down the pitcher, and with shaking hands she lifted the item. The zippered money bag from her bank. The one she had to put her money in for deposits.

She looked around. The metal chair was still wedged

under the doorknob. She'd also placed one under the handle of the back door. Even her windows were locked. How had this appeared here?

Beside the bag was a white piece of paper with small, crisp handwriting lining the width. She picked up the paper and began to read.

> *Dear Jolee,*
> *Here is the money from last night. The bar had a good night, very busy. Sebastian did a great job with the karaoke. The women loved him—no surprise there.*
> *Perhaps you are wondering how I got this into the trailer, as I know you had the place locked up tight, which is understandable.*
> *Jolee, I know you don't want to believe this, but I'm a vampire, too.*

Jolee's hand trembled and she started to put the letter down, but she couldn't. She had to read on.

> *And I can enter your house as a shadow or as mist. It's just one of the abilities I now have.*

She looked around her, a cold chill stealing up her spine. No, this was nonsense. Then she looked at the zippered bag. She knew the bag and the letter hadn't been there last night, and she hadn't slept. So how had she not heard anyone come in the trailer? How had that happened?

> *I became a vampire after Christian attacked me.*

Jolee made a noise in her throat.

> *Please don't let that frighten you. He is not the same Christian now that he was back then. He was*

still under Lilah's influence then. He still believed Rhys had wronged him. And he didn't actually cross me over to vampirism. My beloved Rhys did that, and I'm eternally grateful. He is the love of my life. My soul mate. Just as Christian is yours. I can see that. I can sense it.

Jolee, I know this is hard to accept, nearly impossible to believe, but what he told you is true. Vampires do exist. And they are not evil creatures of the night.

For me, vampires have been the family I never had. And I've never been happier or felt more blessed. Whatever you decide, please know that none of us ever meant you any harm. And I'm pleased to have met you.

Best wishes,
Jane

Jolee read the letter again. She didn't know what to believe. What to think. She set the letter down, and then went through the trailer checking all the windows and doors. Everything was as she'd left it. And she hadn't heard a sound. She had been too agitated to have missed even the slightest noise.

She hurried back to her living room, looking across to Christian's trailer. His heavy shades were drawn and his car was parked in the driveway. Rhys and Sebastian's SUV was beside his Porsche. Did he have those heavy blinds to keep out the sun? Her room wasn't as dark, and he slept in there fine.

She walked back to her room, and realized the room *was* quite dark, especially if the curtains were pulled over the blinds which, now that she thought about it, Christian always did at some point in the night.

Okay, she was losing it. She was actually starting to consider that this ludicrous story could possibly be real. Walking back to the kitchen, she glanced once more at the money and the letter. Those were real and they'd gotten there somehow.

Bang! Jolee jumped as her door shook as if it was going to be ripped from the hinges. She rushed over and peered out the window. Vance stood on the other side, furious.

She hesitated, but then moved the chair. Bad move. As soon as she did, Vance shouldered the door open.

"You little bitch," he gritted out as he stalked toward her. He looked wild and unkempt. His greasy hair spiked from his head. His shirt and jeans were dirty. She backed away from him, but also tried to avoid being cornered.

"Vance, wh-what are you doing here?"

He laughed bitterly. "Like you don't know. First, you didn't give me some money. Not smart. But this last thing, Jolee. Oh, you are going to pay for that."

Jolee shook her head. "I don't know what you are talking about."

He laughed again, his lips curling back menacingly. He stalked forward, and she shifted away, trying to move so that she could reach the door.

"I can't go back to prison."

Jolee realized the police must have questioned him and found some evidence. Or drugs. She glanced at the door, gauging her position. She had to keep him talking, and keep herself moving slowly. If she could get out the door, she could run to Christian.

"I can drop any charges. You can get help."

He laughed again. "I already came to you for help. For money. But you wouldn't give it to me. That wasn't very helpful."

But he stepped closer, stopping her slow sidestep toward the door. "And now I have the damned pigs after me. Not helpful, Cherry. Not helpful at all."

"Vance," she said in a gentle tone, afraid he was going to come closer. "I'll just forget everything. Just let all this go."

He laughed at that. A rough bark. "Too late, sis. They know what I did with that money. They plan to take me in for possession."

"Then you need to go, now," she said, making the fear in her voice sound like it was for him.

Vance nodded. "Yes. I do. But not before I make you pay."

He lunged at her, catching her arm just as she reached the front stoop. He jerked her backward, wrenching her arm. She screamed out in pain and lost her balance, falling hard on the stoop, her body half in and half out of the front door.

Before she could get her bearing, Vance straddled her, his weight forcing her breath out of her. He pinned her arms to the linoleum and loomed over her.

"I'm not letting my trailer trash sister and her cocky-ass boyfriend get the better of me."

Vance hit her then, backhanding her right across the face. She gasped and saw stars. She had to stay conscious. If she passed out, God only knew what Vance might do. He looked strung out, insane.

He hit her again. A bolt of pain shot from her cheekbone throughout her head. She needed help. She needed Christian.

Vance lifted his hand again, and this time his hand was fisted. Maybe he meant to beat her to death.

"Christian," she tried to shout, his name no more than a disoriented cry that he would never hear. She started to lose consciousness.

Christian awoke immediately, hearing Jolee calling for him, feeling her pain. He struggled to his feet, disoriented but desperate to find her. He staggered down the hall, focusing on Jolee and where she was. She was in her trailer. She was in pain.

Her voice reached him again. "Christian!"

He reached for the knob, throwing open his front door. He immediately recoiled as sunlight burned his eyes. He stumbled back out of the direct sunlight and blinked through watering eyes, trying to find her.

He did. Prone on her top step with a man on top of her, hurting her. He saw the man's hand rear back to strike her, and he darted out into the sunlight.

He didn't even feel the rays sear the bare skin of his back, blistering everywhere it touched. All he could focus on was getting to Jolee, protecting her.

He reached them quickly, even though his movements were heavy and awkward. He caught the back of the man's shirt and pulled him off her. Unfortunately, his body was weighted and clumsy from the sun, and the two men rolled down the metal stairs into a heap.

The man rose over Christian, prepared to attack, and Christian saw the man's face. Vance. Of course it was Vance. The bastard. And as Vance saw Christian, he froze, appalled. Christian knew how he must look, blistered and charred. Horrifying.

Vance tried to scramble away backward, on his hands and feet like a scared crab. Christian didn't allow his retreat. He managed to stand in one move, the action costing him much of his energy. But he pushed away the ponderous fatigue and caught Vance's shirt, lifting the man with one arm. Then he punched Vance repeatedly until his nose and lips bled.

"If you come near Jolee again, I will kill you. Do you hear me?"

His voice was raw, grating.

Vance didn't answer. Christian released him, and Vance fell in a crumpled heap on the gravel, unconscious.

Christian fell, too. He tried to stand, to go to Jolee, but the sun stole his strength, just as it was stealing his life. He made it to his feet, only to fall back to his knees in the dirt. He tried again, but couldn't. He was dying.

He fell heavily, face down; he could now smell the burn

of his own skin. He could hear the sizzle. Then he heard a small distressed cry beside him, and he felt Jolee's hands on him. They were blessedly cool on his marred flesh.

He sighed.

"Christian. Oh God, Christian. Please get up." She tugged at him.

At first, he didn't even try. But her pulls became more frantic, and he worried that she'd hurt herself. He used the little strength he had to work with her as she caught him under the arms and dragged him toward the stairs.

After much struggling, she got him into the kitchen, then she managed to pull him down the hall to her bedroom. She left him on the floor to go secure the curtains closed, then she tried to lift him up to the bed, but he had no energy left and she simply wasn't strong enough.

She collapsed onto the floor beside him. Again she touched his face, his hair. "Oh, Christian."

"A fright, aren't I?" he managed to rasp.

"No," she assured him. "No."

She started to stand again. "I have to get your brothers."

He caught her arm; his charred hand looked hideous against her smooth, pale skin. He released her. "No. Will happen to them, too."

She hesitated, then nodded. "But I need to get you to a doctor."

"Won't help."

She shook her head. "Then what should I do? You need help."

"Too late," he breathed.

Jolee shook her head, a desperate sound escaping her lips. No. He couldn't be dying. He couldn't. But as she looked at his horribly ravaged skin, she knew he couldn't survive.

"I'm sorry," she told him. "I'm sorry I didn't believe you."

He shook his head just slightly as if to tell her it didn't matter. Then he smiled, his beautiful lips cracked and blistered. "Showed you."

She knew he meant to be funny, but she couldn't laugh. Instead a desperate whimper escaped her. She couldn't lose this man. This man who risked himself to save her. A woman who'd told him he was insane, who didn't believe him and trust him after all the wonderful things he'd done for her. And now he was dying—because of her.

He lifted a burnt hand to her face, not touching her, just gesturing to her face. "You have bruises."

How could he worry about her? About a few bruises that would heal. He was dying. Her heart twisted, stealing her breath.

"Christian. There has to be a way to save you."

He shook his head. "No."

"But I can't lose you. I love you."

He smiled. "Love you, too." His eyes closed.

She looked around helplessly as if she'd find something to help him in her room. Maybe there was. Maybe she was the thing that could save him.

"What if you fed? Would that help you?"

He blinked his pale eyes open.

"No," he said. In those pale eyes that were sometimes so unreadable, she saw she was right. She could save him with her blood.

"You have to bite me."

"No. Would need too much."

"Would you kill me? Or cross me over?"

"Cross," he stated. "But can't bite."

Her chest squeezed. He couldn't bite. He'd told her that. She couldn't save him, like he'd saved her.

She made a strangled sound, touching his scorched face. She was failing the man she loved. She was losing him.

She stared down at him, helpless.

"Don't cry."

It wasn't until he said the words that she realized tears rolled down her cheeks.

"Then don't leave me," she pleaded. "Please."

He nodded, although she knew he was just appeasing her.

She slid her arm under his back and managed to pull him up, cradling him against her chest, her back braced against the wall. She buried her face in his hair, sobbing helplessly. He shifted, his mouth brushing the base of her throat.

"Don't," he whispered.

"Then stay with me. Make me like you. I want to be with you forever."

He didn't move for a moment, and she feared he was gone. Then she felt the brush of his lips on her skin again. Then a startling pierce at her neck, then tremendous, overwhelming satisfaction. Then nothing.

When she awoke, she was in bed. She sat up, looking around her, expecting Christian to be gone, expecting to discover that the events of earlier were just a dream, a nightmare.

Then she saw him. He stood in the doorway in only a pair of dusty black pants, but the dust was the only sign of his earlier struggle. The charred, blistered skin she remembered was again golden and smooth and perfect.

He regarded her with a worried expression, his eyes clouded with guilt. Only then did she feel the changes in herself. The energy in her veins, the strength in her body. She felt wonderful.

"Am I a vampire?" she asked him.

He nodded, looking pained. She scrambled off the bed and went to him, wrapping her arms around him, pressing her cheek to his bare chest.

"Thank you," she said. "Thank you for not leaving me."

He gently caught her upper arms and pushed her away enough so that he could look at her. "How can you thank me? I used your blood to save my own existence."

"No," she said with a smile. "You used my blood to give us forever."

He stared at her for a moment, then pulled her tightly against his chest. His mouth captured hers.

"Why did Lilah walk out into the sun?" she asked, now knowing that was what she must have done.

Christian frowned, surprised by the question. "She killed herself because she was crazy, and never recovered from the fact she couldn't control Rhys as she did me. She wanted him, and he fought her. He was strong."

She shook her head. "No, you are strong. You risked your own life to save me."

"I love you," he said simply.

"Good thing," she said with a saucy smile. "I don't cry for just anyone."

"You will never have reason to cry again," he promised her. And Jolee knew he was telling her the truth. And she believed him.

Epilogue

For those of you who have read my blog religiously over the past year, I'm sorry that I've dropped the ball in the past few months. I've been busy, and some rather interesting things have happened during that time.

First of all, let me start by saying I've decided that my twelve-step program has worked. Well, sort of. Certain things like Step 1: Honesty, Step 5: Integrity, Step 7: Humility, and Step 9: Forgiveness—those are all huge parts of being a successful human. Actually all the steps (listed in full in my January 15, 2005 entry) are important to being human. And to being a vampire too.

Which, by the way, is what I've managed to become. A good vampire, a happy vampire, a very satisfied vampire. Good, happy, satisfied—not words that I expected to use in conjunction with the word vampire. And especially not in conjunction with myself.

Of course, I didn't do this alone. And this brings me to the most important step of the twelve. The one I dreaded the most, but needed the worst. Step 11: Mak-

ing Contact. That was the one I really did not want to do. The one that I told myself I was doing through this blog. But it wasn't. Sorry. But it's true. I was still hiding. And I wasn't dealing with my past. Things didn't get better for me until I actually got out there and interacted with others being humans and vampires every day.

So, I'm sorry to say this, and again, I do appreciate those of you who read my ranting and whining every day. But this is my last blog entry. I'm simply going to be too busy to write these anymore.

Thanks for listening.

Now, I suggest you go out and make contact.

Sincerely,
Christian Young

Christian applauded with everyone else in the bar as Jolee finished her song. She thanked them, and then returned to the booth to call up the next singer. He watched her as, after she finished starting the music, she approached him. She strolled behind the bar to come to him, smiling. He would never get tired of that beautiful smile.

"Great song," he told her as he pulled her into his arms and stole a quick kiss.

"I know how much you like that one," she said, stealing a kiss of her own.

He liked all the songs she sang, but he did have a particular affinity to that one. Shania Twain, "Forever and Always," a song about keeping with the one she loved forever and always. He felt the same way. He was keeping her. Christian would never grow tired of sharing an eternity with this woman. His Jolee.

"Good lord," Jed muttered around his cigarette. "What does a man gotta do to get a drink around this place."

Christian grinned at the him, then reached for his empty mug. "It's just wrong when a regular can't get served."

"Don't I know it?" Jed winked at Jolee.

Christian placed the mug in front of the man he had come to think of as a father. "You really need to lay off the cigarettes."

Jed snorted at that. "Too late now."

"It's never too late." Christian looked over to Jolee, the woman who'd saved him. Who'd given him back his humanity. They both loved the old man, silently offering him immortality.

"In this old body," he snorted. "I don't think so. I've had a good life, and I'll be happy to go when my day comes."

Christian dreaded that day. He'd miss Jed, but he did understand the man's point. Jed had lived a full life. Christian planned to live a full eternity—finally.

"It's good to have you two back," Jed said, his blue eyes filled with emotions he'd never otherwise let his gruff demeanor show. "I like your brothers, but the place just didn't feel the same."

Sebastian, Rhys, and Jane had watched the bar for the past month while he and Jolee had gone on their honeymoon, a trip around Europe. He'd showed her all the things he'd never appreciated, finally seeing them through Jolee's excited eyes. Finally enjoying them.

"Well, we're glad to be back, too." Christian smiled at the old man.

Jolee leaned into him. "Are you really? Don't you miss the high life? The expensive hotels? And all the luxuries?"

"No," he said readily. "I don't need anything in my life but you."

She grinned. "Ditto." She kissed him, then rushed away to announce another singer.

Christian looked around the old bar with its Christmas lights on the rafters and scuffed wooden floors covered in peanut shells. He looked at its patrons in their dirty jeans and T-shirts. He listened to a woman belt out one flat note after another. He smelled smoke as Jed lit another cigarette.

Then he looked at Jolee. She smiled and mouthed, "I love you." He smiled contently as he filled a mug with beer.

There really was no place on earth he'd rather be than Leo's Brew Pub and Karaoke Saloon.

But he would have to work on Jolee about moving out of the trailer park. He wasn't a completely changed vampire.

He still hated those damned lawn ornaments.

If you liked this Kathy Love book,
you've got to try her other titles
currently available from Brava . . .

FANGS FOR THE MEMORIES

Oh, Brother!

There are Christmas mornings and then there are Christmas mornings like this one: watching my brother, Rhys, swagger through our New York City apartment . . . smiling. We are talking about Rhys, the detached, surly, and annoying; the man who turned brooding into an art form. But he's not brooding now. No, he's practically threatening to pistol whip me for shaking hands with the beautiful, sweet, half-dressed creature named Jane who just tried to sneak out of his bedroom. Weird. And who knew Brother Grim even had a sex drive?

But it isn't just the smiling and the sudden libido that has me freaked out. Something terrible happened last night, something that made my brother break his own rule and save the life of a mortal. Whatever it was, now he doesn't remember anything from the past two hundred years. He wants Jane so bad that he's forcing himself to forget he's a vampire, taking himself back to a time before he crossed over and our family was destroyed. He's sauntering around the place like a Regency viscount with an English accent, saying things like "I behaved like a randy, soused caper-wit." Did we ever really talk like that? So, Rhys doesn't know he's a vampire, and neither does Jane. This is what we call a problem.

All I know is, this mortal woman has managed to touch my brother's frozen heart, and I, Sebastian Young, will do whatever it takes to help him keep her . . .

I ONLY HAVE FANGS FOR YOU

Bite Me

One thing you have to know about my brother Sebastian: he loves being a vampire. After all, what's not to love? He's eternally twenty-five. He's single, and frankly, he's a chick magnet. Yeah, undeath is good. The only thing he's serious about is his nightclub, Carfax Abbey. It's the sort of dark, happening spot where vampires can really let their fangs down. You know, hiding in the shadows, feeding, giving pleasure to unsuspecting mortals, being all cool and vampirey. Whatever. My brother Rhys and I have tried to get Sebastian to clean up his bad-boy ways like we did, but then he went and called us "fang-whipped." Okay, Bite Boy, chew on this . . .

The ultimate righteous reformer, Wilhemina Weiss, is on a mission to shut down Carfax Abbey. She doesn't approve of my bro's biting ways. It seems the spirited, sexy-without-knowing-it vampire is working undercover as a cocktail waitress in his bar while waging a secret war to bring him down. Sebastian's A-positive he can convince Miss Goody-Vampire-Two-Fangs that nothing beats the ecstasy of a good vampire bite. She's certain she can resist him for as long as it takes to reform him. I gotta tell you, the suspense would kill me—if I weren't already undead.

Now, Mr. "Has anyone ever told you you've got a beautiful neck?" is in way over his. He's finally met a girl who may not be his type, but she's way more than his match. Not that he's (cough) fang-whipped (cough) or anything. No, not my baby bro. One thing's for sure, I've never seen Sebastian so completely at someone's mercy in my life. And frankly, I'm enjoying every minute of it . . .

MY SISTER IS A WEREWOLF

The sexy Young brothers may know a fang or two about the art of seduction, but their sister, Elizabeth, is positively mooning over a few issues of her own . . .

Bad Moon Rising

Elizabeth Young's brothers think they have it rough as vampires? Ha! Two words for them: unwanted hair. What werewolf Elizabeth craves is a normal life with a husband, kids, and less shaving. Unfortunately the vaccine she's researched isn't working yet. Worse, she's in heat—and soon every dangerous wolf pack for miles around will be at her door. To buy time, she needs to have sex, and often, with the first human male she can find . . .

Veterinarian Jensen Adler just meant to drown his sorrows, until a stunning, leather-clad brunette made him an offer he couldn't refuse. Now he's caught up in something really weird, definitely dangerous, and, okay, extremely hot. So his new girlfriend's hiding something (and she's a little freaky about the moon), but Jensen knows true love when he feels it, and this time, he's not giving up . . . no matter how hairy things get.

ANY WAY YOU WANT IT

Is That A Treble Clef In Your Pocket—Or Are You Just Glad To See Me?

Maggie Gallagher spends her nights with lots of men. Of course, they're all dead composers, but why nitpick? Her love life is just like the musical compositions she researches—undiscovered. It's time for Maggie to let loose and go wild. In a dive bar on Bourbon Street, Maggie makes a real find in the house band's keyboard player. He's hot. Sexy. Flirtatious. Soulful. And she could swear he's playing an unknown piece she's been researching, which is impossible, unless he's dead . . .

Centuries before he was a badass vampire with a rock-star wardrobe and Big Easy charm, Ren was Renauldo D'Antoni, a composer on the verge of great success until he was betrayed. No one could ever know that, but tonight, the shy strawberry blonde with the big eyes and obviously borrowed outfit actually seemed to recognize his long-lost composition. Now, she wants to know about the composition, and Ren wants to know her . . . intimately. But what starts as attraction—and distraction—just might lead to the biggest discovery of their lives . . .

And here's a sneak peek at Kathy's next book,
I WANT YOU TO WANT ME,
coming in September from Brava . . .

Then she heard it. A distinct bang directly above her head. Her eyes popped open, and she stared at the ceiling she'd painted sky blue when she'd moved in. She remained still, listening.

Just when she'd decided that she must have imagined the loud clunk, another noise echoed from above her head. The scrape of something being dragged across the floor.

She glanced over to her cat. Even Boris stared intently up at the sound. His ear twitched.

For once, the grumpy cat was giving a definite reaction, but of course, it was when she'd much rather have seen his usual bored or apathetic demeanor. She sat up; her eyes still locked on the ceiling as if someone was going to suddenly manifest from the floor above.

There was an apartment over hers. But it was empty. Empty and neglected, since Ren hadn't bothered with the place for several years.

Her heart leapt, pounding in an uneven, breath-stealing way as she heard more sounds. The distinct creak of feet on a hardwood floor. A sound she easily recognized, because the old hardwood in her apartment squeaked the same way.

Careful to make no noise herself, she rose from the sofa and moved to the front door. Her apartment and the upstairs apartment shared the glassed-in front porch.

Her heart still pounding, she peeked out her window. Light from the courtyard illuminated a swath of the porch, leaving the corners shadowed in darkness.

Behind her, she heard walking. She spun, expecting someone to be right behind her. She jumped as she saw a figure in the center of the room. Then she realized it was her distorted creation in the center of the room. Before she'd considered the sculpture to be frustrating, disappointing, and mostly a disaster. Now it looked almost ominous.

She sucked in a deep breath, trying to calm her rocketing pulse. *Calm down. Calm down.*

More footsteps. But overhead—not in the same room. Nothing was going to hurt her. The assurance didn't persuade her heart to stop hammering against her ribcage.

She looked back out the window, trying to angle her head so she could see up the staircase to her right, leading to the upstairs apartment. The stairs, as much as she could make out, just ascended in to pitch black.

Hesitantly, her hand went to the doorknob. She turned it slowly and eased the door ajar. Sticking her head out, she squinted into the darkness. And she listened.

Nothing. Not a sound.

She glanced around the door to Maggie and Ren's. Except for a dim glow from a lamp in the living room, their house was dark too.

She looked back up the staircase, debating on whether she should go up and investigate. Peering into the menacing blackness, she decided that such was a really dumb idea. Instead she pulled the door closed, carefully clicked the lock into place, and went in search of her cell phone.

"See," she said to Boris as she rummaged through her purse, then amongst her art supplies, only to find it buried under a pile of clay-caked rags. She grimaced at the grimy phone, then turned back to Boris.

"See, I'm not that foolish woman in the horror movies, who traipses off to investigate the noise from the attic."

Another creak sounded directly above her head. She quickly swiped off the filth and flipped the phone open. Only to see the faceplate wasn't illuminated. She pressed the ON button. Nothing. She pressed again, harder. Still nothing.

She stared at the useless phone, knowing that even if she plugged it in, the battery would need a while to accept enough charge to even turn on.

"Okay, so I am apparently the foolish woman in a horror movie who has an ancient cell phone that never holds a charge." She snapped the phone shut. "Crap."

Now would be the time to regret not getting her home phone turned on. She glanced toward the windows. She could go to Maggie and Ren's and use their phone. She debated the idea of leaving the security of her apartment, then decided she really had no choice.

"It's dumber to stay in here, listening to someone robbing the place," she told the cat. He blinked, but she wasn't sure if that was in agreement or not.

She rifled through her purse again, looking for her voodoo doll keychain which held Maggie and Ren's spare key. Then she tiptoed to the door.

"Wish me luck."

Boris had already curled back into a black ball of snoozing fur. She shook her head. "It couldn't have been a stray dog that showed up at my door, could it? At least a dog would care if I was going out to greet my imminent death."

She took a deep breath, then unlocked and eased open the door. Everything was quiet, but she didn't take the time to survey the murky corners. Instead she stepped out and rushed to the porch door, which led into the better lit courtyard.

"Hey."

Erika's already tensed muscles reacted on instinct as soon as she heard the male voice close behind her.

She spun toward the faceless voice and hurled the object in her right hand. Without waiting to see if she made connection, she shoved open the porch door and propelled herself out into the courtyard, her legs pumping under her as she raced toward Maggie and Ren's carriage house. She fumbled with the keys, even as she ran. Thank God she hadn't thrown those.

"Wait! Erika!"

The words called out from behind her took a moment to register in her panicked brain. But eventually realized that the disembodied voice had used her name. She stopped, the key poised to enter the lock of the carriage-house door.

Slowly she turned to look over her shoulder.

At first she couldn't locate the speaker in the shadows and greenery of the courtyard. Then he stepped forward into the glow of the courtyard's dim garden lights.

Right away Erika recognized him, even though she's only met him once and very briefly.

"Vittorio?"

Nail-Biting Romantic Suspense
from Your Favorite Authors